MURDER

COMES

HOME

MURDER COMES HOME

A Zane Grayson Mystery

Craig Kingsman

TWISTED DAGGER
P R E S S

Printed in the United States of America.

ISBN 979-8-9937618-0-0

Book Cover Design by the Book Cover Whisperer: OpenBookDesign.biz

To my wife. Love you mostest.

Chapter 1

THE SUN REFLECTED OFF THE turquoise water of Mathoni Lake far below. Zane Grayson stood at the overlook and stared down at the valley. Small fishing boats and canoes looked like black dots on the water. The town of Mathoni wrapped around from the west shore and along the south end.

"They say you can never come home again," Zane said to the wind. Yet, here he was. "More cabins on the hills. I guess I should have expected that."

He exhaled slowly through his mouth. It had been seven years since Zane had last been here. That was for his father's funeral. And much like that day, today was not a day he wanted to see. He'd left Santa Barbara three days earlier, his trepidation increasing as he drove the thousand miles to Utah. Now, worry sat like a rock in his gut. He tried to swallow, but his mouth was dry, and the knot in his stomach tightened.

Growing up, he went to church every week. He had been taught the gospel and read the *Book of Mormon* and the Bible. Everyone in the ward, in the town, thought he'd go on a mission like he'd been taught and expected to do. Then, he told his parents he wanted to play college basketball instead. He knew he'd hurt them. And as the years passed, he'd given up those religious beliefs. His mom had continued to believe.

Now, he was here to take care of her as she went through cancer treatment. *What if she doesn't make it? But at least I'll get some time with her, unlike with Dad. However, she won't be happy when I don't go to church or have my morning cup of Joe, and she will lose it when I have my bourbon and cigar. And what about the townsfolk? Will they accept or ostracize me?* As he left California, that all nibbled at him. A thousand miles later, it took big bites out of him, the anxiety nearly making him throw up.

He rubbed his stomach and exhaled through his mouth again. "I guess it won't get any easier."

Zane squeezed back into his Prius and dropped into the valley, through the switchbacks on State Highway 440. The road straightened out about three miles before getting to the south end of the lake, where the town began. He slowed when the highway made a sharp left at the end of that straightaway and continued on through town.

His breathing got shallower and faster; the knot tightened some more.

The highway followed the shoreline of Mathoni Lake, bending around to the west side. The town's only gas station, now called the Gas & Guzzle, sat on the curve. A convenience store and a Subway had been added.

He drove past the yellow-brick courthouse and then saw the familiar red-brick building with the green and white awning of Lou-Lou's Café. He craved one of their chocolate marshmallow malts. Across the road, a For Sale sign hung from a post in front of the bed-and-breakfast. The wood siding was gray and weather-beaten, and he wondered what had happened to the Petersons. He passed new homes and buildings, some also for sale.

Zane rolled down the window. The air was fresh, warm, and smelled of the lake, farms, and evergreens. *Smells exactly as I remember it.* There was more traffic now. The town was at the height of the summer tourist season; people came to fish and canoe and kayak and camp and hike.

Zane continued north. The town now stretched almost to home.

He made a left turn into the lane; gravel crunched under the tires. He stopped when the house came into view. The house where he'd grown up. The house he was coming back to. He took deep calming breaths and stared for a few minutes, then took his foot off the brake.

When he pulled into the yard, dogs ran out to greet him and barked at the unfamiliar car. He stopped just in front of the house, turned off the engine, and got out. One dog, a brown and white boxer, brave enough to approach, sniffed him and then licked his hand. The other, a black and white Australian Shepherd, barked from a safe distance.

He stood there and looked around; the knots in his stomach tightened even more. The house hadn't changed. It was still white, but needed paint. He made a mental note to take care of that. The Cottage, a smaller home for the lead farmhand, was still there, across the yard from the house. A milk barn and other farm buildings sat behind.

The front door opened, and his mom, Marcia, stepped onto the large wrap-around porch. "Zane," she called. "You made it. You should have called from Vernal, so we'd know when to expect you." She wore jeans and a light blue blouse. A blue and white polka-dot scarf covered her head, hiding the effects of the chemo. Her glasses hung on a gold chain around her neck. Just like always.

Zane walked up the steps and gave her a hug. "Mom, you're looking pretty good, considering."

"I have my bad days, but knowing you were coming home today perked me up. Come in. There's some lemonade in the fridge, and your sister is in the kitchen taking a cake out of the oven."

"You and your cake, Mom. Some things never change." He thought about all the blue ribbons she'd won at the county fair. Even some at the state fair.

Anxiety made it nearly impossible for him to enter the house. He took a deep breath and pushed forward. *Why is this so hard? I've walked through that door thousands of times.*

The house smelled of chocolate cake and Lemon Pledge. He looked around the living room. It was pretty much unchanged except for a new chair and a flat-screen TV where the old console set once sat. The aging furniture still had plastic slipcovers. The fireplace, which was always lit in the winter, looked sad with no fire.

"Mary Elizabeth, look who the cat dragged in," Mom said as they walked into the kitchen.

"Hi Zane." Mary Elizabeth gave her older brother a hug and then stood back to look him over. "You're looking good. I think retirement suits you. And the touch of gray in your sideburns confirms it. You're old. It won't be long and it'll be all gray," she teased. "How was the drive?"

Zane's younger sister had dark, shoulder-length hair and stood five feet five. Zane towered over her. She lived in Portland with her husband, Neil, and three kids. She'd been in Mathoni to help their mom for several months, and Zane knew she was eager to get back home. He'd last seen her five years before when she'd stopped in Santa Barbara during a family trip to Disneyland.

"As long and boring as you'd expect, Sis. That chocolate cake I smell?"

"It needs to cool before you can have some."

How many times did I hear those words growing up? "Mom's chocolate cake is one thing I've missed."

"I heard that, Zane," Mom said. "You'll have to wait until dinner."

Zane shook his head. "I'll always be your little boy, won't I." It wasn't a question.

"Little or big, I'm happy you're back home."

"Tell me the truth, Mom—how are you?" Zane said.

"Really pretty good. It's green week."

"Green week?" Zane asked.

Mary Elizabeth poured them all a glass of lemonade and explained, "Three-week cycles. About two days after chemo, it gets pretty rough for a week or so. That's red week. After that, we go into yellow and finally green when she's good. Then the cycle starts all over again."

"So if we're in green week now, that means another chemo treatment next week?"

"Yes, but enough about me and my treatment. We have plenty

of time for that," Mom said. "What I want to know is the details about that brouhaha with your job."

Zane took a big drink of lemonade and sat quietly.

"Nothing to say?" Mary Elizabeth said.

"I've told you basically what happened. I have no more to say. So, Sis, how are Neil and the kids?" Zane said, changing the subject. "Is Katrina driving yet?"

"They're all fine. And yes, Kat is driving now, and Ash will be this fall."

Mom spoke up. "Zane, you really should talk about the problem you had with the department. It will help you cope with it."

"I've done my coping and don't need to do more. We reached a settlement. I retired. It's over."

Silence fell like a lead balloon. They all picked up their glasses and drank their lemonade at the same time. Zane finished his drink, then rinsed the glass and set it in the sink. Marcia asked for more lemonade, so he refilled her glass. Mary Elizabeth's was still half-full, and she declined a refill.

"I'll get my bags and unload the car." He hadn't brought much. He didn't need it all now. "Tomorrow I'll go to Vernal and get some blue jeans, shirts, and boots. Maybe a hat. My Prius isn't really a farm vehicle, so I should probably trade it in for a pickup." He hadn't thought about trading in his car before, and it hit him hard that he really was giving up his life in California. His Prius was the last vestige of the life he had there. He rolled that thought around for several minutes and finally said, "And I'd like to meet Levi."

"He should be out in the milk barn about now," Mom said.

ZANE WALKED ACROSS THE YARD and behind The Cottage to the milk barn. The white-painted cinder block building hadn't changed. Inside, he found a man pushing a squeegee across the concrete floor. The air inside smelled of manure and disinfectant. "Levi?" he said.

The man looked up from his work. "You must be Zane. Your ma said you would be here today." Levi Smoot was shorter than

Zane's six feet two. He'd been hired to run the farm after Zane's dad died. He was muscular, with a big, bushy mustache and a cowboy hat with a wide brim. Zane guessed him to be about sixty and suspected his picture could be in the dictionary next to the definition of 'cowboy.'

They shook hands. "Nice to meet you, Levi. Mom talks highly of you."

"Mighty nice of her. How was the drive all the way from California?" He pronounced it 'Caleefornia'.

Zane laughed. "Mary Elizabeth just asked me that. I'll give you the same answer. Boring as you'd expect."

"Don't reckon' I'd know what to expect. I've never been to Caleefornia."

"Beautiful there." Zane looked around at the milk barn. "Looks like milking has changed. I don't recognize this barn at all."

"I suspect not. Technology's made it easier now. No buckets to empty. The milk just runs through those tubes and straight into the tank." He pointed to the plastic tubing hanging from the ceiling. "And when the udder's empty, the teat cups release automatically."

"That's impressive. Give me a couple of days to get settled, and then I'll have you show me how it all works. I don't plan just to sit around. Need to stay busy."

"Be happy to, Mr. Grayson, but me, Miguel, and Chilo have it well in hand."

"Call me Zane. I'm not looking to take away anyone's job. Just learn how things work now and help where I can. As far as the farm is concerned, I'll be working for you."

"Thanks, Zane. I appreciate that."

"I just came out to meet you before I unload my car."

"You needin' some help?"

"Nope. I don't have that much."

THAT EVENING AT SUPPER, MARY Elizabeth said a prayer to bless the food, then rolls, a green salad, and a platter of roasted chicken and vegetables were passed around.

Zane looked at his mom and then his sister. They all sat in the same places as when he was growing up. His dad's seat, the mismatched special chair at the head of the table, was empty.

"I'll get fat if you feed me like this all the time," Zane said.

"You should have a special supper for your homecoming. Besides, this has to be better than eating out or TV dinners all the time," Mom said.

"Guilty," he said, his mouth full of chicken. The house didn't feel right, but he couldn't place what it was.

Mary Elizabeth asked, "What are your plans other than helping Mom?"

Zane swallowed the bite of chicken leg he'd just taken. "I'll help with the milking and taking care of the farm. I haven't fished in a long time. I haven't been on a horse for even longer. When I drove in, I noticed the house could use some paint."

"Fishing sounds like a good idea. Maybe catch some trout for dinner. I haven't had fresh trout in a long time." Mom said, then switched topics. "Will you be at church on Sunday, Zane?"

He sighed, put down his fork, and looked at Mom. "No, I'm not. I stopped going to church a long time ago. Remember when Dad passed, and I told you I couldn't dedicate his grave?"

"Now, Zane, you know what will happen if you don't follow the commandments."

"If this will be an issue, I can get in my car and head back to Santa Barbara."

She balled up her napkin, then stood and took her plate to the sink.

Mary Elizabeth stared at him. "Zane, this isn't easy for Mom," she whispered. "Maybe you should give in and take her to church."

He whispered back, "I can't do that." Then louder, "How about a big slice of that cake I've been smelling all afternoon?"

Chapter 2

MARCIA SAT IN THE LIVING room, knitting, when Zane came downstairs the next morning.

"Morning, Mom. What are you making?

"It's going to be a sweater for Olivia."

"I'm sure she'll like it. I'm heading down to Lou-Lou's for breakfast."

"Zane, I can make you something."

"There's no coffee here," he said as he headed out the door.

There was no parking right in front of Lou-Lou's. Growing up, it was the only place to eat in town until Mathoni Pizza opened up down the road. Zane rounded the corner and found parking on the next block.

The bell above the door tinkled as he walked in. The inside was exactly as he remembered. That seemed like a lifetime ago. The smell of grease, burgers, and bacon greeted him, as did the same red Formica tables, same black Naugahyde seats, same bar with the swivel stools, same black-and-white checkered floor covering. Even the Coca-Cola clock was the same. Nearly the same Louise behind the counter. She looked thirty years older. He wondered if her husband, Lou, was back in the kitchen. The couple had owned the place for as long as he could remember.

A man sat alone in the first booth. From his hat and vest, it looked like he'd been out fishing. Two booths down sat a couple and a young boy. He looked about ten. His mother chided him for not drinking his milk. Another man, bald with tufts of brown hair sticking out over his ears, sat at the counter. Two old men, one resembling Zane's high school science teacher, Emmett Young, played checkers in the back booth. The other man had his back to the door. Emmett spoke to the other man and pointed at Zane. The man turned around. Charlie Snow, one of Mom's cousins.

Zane walked to the far end of the counter and sat on the stool, facing the front door.

"Be there in a minute, Hun," Louise said without looking up. She went back to sorting silverware.

"Take your time, Louise," Zane said.

She stopped and looked over at Zane. "Well, as I live and breathe. Is that you, Zane Grayson? Your mama told me you were coming back home. Stand up and let me look at you."

Louise had to be in her late sixties by now. Her hair was gray with some white. She wasn't more than about five feet tall and skinny as a rail.

Zane stood up and slowly spun around, his arms held out from his sides.

"My, my. You have filled out and look fine. I'll bet you can't keep the ladies away. Lou, come on out here and see who I found."

Lou wandered in from the kitchen. He was taller than his wife and had a neatly trimmed white beard. "What you want, Louise. I'm pretty busy back there getting ready for the lunch crowd."

"Now, Lou, looky here." She pointed to Zane. "You remember Zane Grayson."

"Zane. What's it been, five, six years since your pa passed on?" He came around the counter and shook hands with Zane. "You come back for a visit?"

"I retired. Came back to help Mom."

"Retired! You must have done pretty well for yourself. You're still young."

"Well, I did alright. Cops can retire early. Stress of the job and all that."

"What can I get you?" Louise says.

"Coffee to start. Are those pancakes still as good as I remember them? And bacon and eggs, scrambled."

"You drinking coffee? All those godless liberals got to you out there in California," Louise said. She poured him a cup anyway.

Between customers, Louise peppered Zane with questions about life in California.

He was almost finished eating when he looked up and saw a blonde woman at the counter near the register. His stomach flip-flopped again, not from anxiety. It was from seeing his old high school sweetheart, Tiffany. Tiffany Needham. That was her name back then. The two of them had been inseparable. Everyone thought they would get married and settle down in The Cottage. Then he got a basketball scholarship at the University of California, Irvine, and went off to college. She was a year behind him in school. The day he left, she was in tears, begging him to stay. He had a difficult time leaving. It was early morning. A Wednesday. He thought they'd said goodbye the night before, but there she was, sitting on the hood of the car when he came out of the house. She wore jean shorts, a red and white polka-dot top and sandals. She ran up to him and wrapped her arms around him. Her hair smelled like strawberries. Tears streamed down her cheeks. He wasn't sure she would let go. After she finally did, and he and his dad drove off. They got to Las Vegas for the night. He called her from the hotel. She cried again. A year later she went to BYU and ended up married to a guy she met there. Married in the temple. Not until death do you part, but for time and all eternity. He didn't know her surname now.

"Tiffany?" he said.

She looked around to find who had called. Her eyes opened wide, and a big smile appeared when she saw him. "Zane? Is that you?" They hugged tight.

"What are you doing here?"

"Mom needed help, so I moved back to town."

"I moved back too. After Will sold his company, he wanted to do something different. It's Tiffany Massey now. We built a ranch above the lake, and he runs cattle. Been here three years. Time hasn't caught up with you. You're still as handsome as ever."

Zane blushed. "I was about to say the same about you. So you're a rancher's wife now. I can't picture you out riding the range."

"Cattle wasn't my choice, but Will needed a hobby." Zane thought he sensed a tinge of unhappiness in her voice. "But I'm also a mom. Four kids." She held up four fingers on her right hand. "Will Junior is in Chile on his mission, the others are here. August will be a senior next year. The twins, Vince and Ciarra, are fifteen. What about you? Ever get married?"

"Nope. Didn't seem right with my job."

"So, you were a cop in California somewhere?"

"Santa Barbara. I'm retired now. New job is caring for Mom."

"I heard about that. How is she?"

"Seems pretty good, but I just got here yesterday, so not completely caught up yet."

Louise wandered over. "You want anything else, Zane? A slice of pie?"

"No ma'am. It was mighty good."

"Thanks, Hun. Tiffany, your order should be about done."

"Zane, come for dinner sometime," Tiffany said. "You can't miss our place. Other side of the lake and up the hill."

"I might just take you up on that. I need some time to get settled. Give me a couple of weeks."

They hugged again, maybe a bit too long. She picked up her to-go boxes and waved at him as she got into a black Mercedes SUV and drove away.

"I was surprised you and her didn't get hitched." He hadn't seen Louise come back.

"Wasn't meant to be, I guess. Is she happy, Louise?" He'd sensed some tension when she talked about the ranch.

"I suppose so," Louise said, "with all that money."

"Her husband struck it rich?"

"Rumor is he's a billionaire. That's with a 'b', Hun. Built themselves a huge mansion up on the hill the other side of the lake."

Zane looked off into the distance. Was senior prom that long ago? Tiffany was so beautiful in that blue dress. It matched her eyes. He felt like James Bond in that rented tuxedo. They had to go all the way to Rock Springs, Wyoming, for it. He felt like they were the only ones on the dance floor. Then they were named King and Queen and they *were* the only ones on the dance floor as they took their royal dance. Her arms around his neck. His around her waist. He held her close. *Where are the pictures from that night? Does Mom have them?*

He shook his head to return to reality.

"How much do I owe you, Louise?"

"On the house. Consider it a welcome-home gift."

Chapter 3

FOUR A.M. WAS TOO EARLY to wake up. Especially during retirement. Zane had expected to travel. See the world. Sleep late. Waking up before sunrise and doing farm chores was where he ended up.

Zane rubbed his eyes, then dressed in Levis and a snap-button Western shirt, part of the new wardrobe he'd bought in Vernal three days before. He'd also traded in his beloved Prius for a black Chevrolet Silverado club-cab, four-wheel-drive pickup.

The smell of cow manure on the breeze took him back to his childhood, walking across the yard, hand-in-hand with Dad, who'd been buried for seven years. Now, Zane walked alone, except for the dog, Elvis, the Australian Shepherd that had greeted him when he first returned. Marcia had named him after her favorite singer.

He shivered. Despite the calendar showing June, in the elevation of the mountains, it was chilly this time of morning. He didn't look forward to making the same walk in January; with the ground buried in snow and the early morning temperatures well below zero.

The lights were on in the milk barn. Levi was already there with Miguel, one of the farmhands, busy with the milking machines. Levi's dog, Skipper, curled up on an old blanket in the corner.

Milking cows was more automated now than before Zane left. Technology had made it easier. He hadn't forgotten the old way, when it took longer to milk each cow. Growing up, it took about three hours to finish the milking, but they had half the number of cows. Today, it took about the same amount of time to milk the herd and clean up. Then they would do it all again in twelve hours. In between there was tending to the crops, feeding the pigs and chickens, hay for the cows, collecting eggs, fence line repair, and other chores that would fill the day. Then repeat it all tomorrow. And the day after that. And the day after that. And the weeks and months would soon all look the same.

When the milking was done, Zane headed back into the farmhouse, Elvis at his heels again. Zane headed to town later to order paint from the general store so he could get to work on painting the house. Another task on the chores list.

The smell of bacon hit him as he walked through the door, and he realized how hungry he was.

"Morning, Mom, Sis," Zane said.

Marcia set a pitcher of orange juice on the table. He wondered if he'd ever get used to her bald head.

Mary Elizabeth was at the stove. "Eggs are about done," she said.

Zane washed his hands at the sink in the mudroom, then went to the kitchen and turned on the coffeemaker, another purchase he'd made in Vernal. He never drank coffee growing up. It was one teaching of his church to abstain from coffee, tea, alcohol, and tobacco. They called it 'The Word of Wisdom.' He'd discovered his love of coffee shortly after moving to California for college. Now back in his childhood Mormon home, he'd had to convince Mom to allow a coffee maker. As a compromise, he agreed to smoke his cigars on the porch and not in the house.

Levi joined them as he usually did for breakfast and lunch. Mom insisted he have some meals with her. It was better than always eating alone. The hired hands, who didn't live on the farm, had their own meals.

As they all sat at the table, Mom said, "Zane, would you like to bless the food?"

He sighed. "Will you ask me that every morning?"

"I will never give up hope that you'll return to the church, Zane."

"I'll bless the food," Mary Elizabeth said.

Mom and Mary Elizabeth bowed their heads and closed their eyes. Mary Elizabeth said, "Heavenly Father, we are thankful for this food that thou hast provided for us. Please bless it so that it will nourish and strengthen our bodies. Please bless those who prepared it and bless Mom so that she will soon fight off the cancer. In the name of Jesus Christ, Amen."

"Amen," Mom said. Zane and Levi said nothing.

As they ate, they talked about their plans for the day, as they did every morning. It didn't surprise Zane that Mom wanted to make a cake. Mary Elizabeth was going to do some cleaning around the house. Levi mentioned a hole in the chicken coop that needed to be patched. Zane told them he needed to order paint for the exterior of the house, get some chicken feed, and oats for the cows.

"Can you pick up a block of cheddar cheese for the tacos tonight?" Mary Elizabeth said.

Zane wondered how they would compare to the tacos back in California.

After breakfast, Levi headed out, and Zane did the dishes. Then he walked over to The Cottage, where Levi lived across the yard from the large family farmhouse. A light breeze rustled the large cottonwood and Norway maples planted by Zane's grandpa. The front door was open, so Zane knocked on the frame of the screen door.

Skipper barked and appeared at the door. "I'm a-comin'," Levi hollered in his heavy western accent.

"It's me, Levi," Zane called back.

"Come on in, Zane. I'll be right with ya."

It was the first time Zane had been inside the cottage since his return. He took two steps in and stopped dead in his tracks. After years of being a cop, there were signs that said to you, 'Something isn't right.' That sign was now glowing with neon and twinkling lights. It was definitely not what he expected for a sixty-year-old man. Bookcases lined every wall, all filled with Barbie dolls. Hundreds of them. The neon sign in his head flashed 'child molester.'

Levi walked into the living room and chuckled. "I see you spotted my hobby. You must have been a pretty good cop."

"It's impossible to miss. To be honest, it's not what I expected."

"No one does. I grew up on a remote ranch up near Big Piney. There were no boys close enough to play with, so I played with my four sisters."

"You . . . you don't actually still play with Barbies, do you?"

"Hell no. That would be weird. I collect them. Sometimes I resell them on eBay to other collectors. And if I took them out and played with them, well, that would make the box opened and they'd lose value."

Zane still had a creepy feeling. "How much are they worth?"

"Don't reckon I know. Never added them up. Some go for $25,000. The most valuable one has diamonds on it. I read that it's worth over eighty grand."

Zane's jaw dropped.

Levi continued, "I don't have any worth that much." He took one off a shelf. "This here's Pink Jubilee Barbie. She's the one worth the most. I'm thinkin' she'd bring about $2000. She came out in 1989 for Barbie's thirtieth anniversary. They only made 1200."

"How many do you have?"

"Three hundred and seventeen right now. I got eBay bids in on two more."

"I guess everyone needs a hobby." Zane didn't know what his would be now, but he was positive he wouldn't be a Barbie collector.

Levi said, "I reckon' you didn't come here to chew the fat."

"I'm about to go to town. I didn't catch if you needed anything."

"A spool of barbed wire. We need to fix that fence up at the back of the alfalfa field. I'll take care of the chickens and pigs and get some hay out for the cows while you're gone."

"Barbed wire. Check."

DESPITE THE JUNE DAY STARTING off chilly, the sun had warmed up the valley, and Zane rolled down the window of his truck. He missed his Prius and thought about the trip he and Jade had taken in it to San Francisco; going north on Highway 1 as it wound up the coast with amazing views of the ocean. They hit Hearst Castle and the Monterey Aquarium, Fisherman's Wharf, Coit Tower, Golden Gate Bridge, and ate amazing food in Chinatown.

He passed the entrance to the state park at the north end of Mathoni Lake, and the sun glistened off the water. Speedboats weren't allowed; only small fishing boats with paddles and outboard motors could go out on the lake. The fishing was good and there were lots of places for hiking, camping, and mountain biking.

Growing up, the farm was a good five miles away from town. Lots of new cabins now dotted the hills. They were inaccessible in winter except via snowmobiles or snowshoes. In the summer, they added to the number of tourists.

After he finished at the General Store, he wanted something to cool down from the heat. Zane put the purchases in his truck and then walked to Lou-Lou's Café for a chocolate marshmallow malt and some fries. He'd never found a place that made malts as good as the ones at Lou-Lou's. He sat on the same stool he had that first morning back. A high school girl, Emmie, from her name tag, took his order.

A short time later, Zane scooped a spoonful of his malt and noticed a black Land Rover pull up and park in front. Tiffany, got out of the passenger side. He'd run into her a couple of times since his return, and every time he saw her, his stomach flip-flopped just like it did when he was a teenager.

Tiffany screamed at the man who got out of the driver's seat. He was about six feet with light-brown hair. Zane assumed it was her husband, Will Massey. "I don't want a crappy dude ranch, Will. That's our home. I don't want strangers stomping around, making noise, causing a ruckus. Turning our lives upside down."

Will was much calmer. Zane couldn't make out what he said.

"No, I won't calm down. I don't care if people hear us. Call it what you want. It's really just a dude ranch for your rich friends. I've said from the start that I don't like the idea, but you continue to push it."

Will said something unintelligible.

"Stop. Just stop with the idea. It's not the money. We have more than we'll ever need. It's our home. Mine. Yours. The kids. You want a bunch of strangers wandering around. Then it won't be our home. It will be a hotel. I want a home."

Everyone at Lou-Lou's either stared or pretended not to be interested.

Will walked up to Tiffany, put his hands on her shoulders. She pulled back and slapped him. He stepped back, rubbed his cheek.

She stomped up to Lou-Lou's door and pushed it open. The bell tinkled. She continued in and sat at a booth, facing the door. She put her arms on the table, then her head on her arms, gasping for air as she cried.

The bell tinkled again, and Will came in, looked around, and headed over to Tiffany. He sat across from her.

"Tiffany."

"I don't want to talk to you."

"I'm sorry, honey."

"Go. Away," Tiffany yelled.

"Tiffany, let's go home and talk about it." He reached across the table and took her hand in his.

She pulled her arm away. "We've talked and talked." People stared at the couple. "I'm done talking."

Lou showed up at their table. "Will, I think you should leave."

Will looked up at him and then back at Tiffany.

"Now, Will," Lou said.

Will shook his head in disgust before he stood and walked out.

"You alright, Tiffany?" Lou asked.

She pulled a napkin out of the dispenser and wiped her eyes. "I will be."

"Let me know if you need anything," Lou said, then went back to the kitchen.

Zane stood, picked up his food, went to the booth, and slid

into the seat Will had just vacated.

She looked over at him and then put her head down on her arms. "Go away, Zane. This isn't your concern."

"I want to make sure you're okay."

"I'll be fine. Just go back to your lunch."

He leaned forward so that the other patrons couldn't overhear. "Tiffany, I don't really know what to say, other than I'm sorry you're going through this."

"There's nothing you can do about it. Please, just go back to the counter."

He got up to return to the stool, but she called him back.

Zane sat there for a few minutes.

She finally sat up, pulled more napkins from the dispenser, wiped her face, and blew her nose.

"Remember back in high school when we sat here in this same booth—our booth—dipping fries into our malts?" He slid his malt and fries toward her.

She took a fry, dipped it in the malt and ate it.

"Thank you, Zane. Really, I'm fine. I should go."

"Let me give you a ride home."

"No, I'll walk to my mom's and she can take me, but thanks." She stood and left.

Zane turned to watch Tiffany walk out and down the road.

He sat and thought about what had happened. Dude ranch? If he's as rich as everyone says, why does he need a dude ranch? Why was he so insistent?

Zane picked up a fry and went to dip it in ketchup and stopped. It was fry sauce, not ketchup. Fry sauce was just ketchup and mayonnaise, but people in Utah were crazy for it.

"Hey Emmie, can I get some ketchup? I never did like fry sauce."

AFTER THE EVENING CHORES WERE done and supper finished, the sun was setting as Zane, carrying a bottle, went to the kitchen and dropped two ice cubes into a glass, then took it and the bottle out to the front porch. He sat in the rocking chair, opened the bottle, and poured out two fingers of Elijah Craig

Single Barrel 18 bourbon. He took a sip and followed up with a satisfying sigh, then pulled a cigar and a cutter out of this shirt pocket, cut off the end of the cigar, and lit up.

"Ah, shit."

He left his cigar on the table and headed back inside. After a few minutes he returned with an empty can to use as an ashtray only to find Levi on the porch, leaning against the railing, Skipper sniffing around his feet.

"Your mom can't be happy about that." He waved his hand to indicate the cigar and bourbon.

"Mom and I have an understanding." Zane flicked the ashes off the cigar and into the can. "I keep the cigar out of the house, and she lets me have a coffee maker in the kitchen."

"Sounds reasonable." Levi took a leather pouch and a packet of rolling papers from his shirt pocket. He dropped some tobacco from the pouch onto the paper and then used his teeth to pull the cords on the pouch to close it up. He licked the long edge of the paper, rolled it over to seal it shut. Then twisted the ends, struck a match, and lit his cigarette.

"Gotta say, I'm surprised, Levi. Not many people roll their own cigarettes anymore. Want some of this bourbon?"

"Don't mind if I do. Neat."

"I see you're a true connoisseur."

Zane went to the kitchen for another glass. When he returned, he poured a shot for Levi. They sat and watched the shadows settle in, slowly turning into night, and listened to the cows and crickets. Zane took a deep breath. "It's been a long time since I smelled that."

"You mean smell the cow shit?" Levi said.

Zane laughed. "Yeah. That would be it."

They both looked up when the screen door squeaked. "Zane, are you out . . ." Mom stopped when she saw Zane and Levi on the porch with their tobacco and alcohol.

"Ev'nin', Mrs. Grayson." Levi said.

"Hey, Mom. Do you need some help with something?"

She looked around, either confused or worried about the smoking and drinking.

"What about the Word of Wisdom, Zane? You . . ."

"Mom, we have a deal, remember?"

"I worry about you, Zane. Not just here on earth but about eternity and the Plan of Salvation."

Levi downed the rest of his drink and handed the glass to Zane. "Guess I should be checkin' on my auction. Thanks for the snort." He and Skipper headed over to The Cottage.

"You let me worry about that, Mom. I gave up my life in California to be here and help you because it was important and the right thing. You should be able to accept that and allow me my pleasures."

"I just wanted to say goodnight."

"Night, Mom."

Elvis plodded up and laid at Zane's feet. Zane sat back and rocked, and listened to the cows bellow and thought about Tiffany's argument with Will. *I've never seen her so angry.* He wondered just how strong her marriage was.

Chapter 4

TUESDAY MORNING IT WAS TIME to head to Vernal for Marcia's chemo treatment. When she came downstairs, she was wearing a wig. Zane knew she was self-conscious about being seen in public with a bald head.

Zane held the front passenger door of Marcia's Jeep Wagoneer open for her, but she insisted she'd sit in the back seat behind the driver.

Mary Elizabeth whispered to him, "Mom would never tell you, but the seat belt on the passenger side rubs against the chemo port on the front of her right shoulder. Her bra strap hits it too."

They headed south for the hour drive to Vernal. As they climbed into the mountains from Mathoni, the trees quickly turned to sagebrush and junipers. Here and there, a dirt road headed off from the highway to a farm or cabin. Not long after they turned south onto US-191, both sides of the road for miles showed evidence of strip mining for copper, fluorine-fluoride, gold, iron, and lead.

On the way, they filled Zane in with more details of what would happen during the treatment. It would take about an hour. The doctors thought Marcia wouldn't need radiation, but a mastectomy would be required, followed by re-constructive surgery. Those would be done in Salt Lake City. It all sounded awful to Zane.

As they left the mines behind and dropped down the mountains into the Ashley Valley, there was one sign after another about ancient fossil beds that covered the area. Vernal was a stone's throw from Dinosaur National Monument and relied heavily on tourists in the summer.

The conversation morphed into chit-chat, and Mary Elizabeth brought up Zane's job. "You still haven't told us about why you suddenly retired other than there were some problems. What exactly happened? Not telling us makes it worse."

Zane was quiet for several minutes. *Did they have to keep bringing this up?* He decided they would not stop unless he told them. "You remember I told you about my girlfriend, Jade. Her ex, Tyrone, was a forensic tech. They'd had an ugly breakup. He couldn't let her go. He obsessed over her. They'd been split up for months before she and I got together.

"I was called to a murder scene. Tyrone was one of the forensic techs assigned to gather evidence. He thought if I were out of the way, that he could get Jade back. So he planted evidence at the crime scene and made it look like I had done it."

"That's awful. I'm so sorry you had to go through it."

"Thanks, Mom. I was on desk duty for months while it was investigated. Just the allegation hurt my career. It shouldn't have, because I was cleared, but some of the other cops didn't want to work with me afterwards. Even some of my superiors took it out on me. So, when it was over, I sued the city. They paid me a settlement and gave me early retirement with a full pension. Now I'm here."

"But what about Jade?"

"She couldn't deal with any of the bullshit . . ."

"Zane, language."

"Sorry, Mom. Jade couldn't handle it, and we split up. It all hurt me, and my anger is still there. I haven't talked to her for a long time. Since there was nothing for me in Santa Barbara and you needed help, it made sense to come back home."

Mary Elizabeth said, "How much was your settlement?"

"The agreement was sealed. I legally can't tell you, but it was substantial."

They soon passed Steinaker State Park and Reservoir, which signaled they were almost at their destination. Vernal is the closest "big" city to Mathoni. Big was relative. With a population of 10,000, it's ten times the size of Mathoni. Ashley Valley Medical Center was the trio's destination. After all the time that had passed, Zane wasn't surprised at the changes at the hospital. It looked as if it had been completely rebuilt. The old hospital had been brick and mortar. This one was glass and concrete.

They checked in at the front desk at the cancer clinic. A few minutes later, a nurse came out and said, "Marcia."

She stood, and the nurse took her back.

Zane was born here. His first memory of the hospital was when he was eight and had been thrown from a horse and broken his arm. Dad had carried him into the house. He lay on the living room floor, writhing in pain. Mary Elizabeth had said it looked like his hand was falling off. Looking back on it now, that seemed funny, but at the time it wasn't. The drive from Mathoni to the hospital had never taken so long. At first, he was ashamed of the cast as it meant he'd failed at riding the horse. Before he got it off, it became a badge of honor as it seemed everyone in town wanted to sign it.

After Marcia was led back to the treatment room, Mary Elizabeth changed seats to sit next to Zane and gave him a hug. "If you ever need to talk more about what happened with your job, I'm here."

"I'll be fine. I am fine. We just need to get Mom better."

"She will be. The Bishop gave her a blessing before you came home, and the doctors say the cancer is in remission."

He looked at his sister.

"Zane, that look has me worried. What is it? You're not sick too, are you?"

"We need to talk."

She looked at him, her eyebrows drawn together. "Please don't tell me you want to go back to California."

"No, it's not that. I have been thinking about the future.

Mostly mine and what I want to do now that I'm retired, but also about Mom and her future, if she beats this cancer."

"When she beats it. I know she will. She's always been a fighter. Remember when Dad had that first heart attack? Mom jumped in and ran the farm and nursed him back to health at the same time."

"I remember. His heart problems finally caught up with him. Mom's health will surely decline because of age." Zane rested his arms on his legs and leaned forward, his head bowed. He looked over at Mary Elizabeth. "This is really hard to say." He sat up again, ran his hand through his hair and exhaled. "I think she should sell the farm."

"But that's her home, Zane. She's been there for a long time."

"Hear me out. Mom's sixty-eight years old. She has a horrible disease. She can't run the farm much longer. If she sold it, she'd get more than enough for her to live comfortably for the rest of her life."

"Where would she go?"

"Maybe she could get a house in town. Or, move into a retirement community. Visit her sisters."

"I don't know. She loves that house, and there's no retirement home in Mathoni."

"But what happens when she can't take care of the farm anymore? Neil's not a farmer, and it would be an enormous change for your kids, so you won't want it. I don't want it. It's a better option to sell it now."

"She and Levi have been fine since Dad died."

"Levi isn't much younger than Mom. Just think about it. We won't rush into this. Mom has enough to deal with right now. If you agree, we'll talk to her about it when she's recovered."

Mary Elizabeth threw up her hands in surrender. "Alright, I'll think about it, but I can't imagine that I'll change my mind."

Chapter 5

THE MASSEY HOME AND RANCH sat on the leeward side of the hill, but even there the wind blew and whipped through the doorway of the barn. Will Massey walked over from his house and entered the barn. He stopped at a stall and offered a sugar cube to the horse.

"Hello, Will."

Will turned toward the voice. "I was going to call you later today for an update. Where are we?"

"I need more money, Will."

Will's brow furrowed. "What I've given you should be enough."

"But it's not. They're too set in their ways, and we only need one of them. More money will help."

"That's what you said last time—and yet, here we are," Will said.

"I thought it would be enough to sway them, but they're stubborn."

"How do I know you won't just keep it?" Will asked.

"You forget I know all your secrets. Yeah, I'll keep some of it, but I'll have even more if you succeed. That was our deal. You can't do it without my help."

Will laughed. "And I know your secrets. What's stopping you from asking for more money again, and we're still no closer to a satisfactory decision? Or that you'll just keep it all?"

"I'm telling you. I need more! Everyone has a price. I just haven't found their price yet."

"You found mine. It's what I already gave you. You'll have to make it work."

"The amount we've talked about is pocket change for you. Hell, you could give all the change that fell into your couch, and it would still be more than what I need. You won't miss any of it."

"I'm not giving you another penny, and that's final," Will said.

"I'm not asking for a penny."

Will turned and walked away.

"Come back here." Their breathing was noisy, palms sweaty. "You son of a bitch!" They grabbed the closest thing to use as a weapon, a hay hook that was hanging on a post, and ran towards Will.

Will screamed and stumbled as the hay hook impaled his shoulder. The attacker swung again and embedded the hay hook in Will's neck. As they pulled their arm back, a large piece of flesh tore from Will's neck. Blood spurted from the wound, the assailant, the post, a wall now covered in blood spatter. Will fell to the floor of the barn. Blood oozed from the hole in his shoulder and the tear in his neck.

The sight of blood. The smell of blood. The smell of death. The sense of dread. They all saturated the air. It had happened so fast. The horror of it all. No one in sight. "I'm safe."

Then the barn was quiet.

JACOB FAUST, THE RANCH FOREMAN, picked up a wrench and tightened the lug nuts on the ATV. He was almost finished fixing the flat tire and was ready to ride it out to check the herd.

A scream pulled him away.

He ran out of the work shed behind the barn, looked around, trying to locate where the scream came from. He ran to the front of the barn and he saw her. Tiffany, kneeling over a body.

Will was on the floor of the barn, a pool of blood under and around him. Tiffany was kneeling over the body. Jacob got her to her feet and out of the barn.

Her kids ran toward them. "We heard Mom scream. Is she alright?" They stopped when they saw her bloody clothes and looked toward the barn.

"Stop. Don't go in there," Jacob told them. "Go back to the house."

"Why is Mom covered in blood?" Ciarra asked. "Where's Dad?" Then, more urgent, "Jacob, where's my dad?"

Tiffany sobbed. Jacob led her back to the house, making sure the kids followed, then called the Sheriff and Tiffany's parents.

SHERIFF RICHARD RICHMAN ARRIVED SHORTLY after getting the call. He had been elected Smith County Sheriff almost two years earlier. His job consisted mostly of drunks, illegal drugs, domestic violence, and traffic citations. He'd never investigated a homicide. He'd never even heard of a murder in the valley, and he'd lived in Smith County most of his life.

Richman noted that the first deputy on site, Stuart Dodson, had put up yellow crime scene tape to mark off the area. Richman asked for a report.

"I got the call about twenty minutes ago. Came up here and found Mr. Massey over there, dead. So, I put up the crime scene tape and took some pictures with my phone."

Several ranch hands stood behind the tape. The sheriff told them all to wait in the house.

Richman entered the barn. The metallic smell of blood clung to the air. He took one look at the crime scene and threw up. Will Massey was definitely dead. Face down in a pool of his own blood. At least they assumed it was Will. Half of his neck had been torn off, there was another big gash in his shoulder, and blood was everywhere, not just pooled under the body, but spatter covered one wall of the barn.

When the Sheriff recovered, he said, "Stuart, what do you suppose could cause a wound like that?"

"Had to be something big, sharp. A scythe? Or one hell of a

knife."

"That could be." Richman went back in the barn and rolled the body over. "Yup, that's Will Massey."

"Sheriff, should you have done that?"

"What? Oh, probably not. I need to call the state M.E. and the Highway Patrol. Then talk to the family. Get some good pictures and be careful of the blood, and make sure you get some shots of the shoe prints leading away." Richman got back in his car and called on the radio. When he finished, he went to the house and rang the doorbell.

Jacob opened the door and directed Richman to the great room. Tiffany sat in the corner of a sofa, her legs pulled up to her chest, a box of tissues sat on the sofa next to her. Somehow she'd changed her clothes and washed the blood off her hands.

Ciarra, her eyes glazed over, snuggled up next to her mom. August and Vincent sat together in an oversized chair, tears flowing down their cheeks.

"Tiffany," the Sheriff said, "I'm so sorry about your husband."

She stared straight ahead, unaware of Sheriff Richman's presence.

"Jacob, why don't you call her parents? Tell her dad to bring his medical bag. Then I want to talk to you in another room— somewhere private," Richman said.

"I already called Dr. Needham. Let's go talk in the office."

Jacob led the sheriff behind the kitchen to an office. Richman, marveled at the size of the house and took in everything in sight. Richman turned two chairs to face each other, then sat in one and took a notebook from his pocket.

"Sit down. For the record, what is your full name?"

"Jacob Faust. No middle name."

"What exactly is your job here?

"I'm the ranch foreman."

The sheriff was all business. "How long have you worked here?"

"About two years."

"And where do you live?"

"We have a bunkhouse here at the ranch for the workers. I

have a one-bedroom apartment there."

"Workers? Plural? I'll need a list of their names later. For now, tell me what happened."

"I was out in the workshop and heard a woman scream. I thought she'd been killed herself from the sound of it. I didn't know where the scream had come from. When I ran around the barn, I saw her on the floor, bent over Mr. Massey. There was so much blood. The kids were there by then. I sent everyone into the house and helped Mrs. Massey in. She was covered in blood. August helped her change her clothes. She's been like that on the couch ever since."

"Where is the workshop?"

"It's behind the barn."

"And that would be the barn where Mr. Massey was found?"

Jacob nodded.

"Please respond verbally , Mr. Faust."

Jacob said nothing for several minutes.

"Take your time."

Finally, Jacob said, "Yes, that's the same barn."

The sheriff wrote some notes. "How long ago was this?"

"Maybe an hour?"

"And did you see or hear anyone in the barn with Mr. Massey or maybe a car driving away?"

"No, Sheriff. I didn't."

"What were you doing in the workshop?"

"One of the ATVs needed some repairs. I was working on that."

Richman looked at Jacob. "Anyone with you?"

"No. I was alone. Oh God, does that make me a suspect?"

"Only if you have a reason to kill your boss."

"Sheriff, I . . . no, I didn't kill him."

"Did Mr. Massey have an appointment with anyone?"

Jacob shook his head. "Not that I know of."

"Where was Mrs. Massey before she went to the barn?"

"I'm not really sure. It was about noon, so I assumed she was in the house making lunch."

Richman wrote more notes. "Now, I need you to think

carefully. Did Mr. Massey have any enemies?"

"Of course. Anyone with as much money as he has—had—will have enemies, and there were people here who didn't want him to build his guest ranch."

Sirens sounded in the distance.

"Who were they?"

Jacob scratched his chin. "Wayne Hubbard. He was worried about competition, but we were after . . . a different caliber of people. The county commissioners, Jared Snow and Lavell Bateman, opposed a zoning change to allow it and against the helipad. I imagine there were others in town."

"Where are Mrs. Massey's clothes now? I'll need them as evidence."

"In a plastic bag in the laundry room."

"Can you take me there?"

Jacob led the sheriff through the house and upstairs to the laundry. Richman picked up the bag, pulled out a pair of pants and a blouse, bra, and temple garments, all covered in blood. He returned them to the bag.

"Alright, Mr. Faust, I'll have more questions for you later. Right now, you'd best help take care of the family. I need to get back outside."

Sheriff Richman went back through the house and out to the barn. Two more deputies and the Highway Patrol had arrived.

"It looks like someone turned over the body," one of the Highway Patrol troopers said. "Did you do that?"

"The sheriff did."

"He shouldn't have done that."

"What shouldn't I have done?" Richman said as he returned to the barn.

"Disturb the body."

"I had to confirm the victim's identity." He handed the bag to Deputy Dodson. "These are Mrs. Massey's bloody clothes. Please find an evidence box for them."

"Just how many homicides have you investigated, Sheriff?" the other trooper said.

"Counting this one, a total of one."

A car arrived, and Tiffany's parents got out. Sheriff Richman went over and explained what had happened. They both rushed in to take care of grandkids and their daughter. Richman went back to continue the investigation.

One trooper, his hand on his pistol butt, said, "Sheriff, why did you call us in?"

"I haven't investigated a homicide. I need your expertise."

"Well, Sheriff, homicide is not within the Highway Patrol's purview. If you need help, we can call in the State Bureau of Investigation, but they'll have to send a detective from Salt Lake. The medical examiner will have to come from there too."

As they talked, an orange cat walked into the barn. It stopped and sniffed at the blood pool and lapped at it. It only took that one lap, then walked through the blood, leaving grisly, red paw prints on the floor.

"All right. I'll call the M.E. I would like you to help keep people out of the scene. I don't have the manpower. In the meantime, I'll talk some more with the family."

"We can help with that. Where exactly to you want us?"

"I don't want no looky-loos up here. Can you close off the driveway to the house?" The troopers got back in their cars and headed down the mountain to block the driveway.

Richman turned his attention to his deputies. "Dodson, Ambler, Snow, you all stay around here. Make sure we don't get any people or animals wandering around and don't touch anything. I want a bigger area cordoned off. I'll head in to talk to the family."

Back in the house, Richman saw Tiffany wasn't on the couch. "Where is Mrs. Massey?"

"Grandma and Grandpa came and took her upstairs," Ciara said. "They're still with her."

"That's good. We'll be here a while until help gets here from Salt Lake. If you think you can answer some questions for me, it will help. What was your mom doing before she went out to find your dad?" Richman said.

"Making lunch," August said.

"And before that?"

August said, "I dunno. I was texting with friends."

"What about the rest of you?"

Ciarra shrugged.

Vincent said, "I was playing my Xbox."

Sheriff Richman asked if they had seen anyone or heard anything earlier in the day, a car driving away or their dad talking to anyone. No one had.

Chapter 6

WHEN THE TREATMENT WAS DONE, Zane, his sister, and their mom drove down Vernal's Main Street, past the dozens of *Brontosaurus* statues spread around the city, all painted in bright colors, each one different. The biggest, Dinah, a forty-foot tall, pink Brontosaurus, stood on her hind legs, making a suitable welcome to visitors when they arrive at the east end of town.

Vernal's history differed from most of the cities in Utah in that it wasn't settled by the Mormons, and Zane had always been interested in the area's history. The Mormons had tried to settle the area when Brigham Young sent a group in the early 1860s, but they soon returned to Salt Lake City, after declaring the area was only good for nomads. In the same year, Abraham Lincoln declared part of the area would become the Uintah Indian Reservation. It was the late 1860s before Pardon Dobbs, an Indian agent, arrived and built the first permanent cabin. That brought in settlers. They called the area Ashley Valley after fur trader William Ashley, who trapped and hunted there in the 1820s.

The residents selected Ashley Center for the name of the town, but the U.S. Postal Department said it was too close to Ashley, a neighboring settlement, and told them the town would henceforth be called Vernal. History doesn't tell where that name came from.

Zane treated his family to lunch. Then a stop at Walmart for groceries. They had to stock up because it would be another three weeks before they came back. Sure, they could get some of what they needed from the General Store in Mathoni, but it carried a limited inventory, and the prices were better in Vernal.

Mom was none too happy when Zane said they had to stop at the State Liquor Store so he could get more bourbon. "What if someone I know sees us here?" she said as they pulled into the parking lot.

"They'll be just as embarrassed that they got caught too," Zane countered.

Marcia and Mary Elizabeth, both good Mormons, had no desire to go in, so Zane went alone and soon returned with a case of Elijah Craig Single Barrel 18.

On the road back home, Zane's phone rang. It was Tiffany's father, George Needham. Zane thought he sounded strange. Zane pulled over to the side of the road to take the call.

"I need your help, Zane. Will was murdered."

"Oh, my God!" Zane said.

Mary Elizabeth looked over at him.

Marcis, in the seat behind him, said, "Zane, watch your language."

He looked at her reflection in the rear-view mirror. "Sorry, Mom."

Stress, fear, shock. That explained why George sounded funny, Zane thought. "Take a deep breath, George. Tell me what happened."

Mary Elizabeth tilted her head and stared at Zane. He could see Mom in the mirror, leaning forward to hear the conversation.

"I'm so sorry, George. I'm on my way back from Vernal. I'll be there as soon as I can." He ended the call.

"What's happened? Is it Betty?" his mother said.

Zane said, "No, not Tiffany's mom. It's Will. He's dead. Someone killed him."

Mom and Mary Elizabeth gasped at the same time. Zane related what little he knew and said he needed to go to George's after he dropped them off at home. Silence gripped them the rest of the way.

TIFFANY'S FATHER, GEORGE NEEDHAM, HAD been the town's doctor longer than Zane could remember. His home, right in the middle of town, was red brick with his office and examination room on one end.

Zane was happy to see Betty answer his knock. In the years since his dad's funeral, her hair had turned white, and she still had her chubby cheeks, but the smile she'd always worn was now replaced with a frown. Her eyes were puffy and red. Zane doubted it was from allergies. She put her arms around him and hugged him tight.

Other than new furniture, the living room was much the same as he remembered it. Tiffany's kids sat on the sofa. They all looked shell-shocked. Even the comedy movie on the TV didn't lighten the mood.

"George will be right here," Betty said. "Tiffany is an awful mess. George said she's in shock. He's upstairs with her now. Let's you and I go in the kitchen to talk."

They sat at the table, and Betty explained to Zane how Tiffany had found Will on the floor of the barn. The sheriff had questioned all of them, which added to their anxiety. When they finally could leave, she and George had brought Tiffany and the kids to his home.

"I still don't know if they've given some dignity to Will and taken his body to the mortician in Vernal. They left him there on the floor of the barn for hours while the medical examiner came from Salt Lake." Her voice was heavy with disgust for the sheriff.

"It's the medical examiner who takes care of the victim, and every single one I've met is very respectful of the dead." Zane explained. He didn't have the heart to tell her it's standard procedure to do an autopsy on a murder victim before the mortician got the body.

George came in just as his wife finished. He stooped over a bit more than Zane remembered, and his hair had turned white but was still styled with the same flat-top cut he'd always had. Zane stood, and they shook hands, then George pulled him into a hug.

George sat in a chair, his arms on his knees, and put his head in his hands.

"How is she?" Betty asked.

George looked up. "Not good. I gave her something to help her sleep. Zane, I don't know what to do. Betty and I are supposed to go to the Missionary Training Center in a few weeks. I've been called as mission president in Tampa. I don't think we can leave right now."

"I don't envy your position, but why did you want me to come by, George?"

He looked over at Zane. "You were a cop. A good one, from what your mom told us. I'd like you to talk to the sheriff and find out what's going on."

"I doubt they'll tell me. It could compromise their investigation."

"Please," Betty said. "At least you can try."

"I'll do what I can, but don't count on much, if anything. How are the kids?"

"Scared, worried," Betty said.

"In shock," George added.

Zane said, "Have you talked to Will's family?"

"George called them," Betty said. "They live in Sacramento and will be here as soon as they can."

IT WAS DARK BY THE time Zane drove to the other side of the lake. A new moon didn't help. When he got to the driveway up to the Massey home, the Highway Patrol stopped him.

"Trooper," he looked at the name tag pinned to his shirt, "Larsen, I'm a friend of the family. Who's in charge of the investigation?"

Larsen shook his head. "I can't let you up there. The man in charge would be the Smith County Sheriff."

"Call him on your radio. My name is Zane Grayson. I'm a retired Santa Barbara, California, police detective. I have experience investigating homicides. I doubt the sheriff has any experience in that area. I can help." The trooper walked to his car and radioed the sheriff.

Larsen came back a couple of minutes later. "The sheriff is on his way down to talk to you."

Zane raised his eyebrows. He hadn't expected the sheriff himself to come down. He also knew that getting pulled off a murder scene to handle some wanna-be detective inserting themselves into the investigation would anger the investigator more than anything else, but he also thought his experience would be beneficial. Maybe the sheriff would see it too.

Twenty minutes went by before Zane saw car lights come down the driveway and stop near the Highway Patrol vehicles. Zane saw a man get out of an SUV and put on his cowboy hat, but he couldn't make out any real detail because of the darkness. He stopped and talked to Trooper Larsen, looked in Zane's direction a couple of times, then walked over to where Zane sat in his truck.

"Zane Grayson," the Sheriff said, "long time no see. I heard you were back in town to care for your ma."

Zane squinted to see better in the dark, but it wasn't until the sheriff was right next to the truck that he could see his face.

"Richie?" Zane's voice rose and his eyes widened. "You're the Sheriff?"

"Yes, I am. What's it been? Twenty-five, thirty years? I heard you were a cop out in California somewhere."

Richard Richman, Sheriff. He'd always been Richie growing up. His big brother, Sam, had been Zane's best friend. Sam and Zane had been close. They had played on the same sports teams, boy scouts, hiked, fished, hunted, and double dated. Now, here was the little brother. The kid who had often wanted to tag along and was such a geek in school. Small, scrawny, no athletic ability at all. The kid they teased and picked on. He was still on the short side—five feet, maybe six, seven inches—and thin, with a splash of a mustache.

"Richie, I can hardly believe it. Is Sam still teaching economics?"

"Yup, still a big college professor in Missouri."

"What about you? Ever marry?"

"Ugh. Unfortunately, that's an affirmative. Twice. Divorced them both. Before you ask, no kids, and I go by Rich now."

He'll always be Richie to me.

"Are your aunt and uncle still alive?" Sam and Rich were born in Rock Springs, Wyoming. When their parents died in an auto accident, they came to Mathoni to live with their aunt and uncle.

"They're still with us. When they got older, they'd had enough of the cold, snowy winters and moved to Phoenix. I'm kind of busy right now, so enough catching up. I hear you want to come up and help. I can't let you do that as you're not law enforcement in Utah and, from what I hear, not in California anymore either."

"You sure? I've had my share of homicide cases."

"I'm sure, Zane. Now why don't you mosey on home, take care of your ma, and get some sleep." He pointed down the road towards the Grayson house.

"Alright," Zane said. His shoulders slumped, and he stared at Richman for a moment. "What can you tell me?"

"We have one person dead. Nothing more is being released at this time. We're still in the early stages of our investigation."

Zane didn't want to let on that he'd talked to George. "Is Doc Needham still around? I'd have thought he'd be retired by now."

"He's still here. You know country doctors. They never actually retire."

"Yeah, I do. Congratulations on your election. I always thought you'd be a computer programmer." He stuck his arm out of the window, and he and Richman shook hands. Then Zane drove back to town, but his mind didn't rest. Thoughts of murder, blood, and Tiffany swam around.

George and Betty were disappointed when Zane stopped and told them he had nothing new to report. Zane's mother and sister were a different story. Even though it was well past midnight when he got home, they were awake and eager for some news. He told them what he'd learned from George and Betty and about being rebuffed by the sheriff.

When the two women headed upstairs to bed, Zane went out to the porch with his bourbon and cigar. He downed a drink. He thought about Tiffany, George, Betty, the kids, and Will. That fight on the street. *Do I still have feelings for her? The Tiffany I remember would never kill her husband.*

He poured another drink and downed it. Then another. Then he sat and nursed another one, thinking about everything. *What would things be like I were still in California with Jade?*

Chapter 7

IT WAS MID-MORNING ON WEDNESDAY before Zane crawled out of bed. He tried to stand but was shaky and stumbled. He rubbed his eyes as he shuffled into the bathroom for an aspirin. The last time he was this hungover was after internal affairs accused him of planting evidence and then suspended from duty. He shook four tablets out of the bottle and downed them with a glass of water. After he showered, shaved, and dressed, he went downstairs.

Mom put down her knitting and took off her glasses, letting them dangle from the chain around her neck. "Are you feeling ill, Zane? You look terrible. Maybe I should call Doc Needham." She stood and headed to the kitchen. "I'll just get you some breakfast."

"I'll be fine, Mom. The murder and all got to me last night, and I drank too much."

Zane waited a moment for his mom to chide him about abstaining from alcohol, but when she didn't, he said, "Sit back down, Mom. I want to stop at Lou-Lou's and find out what the town's rumor mill says about Will's murder. I'll grab breakfast there."

She sighed and sat again. "Keep me updated." She put her

glasses on and went back to her knitting as Zane walked out.

The late breakfast crowd packed Lou-Lou's, forcing Zane to find a parking spot down the road. A line snaked out the door, and Zane queued up to get inside. Even the checker players, Emmett Young and Charlie Snow, who seemed to always be there at the same table, waited in line.

The primary topic of conversation for the group was the murder of William Massey. Most people, from what he could hear, had already determined Tiffany guilty of the murder of her husband. A few thought it was an intruder. Zane just stood quietly and listened in on the conversations.

"It's always the wife," said a short, bald man with a high-pitched, nasal voice. He stood sideways in line in front of Zane.

"Then why haven't they arrested her?" That, from the woman Zane assumed was the bald man's wife.

"Ha!" Baldy said. "That's easy. M-O-N-E-Y. She has it. I'll bet she used it to pay off the sheriff. Rich people always get away with it."

Zane shook his head in disbelief and looked at Baldy.

Baldy noticed. "You think she didn't off him? She's a rich bitch," he said, poking Zane in the chest with his index finger.

"Rich, yes," Zane said.

"Ah…but now she has all of it. Yup. M-O-N-E-Y."

Zane shrugged and stepped out of the way for a family of four that came out of Lou-Lou's. The smell of bacon and coffee wafted out the door with them, and Zane's stomach rumbled.

Baldy wouldn't let up. "Oh, you don't think so?"

"Frank," his wife said, "that's enough. Stop it. You're upsetting the man."

Zane wasn't sure what Frank would do, so he planted his feet on the ground, ready for whatever Frank sent his way. "For one, the Sheriff has things well in hand," Zane said. He wasn't sure if that was correct or not, but he wasn't about to let Frank Baldy win this.

"Oh, look at Mr. Know-it-all. Thinks he has all the information."

"Small town. Word gets around."

"Well, la-di-da, Mr. Smarty Pants," Frank continued to heckle.

"Frank. Stop. Now." It was the wife again.

"Dorcus, don't get me started with you too," Frank said, shaking a finger at her.

The line moved forward a bit as two more people went in. Zane's stomach rumbled again, and he was grateful his mom had eaten breakfast earlier, so she didn't have to stand in the line.

Zane pushed his cowboy hat back so he could see better and continued, "I know a thing or ten about how an investigation works. I used to be a homicide cop. Retired now."

"Used to be. Used to be. That ain't no good. Used to be. A has-been is more like it. You don't even look close to retirement age."

Dorcus spoke up again. "Frank, if you don't stop, I swear I'll get back in the car and drive home. Without you."

"Best listen to the lady," Zane advised.

"I mean it, Frank," Dorcus said.

"I mean it, Frank," he said in a high-pitched voice, mocking his wife.

That was enough for Dorcus. She pulled her purse straps up onto her shoulder and marched down the street.

"Dorcus? Dang-it Dorcus!" Frank raced after her. "Dorcus. Honey. I'm sorry," his voice was now a high-pitched whine.

Zane laughed. Loud and hard. He wanted Frank to hear it.

With Frank and Dorcus gone, Zane moved up two places. He could hear Gussie Aiken and Zelpha Wells.

"We've both known Tiffany since she was a baby," Gussie said. "Can you imagine her a murderer?"

"No, I can't," Zelpha replied. "That's why I think there was someone there to rob them. Will caught him, and the robber killed him."

The line moved forward.

"Burglar, not robber," Zane said.

The two women turned around and looked Zane up and down.

"Oh, my goodness," Zelpha said. Then she said to Gussie, "See, I told you Zane was back in town, but you didn't believe me."

Gussie said, "What do you think, Zane?"

"I think there's a lot of gossip and few facts."

"You know, he's right, Gussie. All these people here are spreading rumors that Tiffany killed poor Will," Zelpha said.

"They should be ashamed of themselves," Gussie added.

Zane smiled and nodded. He knew they'd never admit they too were part of the rumor mill.

Fifteen minutes later, Zane was inside. The talk was the same as out on the street. The buzz was loud and all about the murder. Some tables claimed Tiffany was guilty. Others that she was innocent. Still others with a split decision. Zane took the only open stool at the counter. When Louise came to take his order, she and Zane talked about it.

"Tell me the truth, Hun. Did Tiffany kill Will?"

"I don't know. My gut and my head," he tapped the side of his head with his index finger, "tell me she's innocent."

"So, we have a killer around town? Are we safe?"

"I haven't thought about it that way, but there's a good chance we do, and yes, I think we're safe."

Louise sighed with relief. "Then if it wasn't Tiffany, my money's on Wayne Hubbard."

"Who's that?" Zane asked.

"He owns the dude ranch down the south side of town past the new county jail."

"Why do you think he did it, Louise?"

"'Cause William Massey wanted to build a dude ranch up on his property. Give Wayne some competition."

Zane rubbed his chin. "Huh. I didn't know there was a dude ranch here. What do you know about this . . . Wayne Hubbard, is it?"

"Nice guy. Goes to church when he doesn't have customers. Came here about the time your daddy passed on. I think he said he was from Roosevelt. Bought some land. Setup his ranch."

"But would he kill someone? That's the big question," Zane said.

"He seems like a nice guy, but I've watched lots of *Law &*

Order. The killers there seem like nice guys, and that's New York, where people are pushy."

Zane chuckled. "Louise, don't take what you see on TV for how cops work—or bad guys either. Now how about some coffee, bacon and eggs, over-medium?"

After Louise brought his coffee, the man on the next stool struck up a conversation. "So, you ain't sure that little lady offed her hubby," he said. "You got some evidence of that?" His voice was deep with a Western accent.

Zane took a sip from his cup and stared straight ahead. He didn't want to get into another discussion about the murder.

"Mister, I's a talkin' to you," the man said.

"So you are, but I don't see where my opinion matters to you."

"And what if my opinion's the same as yours?"

Zane looked at him for the first time. Years of too much sun had tanned and leathered the man's face. He had neatly trimmed his gray and white hair. "Then we're just two guys, here for breakfast, whose opinions don't matter."

The man slammed his hand down on the counter. The dishes rattled a little, startled by the man. Zane jumped too. The other diners stopped talking and looked over at them. "Damn, if you ain't good at philosophizin', Mister."

"Just stating the obvious—and the truth." Zane still didn't look at him.

"Well, Mister," the man hit Zane on the arm with the back of his hand, "you got a way of talkin' some sense. I don't think she done it either. She's too pretty a filly to do somethin' like that."

Zane held his cup millimeters from his lips. "Do you have some evidence of that?" Then he grinned.

"Damn, Mister, if you ain't got some intelligence. I ain't got no evidence, but I knows that family. Mrs. Massey. Ain't no way she done it."

That got Zane's attention. He set down his cup and looked at the man.

"You know the family? How's that?"

"I worked for 'em last year. Ran cattle. That lady's the nicest person you ever knowed. Now, Mr. Massey, he was fine most the time, but get him riled and he'd—well, I'll just say you didn't want to get him riled up."

"What's your name?"

"Homer. Homer Bass."

Zane put out his hand to shake. "Pleased to meet you, Homer Bass. I'm Zane Grayson."

"Grayson. I knowed a Martha Grayson. She ain't your mama, is she? And if I were a guessin', and I am, your pa was a fan of great western literature."

"You got me pegged, Homer. My mom's name is Marcia, and you got my dad right. He was a big fan of Zane Grey, though he liked Louis L'Amour better. He always told me that L'Amour Grayson didn't have a good ring to it, so Zane it was."

Bass laughed. "Your daddy was right. Shit, I didn't even knowed Mrs. Grayson had a boy. How come I ain't seen you around then?"

"Just moved back from California. Why don't you work for Massey now?"

"You might say I growed tired of the cattle business and retired."

Louise arrived with Zane's breakfast. "More coffee, Homer?"

"No thank you, ma'am. I should mosey on and let Zane here eat those vittles. See you around, Zane, ma'am." Homer threw some cash on the counter to pay for his meal, tipped his hat at her, and walked out.

Zane ate his breakfast and thought about what Homer had said. William Massey had a temper. Could he have gotten into an argument with someone? An argument with someone who killed him? Is someone in town a killer? Or was he from somewhere else?

"Zane, you want more coffee? Zane? Zane!"

"Geez, Louise. You startled me."

"I must have asked you three times, Hun. You want more coffee?"

"Yeah, thanks.'

Louise refilled his cup and then turned away to put the pot back on the warmer.

"Hey, Louise, tell me about Homer."

"You don't find them like Homer anymore. Raised to be a real gentleman. He always calls me ma'am or Mrs. Kloepfer."

"So he's honest, too?"

"I never heard anything bad about him, so I suspect so. Why?"

Zane mostly ignored her question. "Did you ever know Will Massey to argue or see him angry or upset?"

"You mean other than the other day when he and Tiffany were having it out on the street here? I've seen him angry many times. He was one of those men who, if you saw him like that, get out of his way. Would take it out on anyone and everyone."

Zane took a sip from his cup. "Huh. Thanks, Louise."

"That's it? I don't get more than 'huh'? What did Homer tell you?"

"Nothing really. I'm just thinking."

"If you want thinking, I'll tell you what I think. You don't get that rich without making enemies. I think he crossed some business acquaintance and was killed for it. When he started talking about his dude ranch, it made Wayne Hubbard an enemy."

Zane shrugged. "Guess it could have been. Richie will figure it out. Not my job anymore." He took another sip of coffee and looked straight ahead.

Louise shook her head and walked away.

But even a retired cop thinks about crimes, and now Zane's thoughts were on the murder. Not just about Tiffany and the Sheriff, but now he had this Wayne Hubbard character who may have felt Will's plans threatened his business. Maybe Louise was right. Was there someone in Will's past who got their revenge?

Chapter 8

IT WAS EARLY AFTERNOON BY the time Zane finished breakfast and drove up to Tiffany's house. He was surprised but pleased to find the Highway Patrol gone. The security gate was also open.

The long driveway wound through a hollow and back behind a hill. From the road, the house was hidden from view. As he went around a bend, the house came into view. Zane marveled at its size. He estimated it was at least 15,000 square feet. All rock and wood, it looked like it belonged at a ski resort.

He walked to the front door. An orange cat lounged in a sunny spot on the porch. Zane rang the doorbell. "Hello," he called. No one answered. He tried the front door. Locked.

Zane walked around the outside. Swimming pool. Five-car garage. Huge patio and balcony. He checked the back door and found it locked.

Off to one side was the barn with a small building and another large one behind it. Zane did not know what they were. One end of a piece of yellow crime scene tape, tied to a tree, flapped in the wind. He looked around, but no deputies were keeping guard. The sheriff had finished processing the scene.

The place was eerily quiet. Why was there no one around?

Had the sheriff just left and people hadn't returned yet? He figured Tiffany was still at her parents' house with her kids. A murder victim's family rarely wants to stay in the house where the crime was committed. Where were the ranch hands? He could see cattle on the hill. Were they out with the herd?

Inside the barn, he looked at the bloodstain on the concrete floor. The spot where William had died. Zane squatted down to look at it. He imagined the body on the floor, the blood pooling around and under it. A cat had walked through the blood while it was still wet, the tracks heading to the back. *The cat by the front door?* The coppery smell of blood was still in the air.

Zane followed the blood spatter across the floor, up one of the support posts, and onto one wall. He took pictures of it all with his cell phone.

From the blood pattern, Zane assumed Will had been stabbed. He acted out the role of the attacker, swinging his arm forward, mimicking how he thought the killer had done it. He pulled his arm back, and imagined how the blood flew from the weapon and created the spatter, then hit again but this time, based on the spatter pattern, with more of a sideways pull back.

The attacker would have been covered in blood. As far as he knew, no one had been arrested. *Did the sheriff find any bloody clothes? How did the attacker escape?*

Bloody shoe prints headed out of the barn. There wasn't much texture on the shoe prints, so likely the shoes had a flat sole with a heel. *Maybe cowboy boots?* From their size, he assumed the killer was a man, but they could belong to anyone. He walked next to the prints. The person's stride was shorter than Zane's, so not as tall as his six feet two frame. He took pictures of the shoe prints.

He followed the path out of the barn, where the shoe prints stopped at tire tracks in the dirt. Straight treads, so not an off-road vehicle like a truck or SUV. He took more pictures.

Zane headed back inside and took some wide-angle pictures of the crime scene, then more of the blood spatter on the wall and post.

Had the killer been lying in wait for Will to come out to the barn? Or did Will meet someone here, have an argument, and then the killer attacked? Perhaps Will surprised a prowler. He looked around for a possible weapon that the sheriff may have missed. A single hay hook hung on a post nearby.

He took his leather work gloves from his back pocket and wished they were latex. He pulled them on, picked up the hay hook and examined it. There was no sign of blood. *This wasn't the murder weapon.* Bales of hay were stacked at the back of the barn. He checked out the stack, where he found two hay hooks stuck in one bale. Zane looked them over but found nothing suspicious.

He also looked over the pitchfork, hoe, and shovel, anything that could have been used as a weapon and create the blood spatter patterns. He wondered if the Sheriff had the murder weapon and exactly what it could be.

Zane walked the entire crime scene again, searching for evidence the Sheriff might have missed, but he found nothing.

A SHERIFF'S VEHICLE SAT IN front of the Needham's house when Zane pulled up. George opened the door and invited Zane in. They went to the kitchen and sat at the same table as the night before.

"Tiffany's in my office with the Sheriff," George said. "Betty took the kids to Vernal. We thought it would help to get them away for a bit. Will Junior is in Chile on his mission. I called Salt Lake and asked them to send him home for the funeral."

"I was surprised when Tiffany told me she had a boy on a mission. She's too young to have a kid that age."

George chuckled. "She's only a year younger than you are."

"You're right. With no kids of my own, I hadn't thought through the age thing. I feel very old right now."

"Now you know how I feel, having a grandson that age," George said.

"I was just up at Tiffany's home and no one was around. Felt creepy."

"The Sheriff told me they were done. I guess Jacob and the other ranch hands aren't back there yet."

"How long have they been in there?" Zane tilted his head toward the closed door to George's office area.

"Over an hour."

Zane thought through the questions he'd ask if he were in charge. They weren't pretty questions either.

Can you walk me through your day yesterday?

Did Will have any enemies who hated him enough to kill him?

What about employees? Former employees? Do any of them hold a grudge?

How are your finances? Although if rumors were true, he knew the answer to this one.

Did you and your husband argue about anything? He definitely knew the answer to this one.

Where were you at the time of death?

Was anyone with you?

How was your marriage?

Was he cheating on you?

Were you cheating on him?

It's always difficult to question the spouse of the deceased. They're not in a good place emotionally, physically, mentally. Statistics showed the killer is almost always family. You can't rule out the spouse until you have evidence to do so. Often enough, the evidence points back to the spouse. The questions have to be asked.

He finally spoke up. "Did the sheriff tell you anything?"

George slumped down. "Only that they believe Will was stabbed. His body's been taken to Salt Lake for an autopsy."

"Based on the evidence I saw in the barn, I think the Sheriff is correct."

"Thank you for looking into Will's death. I knew you'd agree to help. I just knew it."

"I just took a quick look. I came back to Mathoni to help my mom, not to be a cop again."

Tears ran down George's cheeks. "I don't know what to do. Will was a good man. A good husband. A good father. But now —" He trailed off and looked into the distance. He wiped his eyes with a handkerchief and then pleaded, "Zane, we need your help. Please."

Zane rested his elbows on the table, his forehead in his hands, and let out a big breath. "I'd like to help, but I can't do anymore than what I've done. Tiffany should get a lawyer. He'll have people who can investigate."

Zane understood George's desperation. He'd seen it in every homicide he'd investigated. The thought of a family member in prison for the rest of their life was devastating. He wished he could help both George and his mom.

George blew his nose. "Alright Zane. I trust you to tell us what's right. It's just that on TV the spouse is always arrested. I can't believe Tiffany would murder Will."

Zane leaned forward, arms on the table. "It's true that family members are usually the killer, but I don't think Tiffany did it and if the Sheriff is any good at his job, he'll see that too." Did he really think that or was it his hope? Then he continued, "The fact Tiffany hasn't been arrested tells me there's no evidence against her."

Sheriff Richman chose that moment to walk back into the room.

Richman said, "Unfortunately, Zane, it's not that simple. You should know that, after your time in the police department in California."

"You can't be serious. There's no way she killed her husband. She doesn't have it in her," Zane said.

"How could you know?" Richman said. "You haven't seen her in what, twenty, thirty years? People change. But then, maybe you know she didn't do it because you killed Mr. Massey."

"I wasn't even in town," Zane said. "And why would I? I never met him. I grew up with Tiffany. Hell, we both did. We both know her. She did not kill her husband. A good cop shouldn't be blind to other suspects. I've seen what happens to investigations when detectives hyper-focus on one suspect."

"You know that?" Richman said. "Is that from personal experience?"

Zane gritted his teeth. "No, it is not. My cases had a high clear rate. Every single one was a good investigation and a clean collar."

"But you're not a cop now," Richman said. "You are entitled to your opinion, but *I'm* investigating, not you. That's good because while you tell me not to rule anyone out, that's exactly what you did, and I might say, with no evidence."

Zane sat there with his mouth open, not sure how to respond.

"Now, if you'll excuse me," he continued, "I have actual police work to do that doesn't include idle speculation." He walked out.

"Zane, please do something," George pleaded.

"The only thing I can do right now is talk to Tiffany."

TIFFANY SAT ON A COUCH in what was once Doc Needham's waiting room, her eyes red and swollen, nose runny, hair uncombed. When Zane sat next to her, she looked over at him and managed a brief smile.

"You didn't need to come," she said, barely a whisper.

"I know, but I wanted to find out how you're holding up."

"Oh Zane," she leaned over against him and cried. He put an arm around her.

A nervous silence between them hung in the air. After a few minutes, Tiffany was more composed. "Zane," still a whisper. "I don't know what I'm going to do. I didn't kill him, but Sheriff Richman thinks I did."

"Tiffany, I believe you. The Sheriff needs to look at everyone, and they know you argued with him about the dude ranch."

"But I didn't kill him. I'd . . . never . . . ." she broke down and cried again.

Zane waited until she'd recovered. "What exactly did he ask you?"

She looked up at him. "Can you help me? Find who really," she sniffled, "did this?"

"I'm not a detective anymore."

"But you were once. You know how to find out who did this. Richie does not know how to solve this."

"What did he ask you?"

She went through the questions the Sheriff had asked her. When they'd finished, Zane said, "From what you've told me, he doesn't have evidence except a very public argument. If he had, he would have arrested you."

Tiffany sat up and looked at him. "You really think so?"

"Yes, I do."

Tiffany smiled and hugged Zane. "Thank you. That helps me feel better."

"I just talked to your dad about this, it's important. You should get a good attorney. Someone from Salt Lake who defends homicide suspects. This is just in case. My advice is to say nothing to the sheriff unless you have your attorney with you. I'm sure they'll talk to you again."

She nodded. "But I still want you to investigate. You can talk to the sheriff and find out what he knows."

"I'm not a licensed detective. Plus, they won't tell me. It's an open case, and if they tell me anything, the entire case could be compromised."

She laid her head on his shoulder. "Okay."

"But I'll be here for you. If you just need to talk through things. Anything at all."

The silence enveloped them again.

"I'm glad you're here."

"I'll support you as much as I can, Tiff."

"Nobody's called me that in a long time. Will always called me Tiffany." Tears rolled down her cheeks. She pulled a tissue from a box on the end table and blew her nose.

Zane's cell phone rang. He looked at the screen and answered. "Hi, Sis . . . Yes, I know . . . How is she . . . I'll be there as soon as I can."

"Mary Elizabeth needs some help with Mom. Red week is starting."

Tiffany looked at him as if he were speaking Klingon.

Zane thought about when he first returned and had to learn the lingo. "Red week. For about a week after chemo treatment, she has a rough time."

"Thank you. I feel better."

"Let's get you out with your dad before I go. Get some fresh air and food. A shower will help. I know it will be hard, but your kids need you to stay strong."

As they walked out of the office, they could hear voices from the living room. A man and a woman sat on the sofa. Zane didn't know the man, but the woman was his mom's cousin Ruby.

George introduced them. "Zane, have you met Bishop Brough? And you know Sister Bingham, Ruby. She's the Relief Society president."

Bishop. Leader of the local church congregation. His job to console and counsel. Zane shook hands with the bishop and gave Ruby a hug.

"It's nice to meet you, Brother Grayson," the Bishop said. "We came by to see what we can do to help the family, and Sister Bingham brought some dinner over."

"I'm sure you're a comfort to them, Bishop," Zane said.

George spoke up. "Zane was a police detective out in California. We were just asking him to look into Will's—" He took a handkerchief out of his back pocket and wiped tears from his eyes and blew his nose again.

"That's mighty nice of you, Brother Grayson," Bishop Brough said. Zane wished he wouldn't call him that, but said nothing about it.

"I haven't agreed to help. I came back to Mathoni to help Mom. I was just on my way out. It was nice to meet you. Good to see you again, Ruby."

"Tell your mom we're praying for her," Ruby said.

"I will."

The bishop stood and shook Zane's hand. "Please tell your mother hello. I hope to see you at church on Sunday."

Zane wanted to tell him that wouldn't happen, but he just gave some goodbyes and walked out the door.

MARY ELIZABETH WAS TALKING TO her daughter over FaceTime when Zane walked in the kitchen and peeked over her shoulder. "Hi, Olivia."

"Uncle Zane! I can't wait to see you. We'll be there soon to visit. Can you teach me to ride a horse while we're there?"

"Sure, can do. I'll find out from your mom when you'll be here. We have a very sweet horse, Belle, that will be perfect for you."

"Okay, Olivia. Uncle Zane and I need to cook dinner. See you soon. Love you." Mary Elizabeth ended the call.

"So, everyone is coming out?" Zane said.

"Yes. As soon as Neil can get time away scheduled. Likely next week. They'll be here a few days." She looked at Zane. "Then I'm going back with them."

"Uh, all right. I should have the routine down by then."

"Zane, I need you here. You were gone all day today."

"I needed to make sure everyone is—surviving."

"That's a strange way to say it. But, how are Tiffany, her kids, and parents?"

"Betty took the kids to Vernal to get them away from all of it for the day. The oldest is in Chile on a mission. George called the church to see about bringing him home. Tiffany, however, is not so great."

"What does the sheriff know?"

Zane went through the information he had.

"Don't get involved, Zane. Mom needs you here."

"I told them no. I'm not a cop anymore. What's up with Mom that you called me?"

Mary Elizabeth replied, "I just needed you home to help with supper"

They got through the meal, and Marcia settled in for the night. Then, Zane went onto the porch with his bourbon and cigar. *What if Mom doesn't survive? What will I do then?* But his thoughts weren't just on his mom. *George wants me to help Tiffany, but how can I do that and still care for Mom?* Deep down, he didn't know what he should do.

Chapter 9

ZANE STILL DIDN'T KNOW WHAT to do early Thursday morning. He was here to help his mom, but if he got involved in Will's murder investigation, it would mean he might not be home if she needed him.

Zane's best time for thinking had always been while fishing at the lake. Back in high school, he'd been a star guard on the basketball team and received several scholarship offers to play in college. Growing up, he'd been taught that serving a church mission for two years beginning at age nineteen was expected. He'd gone to the lake to figure out what to do. In the end, he took the offer from Long Beach State, which is how he ended up in California. It was hard to tell his parents, his bishop, and his ward members. It was even harder to tell Tiffany that he was going to play basketball instead of going on a mission.

After breakfast, Zane dug through the fishing gear in the garage. It was dust-covered, and probably hadn't been touched since his dad passed. He took his dad's pole, along with an old wicker fish basket, and the tackle box. Then he drove to Mathoni Lake State Park at the north end of the lake. When he was eight or nine, he'd ride his bike down there, the click, click, click of playing cards in the spokes of his bike tires carrying him along, a fishing basket slung over his shoulder, and fishing pole in hand.

The park was busy when he got there. Every campsite was taken, but that didn't surprise him. It had always been this way. The park had grown over the years. More sites had been added. A new park office had been built in the spot where just an old camp trailer had stood all those years ago. Now, a concession stand to rent fishing boats, canoes, and sell fish bait was next to the park office. It wasn't more than a shack with a window to conduct business.

Zane walked up to the window and knocked on the glass.

A man opened it. "How can I help you?"

Zane guessed the man was about thirty. He had greasy, brown, shoulder-length hair and a scraggly beard. An unlit cigarette balanced between his lips as he talked. Pinned to his shirt was a plastic name tag. 'Lance' was written on a piece of masking tape, then stuck to the tag.

"I could use a dozen night crawlers," Zane said.

"Sure. Sure." Zane smelled tobacco on Lance's breath.

"I haven't been here in years," Zane said. "How's the fishing been?"

Lance turned back to the window. "Been alright, I guess. Some people catch fish. Some don't."

Zane couldn't find anything wrong with that logic. "How about today? People have any luck?"

"Oh, I suspect some are and some aren't."

"Can you recommend any place where the fish are biting?" Zane said.

"Well, not exactly. Some places are good and . . ."

"And some aren't," Zane said, before Lance could get it out.

Lance clicked his tongue. "Right on."

Zane paid for the worms, then turned to go back to his truck.

"Hey, Mister," Lance called to him. "I hear the fishing is good down at the other end of the lake."

"Thanks, Lance."

Zane got his gear from his truck and ignored Lance's advice. He walked to the east end of the park. He figured Lance had probably sent enough people to the south end of the lake that he would try elsewhere—his favorite spot where he fished as a kid.

He walked next to the lake for another twenty minutes to the place his dad had always called The Grotto, where the lake kind of bulged toward the mountain. The fishing there had always been good.

Zane sat on a stump and put a leader on the end of the line, then attached a bobber and the hook. He took a night crawler from the box he got from Lance and put it on the hook. Then he cast out.

He hadn't been fishing since high school, and he wasn't sure if the line in the reel was any good as the gear had sat in the garage for years, but the cast was perfect. So far, the line seemed to hold. He sat on the stump to wait.

While he loved the time thinking, he also hated the requirement to stay quiet. You must not make too much noise for fear you'll scare the fish. You can't read or pay attention to anything else because you might miss a fish biting your hook, and it will take off with the rod and reel.

Often his dad or grandpa fished with him, sometimes both. Those were wonderful days for a boy. He'd walk along the shore with his dad, who taught him how to get the line ready, the best way to get the worm on the hook so it would still wiggle in the water.

"That's the real secret," Dad told him. "You've gotta make sure you get the worm on just right. It has to wiggle around so the fish see it and think they can have a tasty dinner. Not that we want to eat worms, but the fish here in this lake love them."

And then the bobber would bounce up and down to let you know a fish had thought exactly what Dad had said. That's when you had to act. Pull the line just right and set the hook, then reel it in. Then let out some line. Play with the fish. Let it think it could get away. Reel it in a bit more each time.

It didn't take much to wear down a trout. If you set the hook right, you could reel in the fish every time. Dad was a master fisherman. To a little boy, your dad is a master at everything.

Since you couldn't do anything else, this was a good time to think. That's what Zane did. Tiffany back in high school. Tiffany now. Will's murder. Marcia and her damn cancer. Life in

California.

The reel sang. He didn't know how else to describe it. He had a fish on his first cast in years. The fish pulled the line. Zane pulled back hard to set the hook, turned the handle to reel the fish in. He did as Dad had taught him those many years ago. He let out some line, then reeled in again. It took only a few minutes to get that beauty. Probably a two or three pounder. He took it off the hook and put it in his basket. Then, he started over again with a new worm.

An hour later, all he had to show for his work were two fish. He moved around the Grotto to another spot and went to work again.

He watched a canoe float by. Two teenage girls were on board, neither wearing a life vest, and both struggling to paddle with little success. It looked easy, but the person in front had to get the strength, length, and depth of the strokes even on each side of the canoe. The person in back had to compensate and paddle to steer at the same time. The two girls obviously didn't know this. They yelled, each blaming the other for the zigzag route across the lake.

"You splashed me," the back girl yelled.

"Only because you can't steer," the other shouted in response.

The girls screeched their frustration and yelled at each other.

Zane turned around for a moment to get his water bottle when he heard a splash. He looked out at the lake. The girls had capsized the canoe and were in the water. They screamed in terror, trying unsuccessfully to use their paddles as flotation devices. Zane realized they were further away from him now. He dropped his pole, pulled off his boots and socks, and ran towards the water.

There was another splash, and Zane saw someone swimming toward the girls from a different direction. He gasped, the freezing water pulling out every bit of air from his lungs. His instincts had come too fast, and he had forgotten how cold the mountain water could be. He tried to take a breath, but his body refused. Would this be his death? Drowned while trying to save someone else from a similar fate?

He tried again. Air filled his lungs, and he headed toward the girls. The cold water enveloped him. It seemed to pull him down toward the bottom, but he pushed on until he finally reached one girl. As a cop in coastal Santa Barbara, Zane had taken many first aid and lifesaving courses, including water rescues. He grabbed the girl and swam backwards, pulling her with him; each stroke stole a little more energy. Where was the other girl? He looked around and saw the other rescuer had her.

As he got to shore, hands reached out and hoisted them onto dry land. Someone wrapped a blanket around each of them. Zane couldn't feel his toes or fingers. He sat on the ground, shivering from the ice-cold water, and tried to catch his breath. He heard a buzzing sound and realized someone was talking to him, but it was all just noise.

It took a few minutes before voices made sense. The blanket was removed and replaced with another. The other man and the girls came into focus. "Are the others alright?" he asked.

Several park rangers were there, helping the girls. A man and a woman held them tight. Zane figured it was their parents.

A park ranger answered, "Yes, they'll be fine." She helped him stand.

The crowd applauded.

He found the other rescuer, and they shook hands.

"Zane. Zane Grayson," he said.

"Marcia's kid? Pleased to meet you. I'm Bruce Colby. I own the insurance agency next to Lou-Lou's. How's your mom?"

"So far, so good, but I've only been back a week."

"Today probably wasn't the welcome home you expected," Colby said.

Zane shook his head. "I wouldn't have expected rescuing someone from drowning back in Santa Barbara either."

Their conversation was cut short. Everyone crowded around to shake hands or slap them on the back and congratulate the two men for saving the girls. Their parents were so grateful they didn't stop shaking hands.

It seemed to Zane that hundreds of people congratulated him, but he'd also made a new friend. He was completely soaked as he walked back to get his gear and thought about the crowd and the girls with their parents. The love the parents showed. He now knew what he had to do about Mom and Tiffany. He just needed to break the news to his mom and sister.

ZANE LOOKED LIKE A DROWNED rat when he walked into the house. After a warm shower and a change into dry clothes, he joined Mom and Mary Elizabeth in the living room. Mom knitted; Mary Elizabeth stopped reading her scriptures. He sat in his dad's old easy chair and related the story of how the girls were saved at the lake.

"Oh, my," Mom beamed. "You're a hero. I'm so proud of you."

"Not really a hero. My police training kicked in. I just did what came naturally. What can you tell me about Bruce Colby?"

"He's very nice. He and his wife Annette have five kids, three boys and two girls. Moved here from Vernal. They're always at church, and he's the second counselor in the Bishopric. I hear he's quite the hunter—deer, elk, ducks, pretty much everything."

"I'll have to talk to him about that," Zane said. "It's been so long since I went hunting."

"Your dad's rifles are still in his office, but they haven't been used since he passed."

Zane scratched his chin. "I think I'd like to hunt deer this fall. Should be more fun than just shooting targets on the firing range. Now, I have something more important to tell you."

Mom put down her knitting, took off her glasses. They dangled on the chain around her neck. She gave Zane an expectant look.

"As you know, Tiffany and her dad asked me to look into Will's murder. I tossed and turned all night, and the reason I went down to the lake was to think about it. Some of my best thinking was done there while I fished."

"I remember," Mom said. "You spent a long time at the lake before you took your basketball scholarship."

"Anyway, I won't take the case. I'm here to help you, and that's what I'll do."

"Good to hear, Zane," Mary Elizabeth said. "Because it won't be long and I'll be back in Portland."

Marcia put her glasses back on and went back to knitting. "Thank you, Zane."

Zane stood and headed for the kitchen. "Those fish won't clean themselves."

He'd finished the first fish when there was a knock at the door. Mary Elizabeth answered and called Zane into the living room.

Sheriff Richman was there. "Is there someplace we can talk?"

They went onto the porch and sat in the rockers.

"What's up, Richie?"

"It's Rich or Sheriff Richman. I came to ask for your help. We're in this murder case over our heads. I want to take you up on your offer. Sure could use your expertise."

"Just stop there, Sheriff. I'm not certified in Utah to be a deputy."

"I can hire you as a consultant."

Zane shook his head. "No Rich. Tiffany and her dad already asked me to help and I declined. I'm here to help my mom. I can't help her and investigate a murder."

"You sure, Zane? I have some budget for another deputy, but I could shift it around for a consultant fee."

"I'm sure."

"Just thought I'd ask." With that, Richman got in his SUV and drove away. Zane went back to his fish.

But later that night, as Zane sat on the porch with his bourbon and cigar, he thought about Tiffany and Will and George and Richman's offer. *I made the right decision.*

Chapter 10

ZANE STROLLED INTO THE KITCHEN Friday morning, opened the refrigerator, and took out bacon and eggs. On the porch the night before, he decided that helping milk the cows was not the best way to help his mom. Making breakfast would prove he was serious about his decision.

As he took the bacon out of the frying pan, Mary Elizabeth came in. "Zane, I'm impressed. Table set, breakfast cooking. I'll have my eggs over easy." She poured herself a glass of orange juice and sat at the table then spread some strawberry jam on a slice of toast. "Why are you suddenly being domestic?" Her voice was thick with suspicion.

"I told you. I'm here to help Mom."

"But I can make breakfast."

"I need to get in practice for when you're back in Portland." He slid two eggs from the pan and onto a plate, added bacon, and set it on the table before her. Then scrambled eggs for himself.

Mary Elizabeth broke the yolks, the gooey yellow spreading across her plate. She took another slice of toast and used it to soak up the yolk. "Mmm. Perfect. You'll make someone a splendid wife someday."

"Ha ha. You forget I lived alone for a long time. Breakfast became a specialty. I often made it for dinner."

"But you and Jade lived together."

"True, but that was only for a couple of years." He turned his head so she couldn't see his eyes watering up thinking of his time with Jade.

"Are you okay?"

He didn't answer. Zane thought about Jade and her last birthday together. It was a Saturday night. They went out to dinner, down on the waterfront at Toma. She had on a sexy black, spaghetti strap dress. He'd ordered the pork chop; Jade, the scallops and shrimp. They shared the tiramisu for dessert. He gave her a long string of pearls. Lab made because it was all he could afford on a cop's salary, but she loved them just the same and kissed him deeply, her tongue hinting at a second dessert when they got home. Then back at their place, once the door closed, she pushed him against it and kissed him again as she unbuttoned his shirt. She wiggled out of her little black dress. When they were naked, he carried her to the bed, her skin soft and her perfume intoxicating. Then she was on top of him. He looked up at her; the pearls hanging down in the valley between her breasts. The contrast of the white pearls against her dark skin was exquisite. They spent hours in bed before falling asleep. Then, enjoyed each other's bodies again the next morning.

"Yeah. I'm fine. The breakup with Jade still hits me hard." He got up, went to the fridge, came back with a jar of salsa, and added some to the eggs. "She was the love of my life. God, she was beautiful. We were so good together, and then her ex, Tyrone, framed me—" He rubbed his eyes.

Mary Elizabeth put her hand on Zane's shoulder. "It's alright. You don't have to talk about it."

He sipped his coffee.

"I'm so sorry. Every time you've talked about her, I could tell she was special. Any chance you can connect with her again?"

"I haven't talked to her in months. She's in the past, and I'm here now."

They heard footsteps above them. "Sounds like Mom's up. I'll go check on her," Mary Elizabeth said.

Zane replayed that birthday again while he ate breakfast alone. The phone rang and brought him back to reality. He went to the phone on the wall. "Grayson residence," he said.

"Mr. Grayson? This is Sheriff Richman."

Zane knew something was up from the formal greeting. "If you think I changed my mind about your offer, the answer is still no."

"Not that," Richman said. "I understand you were up at the Massey place after we finished there. I have some questions for you. Can you stop by my office in the County Courthouse about 10:00?"

"What questions require me to come in?"

"I'm pretty sure you don't want your mom and sister to overhear. At my office would be best."

Zane, convinced Sheriff Richman hadn't told him everything, said, "Sheriff, I saw less than what you saw, and I have a lot of work to do here. It would not be convenient for me to come by."

"Your choice. Either come by on your own or I'll send a deputy out to get you."

Now Zane knew there was more to the request than the Sheriff let on. "I can get myself there, Richie, but I can't promise when." He knew calling the sheriff by his childhood name would get under his skin.

Zane hung up the phone and set about washing the dishes when Marcia and Mary Elizabeth came in.

"Morning, Mom. Can I get you some bacon and eggs?" he said.

Marcia looked at the plate of bacon on the table. "I'm sorry you went to all that work, but I'm not feeling great. Maybe just some toast."

"I'll save this bacon for a BLT sandwich later," Zane said as he popped two slices of bread into the toaster.

THE SMITH COUNTY COURTHOUSE WAS a two-story, yellow brick building in the center of town. Built in the 1950s, it housed county offices, a large room for county commission meetings, the district court, the sheriff's office, and various other county offices.

A deputy led Zane to a conference room with a table and six chairs. A picture of the President of the United States and Utah's governor shaking hands hung on one wall; a whiteboard mounted on another. He looked at the clock next to it, 1:17. He walked to the window overlooking the Mathoni High School football field.

Zane's thoughts went back to the big game his senior year. Mathoni trailed by five points. It was third down with six seconds left, ball on their own twenty-eight yard line. Everyone knew it would be a Hail Mary pass. A last chance for the Mathoni Wildcats to beat their rivals, the Uintah Utes. Zane lined up wide right and looked over at quarterback Sam Richman, then back at the opposing safety. The quarterback signaled to hike the ball and took off in a full run toward the end zone. Zane glanced over his shoulder, the safety a half-step behind. He looked up, saw the ball in the air, then stretched out his arms and pulled them in when the ball hit. He felt a tug on his jersey, knew the safety had a hand on him. A gunshot signaled time expired. He made a spin-move to the inside and freed himself from the hands of the opposing player. At the fifteen-yard line, there was a yank on his shoulder pads. Zane continued his forward progress. The end zone was close. Several hands tried to pull him down. His momentum was slowing. Zane stumbled, almost tripped, but regained his balance. He stretched his arms again, this time hoping to get the ball far enough to break the plane of the end zone. He hit the ground; the ball flew into the air. Zane rolled over onto his back. He looked up as the ball came back down and hit his chest. He wrapped his arms around it. A whistle blew. He saw the referee on his left give the signal. Touchdown! Mathoni won 29-28.

A door closed. Zane looked up to see Sheriff Richman.

"Good morning, Mr. Grayson. Please take a seat." Richman sat at the short end of the table, near the door. Zane watched as he set his phone on the table and tapped the record app.

Zane chose a seat on the long side, to Richman's left.

"I'm Smith County Sheriff Richard Richman, interviewing Zane Grayson. Earlier this week I made an offer to Mr. Grayson to join my team as a consultant in the murder investigation of William Massey. Since that time, additional evidence has come to light. That offer is rescinded. Mr. Grayson is here voluntarily.

Please state your full name for the record."

"Zane Lorenzo Grayson."

"Mr. Grayson, until a few days ago, you lived in California. Tell me about that."

"Ancient history that you know."

Richman leaned forward. "Let's say I don't."

Zane sat back in his chair and crossed his arms. "I'll play your little game." Zane told him about college, the basketball team, his decision to stay in the state after graduation, and life as a cop.

"Why did you leave the Santa Barbara Police Department?"

"The work atmosphere had turned hostile."

"Could that be because you planted evidence?"

"No, it could not. I never planted evidence. I was setup. The investigation cleared me of all allegations."

"But you retired early."

"Part of my settlement with the city."

Richman opened a file folder and took out a sheet of paper. He studied it for a moment. "Full retirement. You also got money in a settlement. How much was that?"

"I can't tell you."

"Can't or won't."

Zane pushed the chair back and stood.

"Can't. The settlement was sealed. Now if we're through with this history lesson, I have more important things to do."

"Sit down, Mr. Grayson. I have some more history," Richman continued. "You and Mrs. Massey had a relationship."

He grumbled and sat down. "Again, thirty years ago. You know all this."

Richman opened the file folder again and studied a paper inside that Zane couldn't see. "You and Mrs. Massey were seen together at Lou-Lou's and another time on the street."

Zane rubbed his hands over his face. "I know where you're heading with this, and it's a dead end. Yes, we bumped into each other. Mathoni is a small town. Yes, she gave me a hug when she first saw me after my return, but there's nothing there. I never met Will, and until I went there after the murder, I'd never been to her house."

"Seems that after thirty years away, you'd have settled in Santa Barbara. Why did you move back?"

"My mom has some health issues and needs help. Here I am. For the record," Zane pointed to the phone, "I was at the hospital in Vernal with her at the time of the murder." He leaned back in his chair. "The only other reason I'm here today is because you think I have information about Will Massey's murder. I don't have any."

"You visited the crime scene after we finished. Why was that?"

"Tiffany's dad asked me to investigate the murder. I wanted to see the scene."

"So, you're working for Mr. Needham." It was more a statement than a question.

"No, I am not. I told him so."

"Yet, you're inserting yourself into an ongoing criminal investigation."

"As I said, I am not investigating."

Richman looked at Zane. "Let me tell you what I think."

"Sure, go ahead and tell me about your misdirected ideas."

"I think you and Tiffany planned Will's murder so the two of you could get back together, and she carried it out."

"And you're basing it on what evidence?"

"Hunches at the moment."

"So, no evidence that points to either of us."

"Not enough at the moment, but it's still early in the investigation."

Zane stood. "In that case, we're done here. Richie." He emphasized the sheriff's name, wanting to get under his skin.

He walked out to his truck and headed back home, his thoughts on the interview. If this were his case, he would have done the same thing and then checked the alibi.

MOM SAT IN THE EASY chair, an old movie on TV. Zane came in and grumbled.

"Are you okay?" she asked.

"I'm fine," he snapped.

"Zane, I don't know what has you riled up, but you shouldn't take it out on me."

He calmed a bit. "You're right. Sorry, Mom. Richie thinks I had something to do with Will's murder."

"You were with me at the hospital."

"I know that. You know that. He knows that." He took a deep breath and slowly exhaled, then looked at the TV. "*High Noon*?"

"One of your father's favorite movies. His birthday is Monday, and he's been on my mind. We used to sit here together on the couch and watch TV. He loved the old westerns, and I'm not ashamed to admit I enjoy looking at Gary Cooper."

Zane chuckled. "You still miss him."

"Gary Cooper?" she teased. "But yes, I miss Robert every day. I miss the sound of his voice, the twinkle in his eye, and the smell of his Old Spice. His beautiful smile."

"We should go to the cemetery on Monday so you can visit him."

"That would be nice, Zane. I hope I feel up to it."

"Something tells me you will be." He smiled at her.

"Oh, Zane, when you smile like that, you look just like your father," Mom said.

"Do you need anything?"

"I'm fine."

Zane stood. "I need to scrape the house so it's ready for the fresh paint."

"Zane?" Mom said.

"Yeah, Mom?"

"Thank you for being here for me."

"You're welcome, Mom."

Zane leaned a ladder against the house and climbed to the top so he could work on the second story and got busy. It was tedious but gave him time to think about the morning as he scraped off the old layer of paint. It was clear he was on the suspect list, even if it made little sense to him. Despite his stomach flip-flopping every time he saw her, there was nothing between him and Tiffany. Zane thought about the argument he'd witnessed, Tiffany, Mom, the sheriff's hunch, and his decision not to look into the murder.

Chapter 11

ZANE DIDN'T GET UP TO make breakfast Saturday morning. His brain hadn't shut off all night. Thoughts of Tiffany, Will, and Mom swirled around, and he hadn't slept. Because of the tossing and turning, he made his decision. Richie saw him as a suspect, and until the actual killer was found, he would remain a suspect. He had no confidence in the sheriff, and if he was in jail, he'd be no help to his mom. It was up to him to clear his name and solve William Massey's murder.

It was quiet at Tiffany's house when he arrived. It reminded Zane of when he had been there the day after George first asked him to solve the crime. He rang the doorbell and turned to look at the view across the hills.

"Hello?" a voice said.

He turned back to the now-open door. A teenage girl, about fifteen or sixteen, stood in the doorway. She looked exactly like Tiffany had at that age.

"Hi," he said. "You must be Tiffany's daughter. I'm Zane Grayson. I saw you the other night at your grandpa's house. I went to high school with your mom. I stopped by to see how she's feeling."

The girl shrugged. "Hi Mr. Grayson. My name is Ciarra. Mom's not too well cause—" She didn't finish but gestured toward the barn.

"I know that's why I'm here. To see if I can help. If she needs anything. How are you holding up?"

"Okay, I guess." But her voice was somber and unsure. "Come in. Mom's in the great room." She called out, "Mom, Mr. Grayson is here."

He followed Ciarra into the cavernous home. A Star Wars movie was on TV. Tiffany sat on a couch, her legs pulled up, arms around them. She looked over at him as he walked in. "Hi Zane."

"Hi Tiff. I wanted to see how you're holding up."

"Let's go to Will's office so we can talk in private."

She led him behind the kitchen, to the office and closed the door. A large desk sat at one end; windows faced out onto the pool. A leather sofa was across from a fireplace at the other end. Tiffany sat there, and Zane sat next to her.

She looked horrible. Eyes red and puffy, hair more tangled. She still needed a shower.

"Oh, Zane. It's so hard. I cry all the time. I . . . I don't know what to do."

He put his arm around her and hugged her. "I know right now it looks bad, but we'll figure this out and it will get better. I came here today for two reasons. First, to find out how you're doing. Second, to tell you I'm going to investigate Will's murder."

She looked at him, eyes wide. "Thank you. I know you'll figure it out."

"There's more you should know."

Tiffany bit her bottom lip and stared at Zane.

"Richie called me into his office. He has this crazy idea that you and I are getting back together and the two of us planned Will's murder to get him out of the way."

"No! We didn't. I had nothing to do with it."

"I know that. I was in Vernal with Mom for her chemo. Unfortunately, he's convinced his theory is the truth."

"He's wrong. How can we prove we had nothing to do with . . . with . . ."

Zane said, "We talked the other day, and it was a big help.

Sometimes people remember things days later. Do you think you can walk through it again with me?"

She nodded. "I think about him all the time. Lying on the floor of the barn. All the blood." Tears ran down her cheeks. "I can't sleep. I see it all over and over. There was so much blood everywhere."

Zane let her talk at her own pace.

"I was making lunch. Will . . ." She pulled a tissue from the box on the table next to her and wiped her eyes. "Will had gone out to the barn to work."

"What was he working on?"

"I don't know exactly. Probably talking to Jacob about something for the guest house he wanted to build."

"How did you feel about that?"

"I didn't want it."

"Why not?"

She pulled another tissue from the box. "I didn't want all his tech buddies here at our home. It would have been a huge disruption every time one of them showed up. He'd be off with them. They'd be wandering around the ranch. I know my kids and I would get pulled in to help."

"Okay," Zane said. "Back to lunch."

"I called to him to come in. When he didn't show up, I gave lunch to the kids and then went to find him." She wiped her eyes again.

"Take your time, Tiff."

After a couple of minutes, she said, "He was face down on the floor of the barn. I saw the blood around him. Jacob said I was kneeling in it, hovering over him. I see that blood every time I close my eyes."

After several minutes, she looked over at Zane. "I remember nothing after that. I'm sorry."

Zane hugged her again. "It's fine. Tell me about your ranch foreman."

"Jacob? You think Jacob . . ."

"Tiffany, everyone is a suspect until they're cleared. Tell me about Jacob."

"After Will sold his company, we had more money than we'd ever need. He had fallen in love with Mathoni the first time he came here with me. For years, he told me he wanted to move here. When we moved here, it was too quiet for him. He always had to stay busy. It started with cattle. He grew up in the city and knew nothing about it, so he hired Jacob. After that, he talked about the guest house. I don't know where he got the idea. Maybe Jacob talked him into it. I just know I didn't want it."

"How did you feel about moving back to Mathoni?"

"I loved the idea. Back here with Mom and Dad. It's a much better place for my kids than Silicon Valley. We don't have all the drugs and crime."

Zane thought of murder as being one of the worst crimes. "Did Will have enemies?"

Silence fell on them again. "I tried to think about that, but I can't. It's like my brain stays on Will . . ." Tiffany pulled another tissue from the box and blew her nose.

"All I can think about is how can I live without him? I know the sheriff is in over his head. Please find my husband's killer. I can pay you anything you want." She looked at him, hope in her eyes.

"There's one more thing. Richie has an ongoing investigation. If I poke around to clear you, I could be arrested for interfering in it. So, I have to do this for me. However, if I do happen to find evidence that clears you too, then even better. I'm not a licensed PI so I can't take payment from you or anyone else. I wouldn't take a penny from you, anyway"

"I think I understand. This means so much to me. Thank you."

ZANE DROVE BACK HOME, WORRIED about what his family would say about him taking the case, especially Mary Elizabeth. He knew she would not be happy and likely would have it out with him.

When he got to the house, Marcia was dozing in the easy chair. He found his sister in the kitchen. "How's Mom?" he said.

"She's tired. Where have you been?"

"Let's sit down and I'll tell you all about it."

They sat at the kitchen table and Zane told her about his thought process from the decision to help Mom and his return home, to the questions from Sheriff Richman, the visit with Tiffany that morning, and not getting any sleep the past few nights.

"And that's why I have to investigate Will's murder. Most importantly, I have to clear my name so I can help Mom." He stopped and looked at Mary Elizabeth, watching for any sign of what she thought, but he couldn't read her.

After several minutes of silence, she went to the sink and poured herself a glass of water. She drank it all then turned and looked at Zane.

"No."

Just one word. It wasn't what he'd expected. He was prepared for her to be angry and yell at him and have a big argument. What he got was calm and collected, and despite the calendar showing mid-June, the air had become frigid. They both left it hanging there.

Finally, Mary Elizabeth broke the ice. "You promised me you'd help. You promised Mom you'd help. We both believed you, and do you know what makes this worse? I knew you couldn't resist. I knew you'd help Tiffany, and I pushed those thoughts aside, thinking you'd changed. You haven't."

"But I have to—"

"Let me finish. When Dad died, it was me who came home and helped Mom. I've been here on and off over the years since while you stayed in California. Except for Dad's funeral, this is the first time you've come home in all those years. You just told me you came back to help Mom, but you've been gone more than you've been at home. It's awful that you're a suspect. We both know where you were, and Rich will confirm that.

"Neil and the kids will be here next week. They'll stay a few days, and then I'm going back to Portland with them. The kids will want to spend time with their uncle. I won't tell them why you don't have time for them. That's on you, especially after you said you'd teach them to ride the horses. You also need to tell Mom. I expect you to do that today. Until I go, I'll take care of Mom, like I always have. After I leave, she's your responsibility.

Don't call and ask for advice. You'll have to figure it out like I did and will be on your own. You have a week."

She walked out of the kitchen. Zane sat there alone. He realized that the frigid air was now arctic. He also knew that the relationship with his sister had changed, maybe forever.

ZANE LEANED AGAINST A POST on the porch and watched the shadows grow as the sun set over the Uinta Mountains. As much as he had dreaded telling Mary Elizabeth about his decision to investigate Will Massey's murder, the thought that he had to tell his mom hung over him. He wasn't sure how to break the news to her.

He saw Levi heading to The Cottage. "Levi," he called, "can you come over here a minute? I need to talk to you about something."

"Want a drink?" Zane asked when Levi got to the house.

"You don't look so good, Mr. Grayson. Means this might not be a good talk. So, I'd better have a belt."

Zane went back into the house and got a glass from the cupboard. When he came back out, he poured the drink and handed it to Levi.

Levi took a big sip. "Alright, I'm ready."

"You know about Will Massey."

"Got himself murdered. Yeah, I heard. Hell, everyone in the valley is talking about it. I think I know what's got you so down. You're pinin' for his wife."

Zane looked at the ground. "No. Maybe. Truth is, I'm not sure how I feel about her, but that's not what I wanted to talk to you about."

Levi sipped more bourbon. "Damn, you buy good hooch."

Zane grinned. "What can I say? I know what I like. I called you over to tell you that when I came back to help Mom, I also wanted to help with the farm, mostly so I would stay busy. I'm not so sure I can help you."

"You lived in the city too long. Lost all the cowboy in you."

"No, it's not that."

"Well, go ahead, I'm listenin'."

Zane finished his drink. "Tiffany and her dad both asked me to investigate Will's murder. I've decided to do it."

"Ah shit. You tell your ma?"

"Not yet, but I told Mary Elizabeth."

"And you lived?"

Zane laughed. "Just barely. Neil and her kids will be here next week to get her. Then she's heading back to Portland with them. I have until they leave to solve this murder."

Levi stroked his bushy mustache. "And if you don't?"

"That, my friend, is a good question. I wish I could answer it."

Levi picked up the bourbon bottle and poured himself another.

"When are you tellin' your ma?"

Zane sighed. "Mary Elizabeth wanted me to do it today, but Mom's in bed now. Problem is, after the way Sis told me off today, I'm afraid to tell Mom, but she's not in the best of shape right now."

"Red week," Levi said.

"Yup. I'd like to give her a couple of days to get her strength back, but not sure Mary Elizabeth will let me."

Levi finished his drink and patted Zane on the shoulder. "You'll find the right time. Don't you worry. I got along fine before you came back. I can handle the farm without you." He headed off to bed.

Zane sat and rocked and stewed about how to tell his mom.

Chapter 12

INVESTIGATIONS START OUT THREE WAYS. The detective has an extensive list of suspects and has to whittle it down. Or they have a tiny list of suspects to which they add more names during the investigation. Finally, they begin with no suspects and need to create a list of suspects from scratch.

Zane found himself in the small-number category. On Sunday morning he wrote his suspect list along with the motives for each person.

- Tiffany Massey - Publicly argued with her husband
- Wayne Hubbard - Guest house threatened his business
- Jacob - Unknown motive
- Unknown intruder - Caught burgling
- Enemy from Will's past - Taking out revenge

That was it—five suspects. He didn't have anyone else, and he was pretty sure Tiffany didn't kill her husband, but until he had the evidence to clear her, she stayed on the list. Wayne Hubbard, however, was a different story. All he knew about Hubbard was he came from Roosevelt, a town about 30 miles west of Vernal, and owned a dude ranch near Mathoni.

Zane opened his laptop and got to work. He typed Wayne

Hubbard into a search engine. The Flying H Ranch had lots of hits, but a ten-year-old article from the *Richfield Reaper* piqued his interest.

Man Sentenced in Spousal Abuse Case

A Richfield man has been sentenced to six months in the county jail after entering a plea deal. Wayne Hubbard had been charged with felony spousal abuse, but in an agreement with the District Attorney, the charges were reduced from a felony to a misdemeanor in exchange for a lighter sentence.

Monday, Sixth District Court Judge Christopher Wellington accepted the plea agreement and handed down the sentence.

District Attorney Derek Johnson issued a statement that he believed justice had been served with the judge's ruling.

Speaking to reporters, Barbara Hubbard's attorney took a different view, saying, "Judge Wellington's ruling is a blow to justice as Ms. Hubbard still suffers from physical, mental, and emotional issues because of the attacks. We will file a civil suit for damages against her former husband in the next few days."

Zane looked for information on the civil suit but couldn't find anything and he wondered if it was ever filed. But now that he had some evidence that Hubbard had a temper, he kept him at the top of the very short list. He also found out Hubbard was from Richfield, not Roosevelt. Two different areas of the state, some 200 miles apart, but he could see how Louise could mix up the two.

SUNDAY IN MORMON TOWNS MEANT people went to church and didn't work. They're taught The Ten Commandments, one that says *Keep the Sabbath day holy.* But in a small farm community, the cows still needed to be milked and fed, and the eggs collected. Add to that a lively tourist trade in the summer bringing in most of the year's income, it meant people worked and there was a late church service with locals and tourists packing the church house.

Zane drove past the church and noted the parking lot overflowed onto the state highway that was also the town's Main Street. He, of course, didn't stop. Normally, Marcia would be there, but she didn't have the energy, so she was home with Mary Elizabeth.

Zane was on a mission. He needed to kick this investigation into high gear. He wasn't ready to talk to Wayne Hubbard yet, so he tackled another item near the top of his to-do list, interview Will Massey's ranch foreman, Jacob Faust.

When he arrived at the Massey ranch, he had no problem finding Faust. He was clean-shaven, early forties, and stood about five feet ten, and wore a black cowboy hat, jeans, and a dusty black button-down cotton shirt. He was ready to check the herd when Zane got to Massey's ranch. They sat in a side-by-side ATV, crossed an alfalfa field, and went through a gate into the sagebrush.

Zane didn't waste any time and got right to the point. "Tell me about the day Mr. Massey was killed."

"It was sunny and warm. I was out behind the barn in a storage shed. As a matter of fact, I was working on the ATV we're riding in now," Jacob said as they drove along the barbed wire fence line. "I heard Mrs. Massey scream."

They crested the hill and headed down into a ravine. At the bottom, cottonwood trees lined a creek. It was cooler in the shade of the trees.

"Did Mr. Massey have an appointment? Did anyone visit him?"

"He had nothing scheduled, but he told me early that morning that he needed to go to Vernal. If anyone was here, I didn't know about it."

Zane took hold of the grab bar as they bounced around. "When did you last see him alive?"

"Around 10:00 that morning."

"And you didn't hear him argue with anyone or see an intruder? No one left in a hurry?"

"Nope. Just Mrs. Massey. I sure wish I had heard something. Maybe I could have saved Will."

The two men bounced into the air as they hit a big hole across the middle of the trail. The toolbox and spool of barbed wire banged loudly against the storage area in the back of the ATV.

"How long have you worked for the Masseys?" Zane asked.

"Just over two years. Before that, I was up in Jackson Hole," Faust said.

"What exactly are your responsibilities here?"

"Originally, I was hired to manage the herd, but planning for the guest house followed closely after I got here. I was supposed to manage it when it opened. That won't happen now as Mrs. Massey is against it."

Zane tightened his grip on the grab bar as they crossed the creek and headed up the next hill. "Those are two very different skill sets. Why did Mr. Massey hire you for it?"

"I was the ranch manager for Harrison Ford up in Jackson…"

"Hang on a minute. Harrison Ford? Han Solo? Indiana Jones? That Harrison Ford?"

"Yes, why? Do you know another Harrison Ford?"

"Well, no."

"So, like I said, I did everything from repair fences to plan menus for Mr. Ford and his guests."

"Sounds like a great job. Cushy too. How did Mr. Massey lure you away?"

"The most common thing. Money. Lots more money. So, here I am."

"How did you feel about the guest house?"

"Other than money, that's one reason I took the job." Faust stopped the ATV next to a downed section of the fence and got out to fix it. Zane followed.

"Do you have a history of working at a hotel?" Zane asked.

"Mr. Ford often had guests, mostly people from Hollywood. I planned the meals and provided everything they wanted. That's the experience Will was after."

"What was the company name for this guest house?"

"Mathoni Ranch Hospitality."

"I hear there was some opposition to Will's plan."

"Yeah, there was opposition. We needed either a zoning change or a variance from the county for both the guest ranch and the heliport Mr. Massey wanted. I think the county commission, which is also the zoning commission, was ready to deny it." Faust made a loop at the ends of the broken barbed wire. "Bruce Colby was for it, but the other two, Lavell Bateman and Jared Snow, were against it. From what I can tell, the townfolk were split about even on the deal."

"Huh," was all Zane said as he thought about this. Mom's cousin was one of the county commissioners. That made his next question harder. He thought about that while he cut three strands of barbed wire off a spool and wound them through the loops Faust had made in the existing fence line.

He finally said, "Do you think either of the county commissioners was against it enough to kill Mr. Massey?"

"That's just it. I don't think anyone in town would kill Mr. Massey." Faust worked the wire stretcher on each wire to pull them tight, then wound the end of the new strands around the old to keep the tension.

"What about Wayne Hubbard? He seemed threatened by it. Maybe he was worried that he'd lose business."

"Now that you mention it, yeah. Hubbard could have done it. He and Mr. Massey had words a few times. If they ran into each other in town, they'd go at it. Hubbard thought the guest house would put him out of business."

"What about other enemies? Massey was a rich man. Surely, he did more than ruffle some feathers to get there."

"If he did, that was before I knew him."

"How many people work here?"

"Nine at the moment. Take shifts so they all get days off." Faust put the tools back in the toolbox along with the leather gloves. "I hadn't thought about this before, but we had to fire Tomás about three weeks ago. He was always late to work. On the day he was fired, he showed up drunk. He swore revenge, but I didn't believe him since he was drunk. Tomás Sanchez. He's related somehow to the guy that owns the Mexican restaurant in town."

"Is Sanchez still around?"

"He could be, but I haven't seen him. There's also your guy, Levi. He applied for a job here. The job paid more money than your mom pays him. So, there's that."

Levi wanted a new job? "What happened with Levi?"

"Mr. Massey knew how much help he was to your mom. It didn't feel right to hire him. Told him he didn't get the job."

The two men climbed back into the ATV and continued along the fence line. Zane was deep in thought about what he'd been told. *Levi certainly didn't seem like the type of guy who would commit murder. Maybe if he felt his Barbie collection was threatened. Still, I have to talk to him.*

Sanchez was an unknown. It seemed extreme to kill someone after for losing a job as a ranch hand. People do strange things when they're angry, especially when they're drunk. He made a mental note to check out Sanchez.

Hubbard was solidifying as a suspect. If not him, could he have sent one of his people to do his dirty work? His list of suspects had just grown quickly, and without a badge he'd have a harder time getting answers to all his questions. Not that it was always that easy chasing down answers, even with a badge.

ZANE KNOCKED ON THE WOODEN frame of the screen door at The Cottage. The inside door was open, and he could hear a baseball game on the TV. When his knock was unanswered, he hollered. "Levi, are you home?"

"Come in, Zane. I'm in the kitchen."

Zane took off his cowboy hat and opened the door. He shivered as he walked past all the Barbies. It felt as if their eyes followed him across the room, and the feeling stuck with him once he got to the kitchen. He laughed when he saw Levi wearing a frilly pinafore apron and washing dishes.

"You never wore an apron while working in the kitchen?"

"I'll plead the Fifth on that," Zane said.

"Thought so," Levi said. "What can I do for you?"

Zane sat at the table. "Why didn't you tell me you tried to get a job with Will Massey?"

"It didn't seem important because I didn't take it. How the hell did you know?"

Zane ignored the question. "You didn't take it, or were you turned down?"

Levi rinsed a plate and set it in the rack to dry, his back to Zane. "You were detecting, and Jacob told you. Truth is, Mr. Massey said he couldn't hire me."

Zane leaned back, stretched out his legs. "How did you feel about that?"

Levi turned and threw the dishrag into the soapy water. "Shit, Zane. You think I'm a suspect. Sure, I wasn't happy. More money would be nice, but kill someone? Ain't no way I could do that. Gotta say, I'm disappointed you think I done it. I like workin' for your ma. She treats me real good, like family. So, after it was all done, I looked at it as something good. Afterwards, I heard Mr. Massey wasn't so great to work for. What I heard was he was demanding, and he fired some kid 'cause he was late for work."

Zane ran his hand through his hair and sighed. "Oh Levi. I didn't think you did it. I had to make sure I could cross you off the suspect list. Why didn't you ask Mom for more money?"

"'Cause I know she's close to breaking even. Didn't want her to lose money on my account, especially with her medical bills."

"I've seen the books, Levi. We can afford to pay you a bit more. It's not much, but how about an extra fifty dollars a week?"

"That's awfully nice of you. I'll take it on one condition. Throw in a bottle of that fine sippin' hooch you drink and you've gotta deal."

"Agreed."

AFTER TALKING WITH LEVI, ZANE sat at the desk in the office and hit the Internet again, looking for information on Mathoni Ranch Hospitality. A state business website showed it was registered as an LLC. The registered agent was named Sal Giovanni.

Giovanni, Zane learned, was a criminal defense attorney in Sandy, a suburb of Salt Lake City, which seemed odd. Next, he looked at court sites. It looked like he represented mostly slimeballs. Everything from drug dealers to hookers to petty thieves. He also seemed shady. The Bar Association site showed his license had been suspended several times.

Why would Will use a slimy criminal attorney for a business venture?

Chapter 13

THE SMELL OF BACON GREETED Zane as he went downstairs Monday morning. He dropped a pod into the coffeemaker and watched as Mary Elizabeth cut canned biscuit dough into four parts.

"Have you told Mom that you can't take care of her?" she said as she mixed the biscuit quarters with chopped and cooked bacon, cheese, sliced green onions, and raw scrambled eggs. She poured it all into a baking dish and put it in the oven.

He took his coffee and sat at the table. "Not yet."

Her shoulders sank. "Zane, you promised. Neil and the kids will be here today."

"I know your deadline. I'll get to it. Do you think Mom will want to go to the cemetery?" He asked, quickly, changing the subject.

"Well, it is Dad's birthday. I hope she's up to it," his sister said. "Either way, today will be difficult for her, but I think it will be good for her to visit Dad. I'll need your help. Do you think you can manage half a day away from your chief priority, the investigation?" Her voice dripped with disgust.

Zane wanted to skip the cemetery. He needed to question,

Wayne Hubbard. He'd lose half a day on the case. However, he agreed with Mary Elizabeth. "Taking Mom to the cemetery is a good idea. If she wants to go, count on me to help," he said.

Mary Elizabeth said, "Really? You're not out trying to find the unknown killer?"

"I think it will keep until this afternoon."

Marcia showed up a few minutes later, wearing a wig and one of her best dresses. "I'd like to go to the cemetery and visit your dad," she announced.

After breakfast, Mary Elizabeth cut some peonies from the yard and put them in a vase with water and then filled a large thermos with lemonade. Zane got some folding lawn chairs and put them in the back of the Wagoneer.

He helped his mom into the back seat so the seatbelt wouldn't rub the chemo port and with his sister in the front, off they went. It was only a short drive, but Mom was exhausted when they got there.

The smell of fresh-cut grass hung in the air as Zane set up the chairs next to his father's grave and then helped his mom into one of them. She walked slowly, more of a shuffle. Mary Elizabeth set the flowers next to the headstone.

Mom said, "Hi Robert. It's Marcia and I have a surprise for you. Zane's here. He's moved back to help around the house and on the farm. Zane, tell your father hello."

"Uhhh…hi, Dad. I retired from the police force, and with Mom's illness I thought I should come back home to help her."

"And Mary Elizabeth's here too," Mom said.

She spoke up. "Hi, Daddy, I miss you. I've been here for a few months helping Mom. Neil and the kids will be here from Portland later today, and then I'll go home with them at the end of the week. I'll be back soon enough in a few months, once the kids are back in school."

"That was nice, dear," Mom said. "Robert, the farm's doing well. Levi's been a big help, and I have plenty of money. Bishop Brough came around a couple of weeks ago and gave me another blessing. I'm so thankful for the priesthood blessings I've been getting, and I know they're helping me get better. I had chemo again last week, so we're in red week again. It really has me worn down. I'll feel better in a few days. We all came down to wish you a happy birthday. I miss you terribly, but I'm glad you're not here to see me go through this awful cancer."

Mary Elizabeth filled plastic Solo cups with lemonade from the thermos. Marcia closed her eyes and dozed off after sipping some of the lemonade. Zane and Mary Elizabeth sat quietly for a few minutes, then Zane got up and walked over to where his dad's parents were buried. He stared at their headstones for a few minutes before walking to the other side of the small cemetery to his mother's parents' graves.

He thought about all the fun times he'd had with his grandparents—fishing at the lake, sledding in winter, and all the dinners they had together, especially the ones at Christmas with the entire family. There were so many people, they had to hold it at the church. He always marveled at all the food. He'd eat until he thought he couldn't have another bite. Then someone would say, "How about some pie?" And somehow, he was able to eat a slice. He didn't care if it was pumpkin, apple, or peach. Just not mincemeat. He always wondered what a mince was, but he knew he didn't like pie made from it.

Thinking about family and Dad, he realized that the strange feeling he got at family meals was because Dad wasn't there. In that moment, he missed his dad more than ever.

"Zane?"

He looked across the cemetery to his sister. She waved him back, so he returned to where they sat next to his dad's resting place.

"Let's get Mom home." She gently shook Mom's shoulder to wake her.

Zane helped her stand, and she leaned against him. "Happy birthday, Robert. I love you. Keep a place warm for me in heaven," she said. Then blew him a kiss.

When they were all loaded in the Wagoneer and on their way home, Mom said, "Thank you, Zane and Mary Elizabeth. I know Robert appreciated your coming along and helping me, and of course, your visit to see him."

Chapter 14

HEADING SOUTH FROM THE GRAYSON farm, the highway took Zane along the west side of the lake and through Mathoni. Where the lake ended, the road curved eastward and continued along the lake's south end. Instead of making the curve, you could continue straight. Main Street became Sheep Creek Road. That's where the town's only gas station, the Gas & Guzzle, was located. Jeremiah Plum had taken it over after his dad passed.

Zane went straight, past the station. He was surprised to find Sheep Creek Road was paved. At least the first two miles of it. A new building, official-looking, now stood near the end of the asphalt. The sign in front said it was the Smith County Jail.

He stopped for a moment to look at it and then continued on his way. The tires on the dirt road created a dust cloud that billowed behind him. He knew his destination was down the road. He just didn't know how far.

After about twenty minutes he found what he wanted, Wayne Hubbard's dude ranch. At the entrance, a sign, high above, stretched across the drive. The words 'Flying H Ranch' adorned the sign, the H with wings on each side.

Zane didn't know whether Hubbard was around or if he was busy with dudes playing cowboy, but he needed to ask Wayne a few questions to either eliminate him or confirm him as a suspect.

The place was impressive. The large main building, built to look like a log cabin. Zane figured it held the guest rooms, a dining hall, and such. There was a large barn to the left, another building off to the right that he guessed was a bunkhouse for hired help, and a house next to that, probably where Hubbard lived with his family, if he had one.

A blonde cowgirl, wearing a pink cowboy hat, walked a horse across the yard toward the barn. Zane pulled up and stopped in front of the main building and got out of his truck. The blonde came up to him. "Can I help you, Mister?"

"I'm looking for Wayne Hubbard."

"He ain't hiring."

"I don't want a job. I have some questions I'd like to ask him."

"You sound like a cop."

He smiled. "That would be a no."

"You wait here. I'll see if he's around. What did you say your name was?"

"I didn't. He won't know me. Tell him it's Zane Grayson."

She continued on to the barn with the horse. A few minutes later, she returned alone.

"He ain't available right now. He'll find you when he wants to talk."

"It's important. Tell him I'll wait." Zane sat on the ground in the shade from his truck, leaned back against the tire and pulled his cowboy hat down over his face.

"Good thing you're settling in. He's gonna be a while," she said, then headed back to the barn.

Someone kicking the bottom of his boot startled Zane awake. He lifted his hat and looked up to see the same woman standing over him. He checked his watch and found he'd been sitting on the ground for over an hour.

"The boss says he'll see you now."

Zane stood, stretched, and followed the woman into the guest room building. To the left was a sitting area. Sofas, chairs, an enormous fireplace, a bookcase filled with books, decks of cards, poker chips, and board games. On the right was the dining area, with several tables and chairs, and a bar with stools. Behind that looked like a kitchen. On one side was a staircase that went up to a second story. Zane couldn't see past that but figured it led to guest rooms.

Behind the counter was a man, mid to late-forties, dark hair, graying goatee, wearing a red plaid shirt and a bandanna around his neck. "Carrie says you wanted to see me."

"Carrie, huh. I wondered what her name was." Zane put out his hand. "I'm Zane Grayson. I've heard a lot about you; thought I'd come down and meet you in person."

"I know who you are, why you're back here in Mathoni, and what you were. What exactly you want with me is what I don't know." Hubbard didn't offer to shake hands.

"Well, you probably heard about Will Massey."

"Don't got nothing to do with me. But, I would like to pin a medal on the guy that killed the son of a bitch. Now, bein' as you're not a cop, you can just get back in your fancy new truck and head back to your milk cows."

"So you had issues with him competing with your ranch?

"None of your business. I'm going to suggest one more time that you get off my land. Now."

Zane held his hands up as if surrendering. "Alright. I'm leaving. I still want to talk to you about it. I know Massey wanted to give you competition. I'm just trying to clear your name."

"My name don't need clearing. Carrie, get Deke and Clay. Tell them we got a varmint."

"Right, Boss."

Varmint? This guy's seen too many John Wayne movies.

"I'm leaving, Mr. Hubbard. You have a nice day." Zane turned and went back outside to his truck, but found Carrie, Deke, and Clay blocking his path. Each wore a gun belt around their waist, complete with a six-shooter, and a rifle in their hands.

Way too many John Wayne movies.

"I was just telling your boss that I'm leaving."

The three held their ground. Zane walked toward them.

Just as he was almost face-to-face with them, they stepped back to make a path for him to pass. As he opened his truck door, one man said, "See you don't come back. Mr. Hubbard don't like people snooping around."

John Wayne movie scriptwriters.

Zane climbed into his truck, started the engine, rolled down his window, and backed up, keeping the three ranch hands on his left side. He tipped his hat to them and then drove off. He believed Hubbard had something to hide. His reaction to Zane was certainly curious. It's one thing to refuse to talk but another to throw someone off your land at gunpoint.

ZANE WASN'T SURE HOW TO proceed. Back in California, he'd had a badge and could get warrants. Now, those weren't options. Could he stake out Hubbard's ranch, follow him when he left, then talk to him in public? He quickly dismissed that idea as it would probably lead to an ugly confrontation. Not only that, but Hubbard might not leave his place for days, and Zane didn't have that much time.

A white Chevrolet Suburban with Oregon plates was parked in front of the house when Zane returned. The Bechtel family had arrived.

Inside, Zane shook hands with Neil and hugged Katrina. He noticed his mom was wearing her wig, something she rarely did around the house. "Where are Ash and Olivia?" he asked.

"They're out with the horses," Mary Elizabeth said.

"That's all they could talk about the entire way here," Neil said.

They all caught up, Neil asking lots of questions about Zane's retirement. Zane went through the story again about being framed and the settlement that he couldn't talk about.

Katrina asked, "Can you tell me about the murder?"

Zane looked at his sister, not sure if he should get into it with Katrina.

"Please, Uncle Zane?" Katrina said. "I listen to lots of true-crime podcasts. I want to study forensics when I get to college."

"Good for you," Zane said. "We could use lots more people solving crimes."

And that took the conversation to Will Massey and his

murder. Katrina hung on every word as Zane went through what he knew, keeping it as PG-13 rated as he could.

Olivia and Ash ran in, shouting for Zane.

"Can you teach us to ride, Uncle Zane?" Olivia said.

Zane said, "Sure, I think we can do that." But Zane wondered how much time he'd have with them because of his investigation.

MONDAY NIGHTS IN MORMON HOMES were reserved for family time. The church called it 'Family Home Evening.' It was supposed to be a dedicated evening spent as a family with no other obligations. There is a lesson about Jesus or *The Book of Mormon*, or something else with a religious tone. Playing games or even roasting marshmallows over a fire was encouraged, as long as the religious lesson wasn't replaced too often.

Zane no longer followed the teachings of the Church, so while everyone else was holding Family Home Evening, Zane refrained. Eventually, he got up from the rocking chair on the porch and carried his bourbon into his dad's old office. Even with the light on, the room was dim because of the dark wood paneling on the walls. After the trip to the cemetery, he missed his dad more than ever.

Zane set his drink on the desk and then lifted the lid on the phonograph. There was already a record on the turntable. Zane wondered if it was the last record his dad had listened to. He turned the power switch and set the needle down. The voice of Waylon Jennings floated across the room.

He sat in his dad's chair, set his drink on the desk, leaned back and closed his eyes. When he was little, he would sit on Dad's lap in this same chair while he did bookkeeping or prepared lessons for church or wrote in his journal.

Zane spun around in the chair and pulled a random journal from the bookcase. He opened it and read.

Saturday, June 14, 1986

Here we are in Salt Lake City. We've been promising the kids all year that once school was out for the summer, we'd bring them here to go to the zoo. I can't believe how big and crowded Salt Lake is getting. The traffic is awful, especially on the freeway. I don't know how people can live here.

After our family prayer, we had breakfast in the restaurant here at Howard Johnson's. We're right by Temple Square, and I felt the Lord watching over us as we walked past the temple. Tomorrow we will go back to see the Tabernacle Choir make its weekly broadcast. How wonderful it will be to hear those heavenly voices in person. I know the Lord will bless us during that time.

But today we went to Hogle Zoo. Mary Elizabeth was excited to see the elephants, and Zane wanted to see the monkeys. I'm happy to see any of God's creatures. It was hot at the zoo, but we had snow cones to cool off and later hot dogs and pop for lunch.

The kids were tired after and we returned to the hotel to put them down for naps.

Marcia and I are blessed with two wonderful children who are learning to love the gospel. How fortunate we are to have been sealed in the temple and can live together forever as a family. I know someday, Zane will serve a mission, bringing the Gospel to more of God's children. And both he and Mary Elizabeth will fall in love with amazing people and be sealed to their spouses forever in the temple. I look forward to being there and later to having grandchildren.

Zane wiped tears from his eyes and said, "I'm sorry I never made it to the temple, Dad. I hope you're not disappointed."

The creak of the door startled him. He looked up to see his mom "Is everything okay?"

"Everything is fine, Zane. I miss your father too. I heard what you said. Robert was proud of who you became and would be proud of you today. You became a good man."

Zane walked to the doorway and hugged her. "Thanks, Mom. I'm happy to hear that."

"The kids sure are excited for you to teach them how to ride a horse."

"I'll get them started tomorrow."

"I hear it might rain."

"Then if not tomorrow, we'll have a chance later in the week. Right now, it's late. We should get up to bed." He turned off the phonograph and the light and they both went upstairs.

Chapter 15

TUESDAY MORNING, THE RAIN CAME down in buckets, which was unusual for June in a desert state. Zane had to turn the wipers on high for the trip to town, where he parked in front of Bruce Colby's office, next door to Lou-Lou's Cafe. A large, plate-glass window on the front announced *Colby Agency - Utah Farm and Ranch Insurance Company*. Zane hadn't talked to Colby since the day at the lake when they rescued the two girls.

Inside the office, there were two desks, filing cabinets, a couple of guest chairs, and a hunting rifle that leaned against the wall in a corner. Colby sat behind one desk, tapping away at his computer. He stood when Zane came in, and they shook hands and exchanged greetings.

Colby said, "Have you heard anything about those two girls we pulled out of the lake?"

"Not a peep. I assume they're recovered, at least physically. They'll never forget that day. Or to go out in a canoe again without life vests."

Colby leaned back in his chair. "If they even get back into a canoe. How's your mom? We missed her at church on Sunday."

"Not so good this week." Zane then told him all about the red, yellow, and green weeks and that it was currently red.

"Somehow though, she pushed through a visit to my dad's grave at the cemetery yesterday. It was his birthday, and she really wanted to be there. Also, Mary Elizabeth's family arrived from Portland yesterday afternoon. The grandkids seemed to perk her up."

"I knew your father. He passed not long after I moved here. Must have been about eight, nine years ago. I believe I met you at the viewing."

"Dad's been gone for closer to seven. I don't remember if we met or not. They say a funeral is to help the family grieve, but I have to admit, it was mostly just a blur, though I remember some of it. How long have you been here?"

"Ten years now. My brother and I ran an agency in Vernal. I would come up here to the lake. We had enough business from here in Smith County to support an office, so here I am. I was elected to the county commission six years ago. Jared Snow, is another commissioner but an old timer. He's been in office for almost twenty years."

"Yeah, I know Jared. He's my mom's cousin. I take it you hunt. Nice looking deer rifle," Zane said, pointing towards it.

Colby swiveled his chair. "I just got it. It's a special order: . 30-06 with added laser scope. Top of the line." Colby picked it up and handed it to Zane.

"It's lighter than I expected." Zane removed the magazine and opened the bolt to verify the weapon wasn't loaded. There wasn't much distance in the office to try out the laser sight. "How does it shoot?"

"Haven't had it out yet. I'm going to the range this afternoon if this rain lets up. You're welcome to come along."

Zane hadn't fired a deer rifle in a while. The last time was the fall of his senior year in high school when he went deer hunting with his dad. He'd brought down a four-point buck.

"I may take you up on that, but I might have to bring Mary Elizabeth's kids along. Her oldest wants to get into law enforcement as a forensic tech, so she may be interested in some target shooting."

He returned the rifle to the corner. They sat and chatted for some time, talking like old friends before Zane got around to the reasons for his visit.

"I wanted to talk to you about Will Massey's murder."

"Terrible thing, that killing. I liked Will." He shook his head. "And I'm not sure how Tiffany will get along without him. What exactly did you want to know?"

"The Sheriff has been listening to town gossip that I'm getting back with Tiffany. He actually named me as a suspect. It's one-hundred percent false that Tiffany and I are getting back together. I was in Vernal with Mom for her chemotherapy the day Will died."

"It doesn't seem logical to me that you're involved. I hope you're not asking me, as a county commissioner, to tell the sheriff to back off, because that's not how I work."

Zane put one leg over the other, ankle to knee. "No, I wouldn't ask you to do that. I've set out to prove my innocence. There was a lot of opposition to Will's guest house he wanted to build. I know you supported the project. Could someone opposed to have wanted to make sure it didn't happen?"

Colby looked around as if making sure no one would hear him. It was just him and Zane in the office. Then, in a low voice, he said, "Sheriff Richman is looking pretty hard at Tiffany. Something about her being set against the guest house being the motive. You didn't hear this from me."

"That's a different motive from what he told me," Zane said.

"What exactly did he say?"

"Tiffany was my girlfriend back in high school. The Sheriff thinks she and I planned it all so we can get back together. It's all bullshit."

Bruce rubbed his chin. "Classic motive. I personally don't see Tiffany killing her husband, even with her being against his guest house."

"Why was the county commission involved in it?" Zane asked.

"His land is zoned agricultural," Colby said. "He petitioned the county commission to change it so he could build the guest house. He also wanted to put in a helipad to fly in his guests."

"Other than Tiffany, can you think of anyone who is opposed to it?"

"I supported it because it would bring in some tax revenue. A small county like ours could sure use it. There's a lot of people opposing it and a lot of people supporting it. But against it enough to kill a man? No, it makes little sense."

"I take it the commission was split?"

"I was the lone supporter. The other two, Jared and Lavell, were against it. Those two couldn't have killed him. In the end, they're politicians."

"What about Wayne Hubbard? He could have worried about his business."

"Oh, I didn't think of him. Yeah. Maybe?"

"What's your impression of him?" Zane said.

Colby picked up a pen and tapped it on his desk. "Wayne could be ornery, but I got along well with him despite our differences about Will's business. He's a client, you know."

Zane put his leg down and sat forward. "No, I didn't know that."

"Oh yeah. Ever since he moved in and built his ranch."

An inkling of an idea formed in Zane's head. It was just a spark, but Zane hoped it could catch fire. "Tell me about him. Is there a Mrs. Wayne Hubbard?"

"Dear no. He told me he had been married once, but never again. I took it that his marriage had a nasty end."

Zane knew from the newspaper article how it had ended. "And his business? Doing well?"

"That I don't know. He pays his premium on time. So, probably?"

"Does he have friends in town? People he might go hunting or fishing with?"

"Oh yeah. I've gone out with him a few times. So you have me, and the mayor. Let's see , who else? Oh, Bishop Brough."

Zane smiled, and his eyes grew wide as the spark ignited.

"Would you say you're good friends with him?"

"Probably as good as anyone."

The spark grew into an idea that fully engulfed him.

"I was out at his ranch yesterday. Tried to talk to him about Will's murder. Not only did he refuse to talk to me, but he had his ranch hands run me off at gunpoint."

"What? Did you tell the sheriff?"

"Nah. He doesn't need to be bothered with that. However, I do have an idea. Maybe you can talk to him about it. Just don't let him know I asked you to do it."

Colby did a double-take, his eyes wide. "Me? Snoop around?"

"It's not snooping. Just ask him some questions. Tell him about your new rifle over there and invite him shooting, then bring up Will's murder in normal conversation. Be real friendly."

"I don't know, Zane."

"Ah, come on, Bruce. I can tell you're good at talking with people."

Colby stood and paced the floor.

"I'll give you a list of questions to ask him. You'll just need to memorize them. If you read them off a list, he'll know something's up."

"You sure I'll be safe? You said he ran you off his land at gunpoint."

"Truthfully, I think he's like a small, yappy dog. All bark and no bite," Zane said.

Colby exhaled and ran his hand through his hair as he continued pacing.

"Bruce, this may be the only way for me to get any information out of him."

He stopped pacing and shrugged in resignation. "Alright, I'll do it. We'll go this afternoon, assuming the sun comes out. You can join us."

"Hold on. He won't open up if I'm there. Hell, he probably won't even show up if I'm there."

Colby slid a yellow legal pad and a pen across the desk, and Zane wrote out half a dozen things to ask Wayne Hubbard. When he finished, he slid the pad back. Bruce looked over the list and then called Hubbard to get it scheduled.

ZANE DROVE OUT TO SEE Jared Snow, one of the two county commissioners opposed to Will's guest house. He knew the man fairly well since he was part of the family. They saw each other regularly at family reunions and holidays when Zane was growing up. He lived out in Snowden, ten miles up the highway.

At family gatherings, Jared would sit on the floor and play Monopoly with Zane and some of the kids. "Nobody buys Body Odor Railroad. That one's mine," Jared would say. That's what he called B&O Railroad, and the kids would all laugh. It was always a miracle if they could get through the game without someone getting mad and flipping the board over.

Zane was surprised the big maple tree in front of Jared's house was gone. He figured it had probably died. In the summer, he'd try to climb it and Jared would always tell him to get down. He'd never made it up very far.

The house was different. The carport was gone, replaced with a garage.

Jared answered the door. He was a big man with gray hair, a big beard, and a bushy mustache combed sideways. Zane had never seen him wear glasses, but he now had a pair with round lenses and a wire frame. He pulled Zane to him in a bear hug.

"Come in and sit," then called, "Linda, Zane's here."

A clatter sounded from the kitchen, then Linda came into the room and hugged Zane. "Marcia told us you were here. We thought we'd see you sooner," she said.

Linda looked the same as when Zane last saw her at his dad's funeral. Some would call her stout; others, plump. She had cat-eye glasses, and her curly, gray hair cut short.

"I've been surprisingly busy since I moved back."

They spent a long time catching up on the past twenty-five years. Linda went to the kitchen to get some cookies for everyone. Finally, Jared brought the conversation back to the present. "I hear the sheriff thinks you're involved with Will Massey's killing."

"I am, in a way. Richie seems to think I was in on it with Tiffany. I'm out to clear my name."

Jared laughed. "I haven't heard him called Richie since he was a little kid. As for clearing your name, you weren't arrested. Wouldn't you be in jail if he thought you were guilty?"

"Only if there was enough actual evidence. He doesn't have that because I didn't do it. That's why I'm here. You had dealings with Will. Did he have any enemies?"

Jared stroked his beard. "You mean here in the area? I guess anyone opposed to that hotel thing he wanted to build. Not a dude ranch."

"A guest house," Linda said.

"Yeah, that's it. A guest house. He was pushing hard to get a zoning change for his land so he could build on it. He also wanted to put in a place for helicopters to land. Make it easy for his rich friends to get here. I think that's what people objected to the most. Didn't want all the noise."

"Is that why you opposed it?"

"That's one reason. The other is he came waltzing into town with all that money. Built that giant mansion. Threw money around like he owned the town. I wanted him to know he didn't. He was arrogant. Thought he was better than the rest of us."

"Sounds like you didn't like him much."

"You got that right."

"How do you feel about his wife?"

Linda spoke up. "She's changed since she was a kid."

"She definitely likes the money they have. Expensive clothes, jewelry, cars, but she doesn't have her nose up in the air like Will did," Jared added.

"Now, I have to ask you—where were you at the time of Will's murder?"

The question startled Linda. "Zane, you know us better than that. How can you ask such a question?"

"I hate doing it, but I have to ask to confirm what I think."

"We left early that morning and went to the temple in Vernal," Jared said.

"What about the other county commissioners? I understand Lavell Bateman opposed the zoning change, but Bruce Colby supported it."

"Bruce was Will's biggest cheerleader. Kept trying to get me to change my mind. He'd tell me how it would bring tax dollars into the county, spur more visitors and more cabins. There are too many now. Lavell was one-hundred percent with me."

Zane got up and looked at family photos covering one wall. He found one with his great grandparents and all their descendants. His mom looked about four. "Which one is you, Jared?"

"Third from the right on the second row. That's Marcia there on the left, first row."

Zane squinted to see better. "Ah, thanks. Now what about Wayne?"

"He hated the idea more than I did, and I can't blame him. It would have cut into his livelihood. I think it's a pretty good business too. He's busy down there most of the time."

Zane sat again. "Do you know him, Jared?"

"Not too well. He comes to church and sits in the back and then leaves after Sacrament Meeting. People seem to like him. You don't think he's the killer, do you?"

"Everyone's a suspect until they're not. Yes, that includes you."

Jared laughed. "You were a cop too long, Zane."

"That might be true. But Hubbard ran me off his land at gunpoint."

"What? At gun point? I knew he could be ornery, but that takes the cake."

Zane related the story of getting thrown off Hubbard's ranch.

"Zane," Linda said, "thank goodness he didn't kill you, too."

"We don't know that he killed anyone. All we have are hunches," Zane said. "I think you told me enough to scratch you off my suspect list." He stood to leave. "Thanks, Jared, Linda. Thanks for the cookies. They hit the spot."

"Don't leave just yet. I have something for your mother." Linda went to the kitchen.

"Be careful, Zane," Jared said. "If Wayne did it, he's dangerous."

"Don't worry. I'll be fine."

Linda returned with a paper bag and handed it to Zane. "Some more cookies I just baked."

"Thanks, Linda. I'm sure Mom will like them."

IT WAS MID-AFTERNOON BEFORE THE rain finally let up. Ash and Olivia again asked Zane to teach them how to ride a horse. Unfortunately, the corral had turned to mud, so they stayed indoors and played board games. Zane's mind was really on one thing—Bruce's meeting with Wayne Hubbard. Throughout the afternoon he wondered how things were going. As evening set in, concern grew with the shadows. Bruce should have called by now.

It was after 10:00 before Zane got the call he was expecting. "Wayne showed up right on time. I did what you said and worked it into the conversation. We were just shooting. That new .30-06 is sweet."

"But did you get the information I wanted?" Zane asked.

"Well, we were between rounds, checking and replacing the targets, reloading, you know."

Zane walked around the yard to work out his anticipation. He just wanted the information, not a life story.

Colby continued. "I said to him, 'Wayne, I'm sure you've heard the scuttlebutt going around about you and Will Massey.' He stopped what he was doing, a box of shells in his hand, and stared at me. The look on his face frightened me. He was all steely-eyed. I was terrified. It was quiet for what seemed like forever. I didn't know what to do. Finally, I said, 'I don't believe a word of it.'"

Zane said, "Good response."

"But he didn't say a word. He just closed that box of shells, picked up his stuff and left. Not a single word. Not a thanks. Not a goodbye," Bruce continued. "Took me some time to calm down. That's why I didn't call earlier. But the look he gave me. He did it Zane. He didn't say it, but it was the look in his eyes. Wayne Hubbard killed Will."

"You did fine, Bruce. How are you feeling now?"

"Still a bit shaken, but I'll be fine. I've never been face-to-face with a killer before. I need to call the sheriff and tell him."

"I'm sure Richie has already interviewed him. Talking to the sheriff won't do anything. Your feelings aren't evidence. Get a good night's sleep and in the morning, you'll see I'm right."

Bruce sighed. "Alright, Zane. I'll sleep on it."

"Thanks for your help."

The call ended. Zane didn't know what he would do now. He couldn't go to the sheriff without proof. All he had was hearsay and gut instinct. There was no evidence to prove Wayne Hubbard was a murderer, and he didn't know how to get it.

Chapter 16

THE FOYER OF THE MATHONI church house was an entry area that more resembled a doctor's waiting room than a church. Simple brick walls, painted white, and tightly woven carpet covered the floor. A sofa and chairs lined the walls. It hadn't changed since his dad's funeral. A hallway to the right led to the bishop's office, classrooms, and an area to hang coats. Directly across from the front doors, another hallway led to the kitchen and gym. On the left was the chapel where Will's funeral would be. Propped-open double doors provided easy access to the chapel.

The simplicity of the building was typical of a Mormon congregation. Instead of members attending whichever congregation they wished, wards, as local congregations were called, were assigned geographically; a member attended the ward that covered the area where they lived. Each ward could have up to five hundred members. Mathoni had two wards; both used the same building. In a heavily populated area, Salt Lake City, for example, a ward may only be a few blocks in size. A group of eight to ten wards were organized into a stake. Mathoni's wards were in the Vernal North Stake.

Organ music flowed through the open chapel doors, setting a

tone of reverence. Marcia followed the music into the chapel.

A TV in the foyer played a presentation about Will's life. Zane stood and watched it cycle through pictures of Will as a child to an adult. He too had played basketball in high school, and he'd been a missionary in Paris, France. Other pictures rotated through of his college graduation from BYU, wedding reception with Tiffany, Shaking hands with Bill Gates, the founder of Microsoft, Will and Tiffany at the Eiffel Tower with their children, then at the Coliseum in Rome, and London with Big Ben behind them. *It's just as well that we didn't marry, like everyone thought we would. I couldn't have given Tiffany anything like that.*

Funerals were often proceeded by a viewing where friends and loved ones could file past the open casket and give condolences to the family. Zane thought of the viewings for his grandparents. The first one he remembered was when he was eight. It was creepy to see the dead body of his Grandpa Snow in the casket, eyes closed as if asleep. He'd tentatively touched Grandpa's hand. It was ice cold. He'd thought about war movies where the dying soldier would always say he was cold, and he had wondered if he would feel the cold when he died and if that's why his grandpa was cold.

At his dad's viewing, he'd stood in the receiving line, and it seemed he shook hands and got condolences from the entire town. He'd had to speak at the funeral and was uncomfortable about it mainly because he was no longer active in the church. He wondered if he'd feel out of place again today.

There was no viewing for Will. Did that mean that the body was not in good condition? Or maybe the family wanted to limit Tiffany's public exposure? Perhaps some of both?

Ward members flowed in, some stopping to welcome Zane back home. He wondered if they could sense that he no longer followed the tenets of the church.

When the presentation on the TV circled back to the beginning, he turned and entered the chapel. An usher handed him a small, folded paper that was the program for the funeral. On the front was a picture of Will with the dates of his birth and death printed below. Will was about a year older than Zane.

Finding his mother, he slid into the pew and sat next to her. More people filed in and welcomed him. He opened the program.

On the left-hand page, Will's family was listed—his wife, children, parents, and the pallbearers. On the right-hand side was the program agenda for the funeral. Zane scanned the page and saw the names of people who would speak, including his children and a brother, and the names of hymns that the congregation or family members would sing. He was surprised to see that the burial would be in the Mathoni cemetery rather than Sacramento, where he grew up.

A few minutes later, the congregation stood as the mortician wheeled Will's casket in. The casket was closed, but it always was at this point. Will knew the family had been sequestered in the Relief Society room. The casket was normally open then so the family could say their goodbyes. Will and Tiffany had been married in the temple, or sealed as the Mormon church called it, for time and all eternity. The goodbyes were really 'we'll see you agains.' Then there would be a family prayer, meant to console them, and the casket would be closed.

Whispers from all around Zane began when Tiffany came in behind the casket, followed by their children and then other family members. Zane couldn't make out anything specific but knew it was a mix of 'She's guilty', 'She's innocent', 'Do you think she did it?', 'Shouldn't she be in jail?', and 'How dare she show up.' The Massey and Needham families snaked down the aisle to sit in the first rows of pews that were reserved for them. Tiffany's parents sat on one side of her with her kids on the other. An older couple, who Zane assumed were Will's parents, sat away from Tiffany. *A subtle sign they thought she was guilty?*

Zane looked around the chapel. The pews were only about half full, and of that, about a third were family of the deceased. *Were people staying away because they thought Tiffany guilty or were they busy with their farms and everyday life?* Mathoni was a small, conservative community, and Zane suspected it wasn't the latter.

There were several people in attendance that Zane recognized: Mayor Curtis Hale, county commissioners Jared Snow and Bruce Colby, and Jacob Faust, the Massey ranch manager. Rich Richman, wearing a suit and tie, sat near the back.

Bishop Brough stood, and the organist finished the prelude hymn she was playing. "Welcome all to this service honoring the life of Brother William Massey. I'm Bishop Brough of the Mathoni First Ward, and I will be conducting." He acknowledged several other ward and stake leaders sitting behind him on the stand. The congregation sang a hymn, and Will's cousin Kenneth offered a prayer.

Will's youngest son, Vincent, read his dad's obituary and gave a brief history of his dad's life. Will grew up in Sacramento, California. It was a large family with six brothers and sisters. He and Tiffany met at BYU. After college, he and his best friend, Brian Christian, had created a computer security company that was eventually sold to Microsoft. He'd been in the Bishopric in California before they moved to Mathoni. He loved to ski at Deer Valley, a resort next to Park City.

Zane felt an uneasiness come over him, much like he had at his father's funeral. He looked back at the podium and realized the speaker was someone different. The program said it was Charles, Will's older brother. He was saying something about a family trip to Seattle while growing up. Will had enjoyed the otters at the Seattle Aquarium, but liked the Space Needle the best.

The Massey children then sang a Primary song, *Families Can Be Together Forever,* and then Will Jr. got up to speak next.

But Zane couldn't shake the uneasy feeling. He knew the sheriff was a few rows back. Maybe that was it. He turned and looked. Richie Richman stared, steely-eyed at him. Zane nodded and then turned back to focus on the speaker.

The Bishop was up next, emphasizing the importance of family, both near and far, and how neighbors can be family too. He talked about being together again as a family in the afterlife. Another hymn was sung by Will's sisters, followed by another prayer to end the funeral.

Everyone stood while the pallbearers went forward and escorted the casket out to the hearse to take it to the cemetery. After the family was out the door, the congregation left too.

"That was a nice ceremony," Zane's mother said to him.

"I hope the family can get some peace, but I'm afraid that won't happen for some time. Murders are vicious crimes, and it can take years for the victim's family to get closure," Zane said.

"We should do something nice for the family."

"I'm sure the Relief Society has it under control," Zane said.

"Still, I'd like to do more. I'll have to think of something I can do to help."

When Zane and his mother got to the Wagoneer, he looked across the parking lot and saw Sheriff Richman watching him.

BACK HOME FROM THE FUNERAL, Zane was in a somber mood. *Why can't funerals be more of a celebration of life?* He thought about that as he changed out of his suit. *Why not have a big party where people laugh, dance, and have fun?*

Because his sister was off at the lake with her family, Zane was home in case Marcia needed him. He sat at the kitchen table, digging through the Internet for information on Wayne Hubbard. Everything he found led back to the Flying H Ranch. The Yelp reviews were all positive with comments. One commenter wrote 'Wayne is a great host. I felt like a real cowboy.' Another, 'I can't recommend this enough. Sitting in the saddle and herding cattle was the best time of my life.'

Seems that people like Wayne. Why was he so upset when I was there?

Zane didn't have an answer to that question, so he switched to finding information on the victim. Maybe there was someone in his past who had it out for Will. He and Brian Christian had founded a company in Lehi, Timpanogos Security, that specialized in computer security. Later, they moved the company from Utah to Silicon Valley to "be closer to funding sources." According to a magazine article he found, shortly after that, Christian left the company and Will became president, chief executive officer, and founder. The following year, Microsoft bought the company for $2.3 billion. That was about the time the Masseys moved to Mathoni.

Zane had heard rumors that Will had got a billion dollars in the sale. He couldn't even imagine that much money and wondered how much they really got. He added Brian Christian to his suspect list and then made another list of questions for Tiffany.

What can you tell me about Brian Christian?

How did you feel about moving to Silicon Valley?

Why did Brian Christian leave the company?

How much did you and Will get in the sale?

Did Christian get any money from the sale? If so, how much?

How was the relationship between Brian and Will before Brian left?

After he left and after the company was sold?

He found that Christian and his wife Janis had made several large donations after that. Five million to Santa Clara Medical Center, ten million to BYU, and another five million to Mercy General Hospital in Sacramento.

Zane looked at his watch and found two hours had sped past. He went to the living room to check on his mom and found her asleep in a chair, her knitting in her lap and her glasses still perched on her nose.

Back in the kitchen, he dropped a pod into the coffeemaker. When it was ready, he added cream and sugar to the mug, then sat again at the table to do research on Brian Christian. Just as he clicked into his search engine, he heard the front screen door slam shut.

"Shhh. Ash, I told you to be quiet. Grandma's asleep in her chair." Mary Elizabeth said.

Zane got up, and they went to the porch. "How was the lake, Ash?" he asked.

"The water is too cold, Uncle Zane. We couldn't go in it." Disappointment dripped from his words.

"How about we go ride the horse?"

Ash said, "Can I, Mom?"

"Go change into your blue jeans first," she said. "But remember, be quiet so you don't wake up Grandma."

Ash disappeared into the house.

"How's Mom doing, Zane?"

"She's been asleep for a couple of hours. The funeral really wore her out."

"Thank you for being home with her today."

Did she just thank me? "You're welcome, Sis."

Neil and the other kids appeared.

Mary Elizabeth said, "Olivia, if you want to ride, go put on some blue jeans. Your uncle will meet you out in the barn."

Chapter 17

AFTER THE SOLEMNITY OF WILL'S funeral, the next day was a big shift. Founders' Day traditionally brought out the entire town and even tourists who were there just to have fun.

Zane and family were up and out the door before 7:00 to head to the city park to kick off the festivities with a pancake breakfast. This was one of Zane's favorite days when he was young, even though the pancakes and eggs were always cold by the time he got his plate loaded up. He wondered whether today would be any different.

In 1899, Mormon Church prophet Lorenzo Snow sent his son Mansfield to settle the area. Their first winter in the area was harsh, and three members of the group, including Mansfield's youngest child, died. However, they persevered, and now every year the town celebrates the day the settlers first arrived. When Zane was born, he was given the middle name of Lorenzo, in memory of his ancestor.

At the city park, Zane got Marcia seated at a table and then he queued up to get breakfast for both of them. Bruce Colby flipped pancakes onto the plates. Mayor Curtis Hale was on egg duty. Parley Brough had hash brown duty. Even Lou Kloepfer was pulled away from Lou-Lou's and manned the fry grill for the bacon. The plates were loaded, just as Zane remembered. When he returned to the table, the food temperature was as he expected —cold—but he still ate it. Mary Elizabeth's family sat with them, Ash's plate piled twice as high as the others.

"Ash," Zane said, "you going to eat all that?"

The kid blushed. "I'll bet you ten dollars I'll eat it all, Uncle Zane."

Zane chuckled. "Deal."

Ash started eating in a way that made Zane wonder if he would be out ten dollars.

Little kids ran around screaming and laughing. Zane remembered being one of them. Playing chase or hide-and-seek. His father yelled at him over the noise to be careful. One year when he was five or six, he was pushed from behind and fell to the ground. He tore a hole in his pants and got a big scrape on his knee that bled. It hurt so bad and he cried for his mom. She was soon there and sat on the ground with him, holding him in her arms. Someone showed up with a first-aid kit and water. They washed off his knee and put alcohol on it. That stung worse than the wound. They put a big bandage on the wound, and Mom held him until he stopped crying. He was soon up and running around again as if it had never happened.

He looked over at his mom, and thought of the love she had for him. He didn't get emotional much, but his eyes teared up. "Mom, remember the year when I fell here and scraped my knee?"

"You were so little. How do you remember it?"

"We remember traumatic stuff. I don't know if I ever said thank you for being there for me that day."

He looked at his mom, her eyes also tearing up. "You're welcome. It's what moms do."

They sat for a few minutes in silence, Ash still working on his breakfast.

The squelch of a bullhorn pulled them back to reality.

"Thank you all for coming out for this year's Founder's Day," Mayor Hale said. "The horseshoe-tossing contest will get underway over on the north end of the park in fifteen minutes."

"Just like old times, isn't it, Mom?"

"Not quite, Zane. Your father isn't here."

And Zane knew how much she missed his father. Her husband. Her partner. His eyes watered up again. He missed him too. "Are you doing okay, Mom? Need anything?"

"I'm fine right now. Just thinking about Robert."

"Me too."

She smiled at him. One of those smiles from a mom to a son that said how much she loved him. That said everything. He was sure she'd smiled at him that way when he returned home. Hadn't she?

He took her hand. "Thank you for everything, Mom. I love you."

"I love you too. I always have. I'm happy you're back here."

Zane blushed. Ah, shit, he thought as more tears filled his eyes.

A clank sounded across the park and was followed by cheers. Someone got a ringer at the horseshoe pitch. Then more clanks and cheers.

"Do you want to go watch, Mom?"

"You go. I'll be alright here."

He got to the pitch in time to see Bruce Colby declared the winner. Then, the mayor awarded him a championship medal on a long ribbon. Colby put it over his head, the medal resting in the center of his chest.

Mayor Hale came on the bullhorn again. "Now, if you'll head over to the west end, we'll have the tug-of-war. The crowd headed in that direction. Zane wondered how big the mud pit would be this year.

It turned out it was quite large and very gooey. Bruce Colby was the designated judge. There were eight teams, with five members on a team. The team with the largest members comprised linemen from the high school football team. If there had been wagering, Zane would have bet on them to win. In the end, they were the only team to come out clean. They jumped and hollered as if they'd just won the state football championship. Each team member got a medal from the mayor.

Zane went back to check on his mom. Someone had brought

out a lawn chair from the Wagoneer, and she was sitting in the shade of a maple tree talking to Neil and Mary Elizabeth. The kids weren't around, except for Ash, who was still working on his breakfast. Zane was impressed. His nephew had nearly finished clearing his plate. He checked his wallet to make sure he had a ten-spot.

Heading to the arcade, Zane found his nieces at the ring toss. He watched them for a few minutes, and then they went to the basketball shooting booth. Zane took a turn, hit every shot, and won a stuffed bear for each of his nieces.

He then wandered through the arts and crafts area, where people sold stuff they'd made. When he was a kid, there were only a few booths. Now there were dozens. One man from Vernal had amazing clay pots. A woman made caricature sketches of people. A Native American woman had silver and turquoise jewelry. Others sold fresh berries, jam, pies, cinnamon rolls, macrame, 3-D printed toys, kid's face painting, and more. Zane realized how much this part of Founder's Day had grown.

At the end of one row, the mayor sat on the dunk tank, and a long line had formed to drop him into the water. It was his own son who finally got him—and on his first try. Zane later found out the kid was the pitcher on the high school baseball team.

Bruce Colby replaced the mayor on the tank. Several losers in the tug-of-war were ready for him. Zane watched and laughed as they dunked Colby time after time after time, shouts of victory from the crowd whenever Colby dropped and got wet. Colby was laughing along with the crowd. He was a good sport.

Zane needed to use the restroom and walked behind the rodeo ground bleachers. The noise of the crowd faded away, and he passed a woman with a small girl heading back to the crowd.

Out of the corner of his eye, he spotted some movement in the shadows under a bleacher, but when he looked, no one was there. Zane continued toward the restrooms. Next thing he knew, he was on the ground, pain surging in the back of his head. He reached back to rub the spot and felt something wet. He looked at his hand. Red liquid covered his fingers. Then everything went black.

* * *

ZANE SLOWLY CAME TO. HIS face was in the dirt. His whole body ached; the back of his head hurt the most. He rolled over, spit dirt out of his mouth, and groaned. He hurt everywhere and struggled to his feet only to stumble and fall to his knees. When he got up again, he staggered toward the crowd. Everything looked fuzzy.

Some teenage boys pointed at him and laughed. "Look at that dude. He's drunk."

He fell again.

Zane felt arms around him, lifting him and dragging him forward. Zane couldn't see their faces, and he still couldn't focus on anything. He was in the grass and heard someone call for medics.

He heard sirens and someone calling his name.

The next thing he saw was light shining in his eyes. Beeps and buzzing seemed to come from all around him.

"Zane, can you hear me?"

Someone squeezed his hand.

"Zane?"

He blinked.

"My mom. Is she okay?" Zane barely got out a whisper.

"She's fine," someone said.

"Where am I?"

"You're at Ashley Valley Hospital in Vernal. You've been badly beaten. Nothing broken—one cracked rib. No internal bleeding. Do you understand?"

Zane nodded.

"We're keeping you . . ."

He tried to sit up, but someone pushed him back and said something to him, but he didn't understand.

He woke again in a bed and groaned. There were footsteps nearby.

"Nurse!" Marcia called.

He heard more footsteps getting louder as someone approached. "I'll get the doctor." Zane assumed that was the nurse his mom had called.

Zane blinked. He thought he saw the ceiling, but the light was dim. What the hell is that beeping?

"Zane, it's Mom. Can you hear me?"

"Yes." It was just a whisper. His throat hurt; his mouth was dry. Someone pushed a straw between his lips. He sucked at it, the liquid cooling his throat.

"Yeah, I can hear you," his voice stronger now.

"Oh, Zane. I was so worried about you. The doctors say you'll be alright. Just a few days of bed rest."

"I was heading to the restroom behind the rodeo bleachers and felt a sudden pain in the back of my head. I was dizzy. Then woke up here."

A man said, "Mr. Grayson?"

Zane looked in the direction of the voice. He didn't recognize the man in the white coat.

"I'm Dr. Zobell. You're in the hospital in Vernal."

Zane looked around the room. The smell of disinfectant was heavy in the air.

A cold stethoscope pushed against his chest.

"Sounds fine," Dr. Zobell said. "You had quite a beating. Our guess is you were kicked and punched multiple times."

"Zane, who did this?" Marcia asked.

He looked to his right, where Mom was sitting next to the bed. "I don't know. Never saw them. What time is it?"

"10:24 p.m. They're keeping you overnight just to make sure you're okay."

He nodded. "Did Ash finish his breakfast?"

Marcia shook her head. "That's what you're worried about?"

"Well, did he?"

Mary Elizabeth said, "Ash asked me to tell you that you owe him ten dollars."

Zane smiled and then winced from the pain. "Mom, go home and get some rest."

"I'm staying," she insisted.

Mary Elizabeth said, "Neil and the kids are at the house. I'm stepping out to call them with an update."

"Mr. Grayson, we didn't find any signs of a concussion," Doctor Zobell said. "But you took a pretty good blow to the head.

You'll have some nasty bruises for a while along with aches and pains."

"Who found me?"

Marcia provided the details. "Bruce Colby. He got some help and called for the medics. They brought you straight here. Zane, they found a paper in your pocket that said, 'Stop your investigation.'"

"I can't stop, Mom. I'm on to something."

Chapter 18

ZANE HAD NEVER FELT SUCH pain as when he woke up. He tried to shift a bit in the bed, but it didn't help. Every inch of him screamed out. Even his hair hurt.

He groaned and Marcia appeared at his bedside. Her eyes were swollen and red, and her dress wrinkled.

Sunlight streamed through the window.

"Have you been here all night, Mom?"

"I wanted to stay, but they wouldn't let me. Mary Elizabeth drove me here first thing this morning. She just stepped out to call Neil. You must be hungry. We should get you some breakfast."

Zane coughed and wrapped his arms around himself.

"Maybe something for the pain, too," Marcia said.

He wanted to tell her he'd be fine, but he couldn't lie. Not to Mom. "Hurts like hell." He sat up so he could get out of bed and winced.

"Zane, lie down. You need bed rest."

"I have work to do. You need to rest at home." He pressed the button for the nurse.

"You should wait for the doctor to discharge you," Marcia said.

Zane groaned again. "Fuck, it hurts to breathe."

"Language," Marcia chastised him.

A nurse walked in, saw Zane sitting on the edge of the bed. "You shouldn't be out of bed, Mr. Grayson."

"I need to leave."

The nurse shook her head. "Dr. Zobell left instructions for you to stay on bed rest. You were badly beaten."

"Just get me some pain killers and I'll be on my way. I'm sure you have some papers for me to sign."

The nurse let out a heavy sigh. "It will take some time. I'll be back. By the way, there's a Sheriff's Deputy here to see you." She left Zane and Marcia alone in the room.

Zane tried to stand, nearly collapsed, then sat on the bed again.

"Now do you see the doctor is right?" Marcia shook her head. "You haven't changed in all these years. You're as stubborn as your father was. You should lie back and rest."

"I just need some pain meds, preferably Ibuprofen. I don't want anything that will make me sleepy. There's a killer out there and I need to find him."

A knock on the door drew their attention. "You can come in," Zane said.

The door opened and Deputy Ambler from the Smith County Sheriff's Office came in. "Mr. Grayson, I have some questions for you about the attack if you're feeling up to answering them."

"Let's get it over with."

Ambler looked over at Marcia. "Ma'am, could you excuse us while I talk to your son?"

"I'll step out and find Mary Elizabeth," she said.

Once Zane's Marcia left, Deputy Ambler took a notebook and pencil from his pocket. "Tell me what happened yesterday at the Founder's Day celebration."

"I was walking through all the vendor booths and needed to use the restroom. The one behind the rodeo arena grandstand was the closest, so I headed that direction. I remember falling and my head exploded. I don't remember anything after that."

"Did you see or hear anyone?"

"Nope."

"We found a note in your pocket."

"My mom told me about a note. Where is it?" Zane said.

"It's locked up as evidence, but it read, 'Stop your investigation.' I assume it was a warning for you to back off your snooping around Will Massey's murder."

"I'm not snooping. I'm clearing my name."

"Alright. If that's what you want to call it. Anyone you can think of that could be the attacker?"

Zane coughed and groaned. "Anyone that wants me out of the way."

"Anyone in particular?"

"I don't know. Maybe the killer?"

Ambler scribbled a note. "Why is that, Mr. Grayson?"

"You tell me. Who is on your list of suspects for Will's murder, besides me?"

"You know I can't answer that."

"My assumption is that . . ." Zane coughed again, "anyone on your suspect list could have attacked me. You can start there."

The deputy closed his notebook and handed Zane his business card. "If you think of anything, please contact me. I recommend you do exactly as the note warned or you could find yourself in a jail cell. The murder of Mr. Massey is an ongoing investigation." He turned and left.

Marcia returned with Mary Elizabeth and asked about Ambler's visit. Zane was updating them when a doctor walked in.

"I hear you want to leave. I strongly advise against it," Dr. Zobell said.

"Message received, but I need to get out of here."

The doctor looked at Marcia for some help. She held up her hands in surrender. "Very well. Let me have a last look at you before you're released."

He examined Zane then left. A few minutes later, the nurse came back and unhooked his IV. Another woman soon arrived with discharge papers.

Two hours later, Zane had a bottle of prescription strength Ibuprofen and they were on their way home, Mary Elizabeth behind the wheel.

Back home, Zane again told the story of how he walked behind the bleachers and was attacked. He had no memory of anything else. He headed upstairs to clean up, but Mary Elizabeth intercepted him just outside his bedroom.

"Did you tell Mom yet?"

"Not exactly."

"What does that mean?"

"I haven't told her, but she knows. What happened to me made it obvious."

"I'm going home. Tomorrow. So you'd better tell her rather than her assuming that you won't be helping her. Tell her now." She walked away.

Zane washed up a bit with a washcloth and shaved. After he dressed, he headed downstairs. Marcia was alone in the living room, knitting needles in hand.

"Mom, I have something to talk to you about."

She took off her glasses and looked over at Zane. "You know you can tell me anything."

"Yeah . . ." He couldn't get the words out.

"Zane, what's wrong?"

He sighed. This was harder than he'd expected. "So, I've been putting off telling you this. I'm not sure how much I can help you out after Mary Elizabeth goes home."

"Is that what's been worrying you?"

He took a deep breath and winced. "I'm all in on finding Will's murderer. I'll be out following up leads and trying to solve the crime and may not be here when you need me. My name also needs clearing, and Tiffany's too. She could be fighting for her life."

"So am I."

Zane stared at her. He knew there was a chance she wouldn't survive, but hearing his mom made it hit home like it never had before. "I know, but you're doing well. The doctors said that you're doing great. She's not."

"Oh, Zane. I've known all along that you would move heaven and earth if you thought it would help Tiffany," she said. "You still love her, don't you." It was more a statement than a question.

"I honestly don't know. However, I do know she didn't kill her husband."

"But someone did, and now they're after you. That has me worried."

Zane walked over to Marcia, bent down, and hugged her. "All killers are violent. I've chased them before. I'm on the right trail, and the killer is running scared. That's why someone attacked me."

"You do what you need to do . I'll be fine. It's yellow week, so I won't need much help." She went to hug him back, then stopped. "I don't want to hurt you, so I guess I better not hug you right now."

"Thanks, Mom. Where's Mary Elizabeth?"

"She's out teaching the kids to ride a horse."

"Shit. I promised to do that." He headed out to find his sister and located her in the barn and pulled her aside.

"I told Mom."

"And?"

"She said she knew all along that caring for her would take a backseat to finding the killer, and she'll be fine."

"That's so like her," she said.

"I need to go. I have a suspect to interview."

ZANE'S MISSION WAS TO TALK to Lavell Bateman, the third county commissioner. He had never met the man because he moved to the area after Zane left, but he knew he lived north of town, almost to Daggettt County, much of the travel on a winding dirt road. He never would have found the place if not for Bruce Colby's directions.

Winters in Smith County could be harsh, and he wondered how Bateman got in and out when the snow blew in. He had his answer when he finally got to the ranch. An old, orange Thiokol Snow Cat, like the machines used by ski resorts to groom the runs, sat parked near the garage. The Snow Cat has large tracks, similar to an Army tank, but instead of a cannon, it had a cabin that could seat several people. He hadn't seen one since he was a kid.

The house was a single-story, yellow brick rambler. He knocked on the door and waited, then knocked again. With no answer, he shouted. "Hello?" It was obvious no one was home. He wondered if he had the right house.

He got in his truck and headed back towards town. About half-way down the dirt road he saw a dust cloud ahead and knew someone was coming in the other direction. They soon met up. It was a white, 1970s Ford Bronco.

The two vehicles stopped when they got next to each other. The sun reflected off the other car and into Zane's eyes, so he couldn't see the other driver, but he said, "You must have been out looking for me. Just follow me back."

Zane waited long enough for the dirt cloud kicked up from Bateman's Bronco to dissipate, then turned around and headed back.

As he slid out of his truck, Zane groaned in pain. He glanced over at Bateman's SUV and noticed the rifles in the gun rack behind the seat. Looking back at the house, he saw Bateman was already on the porch, leaning on a cane. He was as tall as Zane, with a large build. White hair poked out around his cowboy hat, and rectangular wire-framed glasses sat on the top of the largest nose Zane had ever seen. *Grandpa Grayson would have called it 'a large proboscis.'*

Inside was cozy with furniture covered by worn slipcovers. Crocheted doilies sat underneath a couple of lamps on end tables.

Zane sat on the couch and Bateman in an old wooden rocker. Across from Zane was a fireplace stacked with logs. When Bateman set his cane on one of the end tables, Zane saw it wasn't a cane but a walking stick with an ornate brass knob as a handle.

After exchanging introductions, Zane asked, "Is it just you or is there a Mrs. Bateman?"

"It's just me. Sandra passed last year. I retired from farming and sold most of my land. I just kept this parcel with my home," he said, sadness in his voice.

Zane pointed to a photograph of Bateman and a woman hanging on the wall. "Is that Sandra?"

Bateman looked up at it. "Yeah, that's her. That photo was taken about three years ago. Back when she was full of life, before she got sick."

"I'm sorry to hear about her passing."

"Thank you kindly."

"Why are you still way out here? You could have moved closer to town."

"It's not so bad, except in the winter." Bateman took a handkerchief from his back pocket and wiped his eyes.

"I saw that Snow Cat out there. Does it still run?" Zane said.

"It's persnickety, but it runs. In the winter, I park the truck at Carl Snow's place and then take the Cat in and out. You probably know Carl. He's been here forever."

"Yeah. He's related, but you know after some point, you lose track of who is who in the family. There were so many aunts and uncles, who had kids, then they had kids. Pretty soon, you give up trying to match family members."

"Well, I guess so. Sandra couldn't have kids." Bateman frowned and looked away. Zane thought he saw a tear. After a minute, Bateman wiped his eyes again, blew his nose, and returned the handkerchief to where he'd pulled it.

"Sorry, Mr. Bateman. I didn't mean to bring up memories."

"I'm okay. Just miss my wife sometimes being all alone. Now, what brings you all the way out here to see me?"

Zane thought about Mom being alone since Dad's death and wondered if she was lonely. "Well, as you know, William Massey was killed."

"Yeah, I know." There was disgust in Bateman's tone.

"I'm investigating his murder and . . ."

"Just a minute now. What got your nose poking into it?"

Zane held back a smirk. *If anyone had his nose in it, it would be you.* "The Sheriff seems to think I was in collusion with Tiffany."

"Tiffany, huh. You just come into town and already call her by her first name. Seems to me, the sheriff may be right."

"I had nothing to do with it. Tiffany and I are old friends. We went to high school together, along with the sheriff's brother. We all hung out."

"So, if you had nothing to do with the murder, why are you still investigating?"

"Because the sheriff hasn't said that I'm not a suspect."

"He suspects you, but you haven't been arrested? Seems wrong to me. As a county commissioner, I think I'll have to talk to the sheriff and find out why you aren't in jail."

Zane didn't expect that line. "I can tell you why."

Bateman looked at Zane, suspicion in his eyes. "Sheriff Richman's big brother was my best friend. Rich wanted to do everything with us, but he was younger, and we wouldn't let him tag along. We would tease him because he was small and scrawny. I'm a suspect because he's getting back at me for that. However, there's no evidence I murdered Will because I wasn't even in town. I was in Vernal at the hospital with my mom. Easy to prove."

"Again, why the hell are you poking your nose into something that ain't your business?"

"The sheriff still thinks I'm connected, and that has me looking for the actual killer."

Bateman laughed. "And you're here because you think I did it?"

Zane ran his hand through his hair. This clearly was not going as easily as he'd hoped.

"Mr. Bateman, before I moved back here, I was a police detective in California. I solved homicides. I know what I'm doing. I know cops sometimes think they know who's guilty and fixate on them, ignoring the actual killer."

"And you think that's what the sheriff is doing?"

"Not completely. Tiffany and I were . . . an item back in high school, so we have some history."

"Nothing you've told me . . ."

"Let me continue. A good cop will suspect everyone until they are all eliminated, or he gets enough evidence to prove one of them is guilty. What I'm trying to do is eliminate you from the suspect list. I know Will was pressuring you to approve his zoning change request. So maybe you are, and I'm not saying I'm right, I'm eliminating everyone I can, but maybe there was enough animosity between you and him that caused you to break and well, kill him. But maybe not."

"Jared Snow was against the zoning change. You suspect him, or did you automatically dismiss him because he's your cousin?" His voice was full of anger.

Zane rubbed the back of his neck and then crossed his arms. "Second-cousin actually. As I said, everyone is a suspect until I can eliminate them. I didn't dismiss him because we're related. I already talked to him, as a matter of fact." He wondered if he should move Bateman up the suspect list.

"You talk to that man, Hubbard? He had quite a bit to lose."

"I haven't talked to him yet. It's not from a lack of effort. He ran me off his property at gunpoint before I could begin questioning him."

Bateman let out a loud, hearty laugh. "Did he now? Sounds like he had a good idea. Alright, I guess I'll tell you. I had nothing to do with the murder. Personally, I liked Will Massey. I just thought his idea wasn't good for the county. Sure, we could use the tax dollars, but if he gets a zoning change to build a luxury hotel up there—and that's what it really was—then others will come in and ask for the same. We've got enough rich, city folk putting in cabins now. Don't need no more. Including that damn luxury hotel. I told him I'd do everything in my power to stop the damn thing."

"Everything?" Zane said.

"Everything in my power as a county commissioner."

Or everything, including murder? "So, where were you when Will Massey was killed?" Zane asked.

"Right here at home. Before you ask, I was alone."

Zane wanted to ask him if he could think of anyone that would kill Massey, but after the belligerence he'd faced, he was ready to leave. "Thank you, Mr. Bateman. That's all I needed to know." He stood and started toward the front door.

"Grayson," Bateman said.

Zane turned to look at the older man. It had been months since he'd been called only by his last name.

"I'm still going to talk to Sheriff Richman about this."

"Do what you have to, Mr. Bateman." And with that, Zane left.

As he drove down the dirt road back to Mathoni, Zane wondered what had happened to the friendly little town where he grew up. Lavell Bateman was anything but agreeable to answering questions. Wayne Hubbard had forced him off the land at gunpoint, and quickly rose to the top of his suspect list. Bateman wasn't far behind.

Chapter 19

MOM WAS NOW ZANE'S RESPONSIBILITY, and his alone. Mary Elizabeth and family left at 5:00 a.m. for the fifteen-hour drive back to Portland, and the house was quiet Saturday morning.

Zane sat at the kitchen table with his coffee, his body racked with pain from the attack, and contemplated how he'd be able to help his mom with his body bruised and barely able to move, in addition to working Will's murder. Maybe they could get help from the church. He was sure the Relief Society, the church's women's organization, would help. After all, helping people in need was one of its purposes.

Then he turned to his list of suspects. First there was his primary suspect, Wayne Hubbard, whose entire livelihood was threatened by Will's guest house. The way he ran Zane off also made him look more guilty.

Then Will's ranch manager, Jacob Faust, was an unlikely suspect as he would probably lose his job now, but Zane couldn't eliminate him. He said he was in good with Will, but was he really?

Next were the county commissioners. Zane eliminated Bruce Colby because he supported Will's plans. Mom's cousin opposed the guest house, but his gut told him Jared didn't do it. That left

Lavell Bateman, who liked Will but opposed the guest house. The more Zane had thought about him, the more he thought the man belonged on the list. His attitude didn't help him seem innocent.

His own farmhand, Levi Smoot, who was turned down for a job working for Will. Zane ruled him out.

Following Levi was Tomás Sanchez, who Will fired. Of all the suspects still on the list, Sanchez was at the bottom. It seemed unlikely that he would kill because he lost a ranch hand job. Just the same, Zane still needed to follow up on him.

Will's lawyer, Sal Giovanni, who apparently was something of a slimeball, came next. He didn't seem like a suitable candidate, but his connection to the guest house was unusual.

Then there was his old girlfriend. The Tiffany from thirty years ago couldn't have killed her own husband. She couldn't even step on a spider. She'd urge them onto a sheet of paper and release them outside. Today's Tiffany didn't want the guest house, and there had been that huge public argument that Zane had witnessed. That didn't make her look good. She had slapped him so she could get violent. He still didn't completely understand why his stomach flipped-flopped every time he saw her. Did he still have feelings for her? Were they clouding his judgment? She didn't have a solid alibi, but he believed she was innocent.

Finally, he had Brian Christian, Will's former business partner, who'd been left like a bride at the altar when Will sold the company to Microsoft for billions of dollars.

Zane had taken this case based on his gut and the sheriff trying to force the Zane piece to fit into the puzzle. A piece that would never fit.

Going through this list, he realized he had four good suspects. Wayne Hubbard, Brian Christian, Lavell Bateman, and Sal Giovanni. He still needed to track down Sanchez.

He decided that today he'd talk to Tiffany about Brian Christian. Then, not having another way to talk to Hubbard, he'd do something he had decided against earlier—set up surveillance on the Flying H Ranch and hope for the opportunity to question the man. He also knew he could be there a long time, so he'd take something to eat. He was in the middle of making sandwiches when his cell phone rang.

He tapped the button to answer. "Grayson."

"Zane, it's George Needham."

"Morning. What can I do for you?"

"I'm at Tiffany's house. The sheriff is here with a search warrant."

"I'm on my way," Zane said.

THREE SHERIFF'S VEHICLES WERE PARKED in front of the Massey home. Zane rang the doorbell, then clenched and unclenched his fists. George opened the door and led Zane inside to the great room, where a sheriff's deputy stood watch from a corner. Zane headed straight to Tiffany, who sat in a chair staring out the window, a blue throw pillow clutched tightly to her chest.

Zane crouched next to her. "Tiff."

She looked at him. "They're in my house. Again. Get them out."

Zane winced as he stood and walked to the deputy. "I'd like to talk to the sheriff."

The deputy clicked the microphone hanging on his shoulder. "Sheriff, can you come out here? Mr. Grayson is asking to see you."

Zane looked around the room. "Where are the kids?" he asked.

"Will's parents took them back to Sacramento for a few days," George said.

Sheriff Richman came into the great room from the master bedroom, his hat in his hand, and said, "Zane, why are you here?"

"I got a call from George that you were here with a search warrant."

Richman fidgeted with the hat. "If you keep inserting yourself into this investigation, you'll be the one we're arresting. I know you talked to everyone on the county commission. Treated them all as suspects."

"I assume Lavell Bateman told you," Zane said.

"It doesn't matter where I got my information. Only that you know better than to get involved in an active investigation. Now, how about you get out of my crime scene?"

Zane walked over to Sheriff Richman and spoke in a low voice, "What exactly are you looking for?"

"That's all spelled out in the search warrant."

His radio crackled. "Sheriff, you better come back here. We found something."

Richman turned and walked back to the master bedroom.

"George," Zane said once Richman was out of earshot, "did the sheriff give you a copy of the search warrant?"

"I didn't see one," George said.

The sheriff returned a few minutes later. "Seems we have the murder weapon." He walked over to Tiffany. "Mrs. Massey, please stand up."

She looked up at him. "I've had enough of you. Get out of my house."

Richman took her by the elbow and coaxed her to her feet. "Tiffany Massey, you're under arrest for the murder of William Massey."

George collapsed.

She looked at Zane, tears streaming down her cheeks. "Please help me. I didn't do it," she pleaded. The deputy from the corner took her out to one of the Sheriff's Department SUVs.

Zane kneeled on the floor to help George. "I think he just fainted. Rich, let's him onto the sofa." They laid George on the couch and got his feet elevated.

"Sheriff," Zane finally said, "what did you find?"

Richman put on his best 'I'm in charge here' voice, and said, "An anonymous call pointed us toward where the murder weapon was located. Upon obtaining a search warrant for the premises, we began our search. In the back of a closet in Mrs. Massey's bedroom, behind some towels, we located a hay hook that appears to have dried blood on it. Blood that should prove to have come from the victim."

A groan came from the couch. Zane helped George sit up.

"I'm fine. Things just hit me hard, and I fainted. Nothing more. Where's Tiffany?"

"We've taken her to the county jail," Richman said. "You'll be able to see her later, after we finish processing her. Now, if you'll excuse me. I need to inventory this new evidence." He turned and walked away.

Zane told George to call his wife so he wouldn't be alone after fainting. After talking to his wife, George called Tiffany's attorney.

ZANE STAYED WITH GEORGE UNTIL Betty showed up before he headed out for the day's mission, the surveillance of Wayne Hubbard's ranch. He did not know whether Hubbard would leave his ranch or if he was there. Somehow, he had to find a way to question him.

There were no side roads or trees to park behind at the entrance to Hubbard's ranch. The hills were mostly covered in sagebrush. He decided there was no reason to be discreet. He parked across the road from the entrance to Hubbard's place, where he could see anyone coming or going from the Flying H Ranch, then settled in for a long afternoon.

He had downloaded a Louis L'Amour collection of audio books narrated by Willie Nelson, Waylon Jennings, Johnny Cash, and others. Something to concentrate on would help him stay awake. He took Ibuprofen caplets, unwrapped a tuna sandwich, and turned on book one, *Riding for the Brand.*

An hour later he was still there and had seen no one on the lonely stretch of road. He did not know what was happening with Louis L'Amour as his mind had been on Tiffany, the arrest, and that hay hook that Sheriff Richman claimed was the murder weapon.

The mysterious anonymous call weighed heavily on him and caused him to think the hay hook was planted. Only the family or the actual killer would know it was there. He couldn't imagine any of Tiffany's kids as murderers. He wondered if Tiffany really was guilty, then quickly dismissed it. Her reactions on the day of the murder and at the time of arrest were real. Her participation in high school plays told him she was no actor.

Either the killer was at the house on the day of the murder or had access afterwards. Other than the family, only Jacob, the other ranch hands, and law enforcement had access to the house. *It wouldn't surprise me if Richie did a sloppy job searching the house.*

What about afterwards? There were several days when the

family was staying at George's and the Massey home was empty. Could someone have gained access and planted the hay hook then? He needed to talk to Jacob.

However, new issue had come up. One of the biggest problems of being on surveillance. He had to pee. Being alone meant holding it or risking missing the suspect while stepping away to take care of business. The nearest public restroom was several miles back at the Gas & Guzzle.

He looked up and down the road, checking for a dust cloud indicating someone was coming. Seeing no one, Zane opened the door and slowly got out of his truck. He groaned and hobbled around to the passenger side, away from the road, and opened the door to the front seat and the one to the crew cab, then stepped between them and unzipped his fly. He hoped the cover of the two doors and the truck itself would be enough to keep him hidden should someone drive by.

A dust cloud rose in the distance. Now he panicked, only that made him nervous, and it became more difficult to do his business. Up the road, the dust cloud was closer—it was just over the hill now. The driver would see him when they crested the top.

Zane willed things to move faster, but nature has its own timetable. He looked towards the dust cloud. A white pickup truck was heading down the hill. It would pass by him and see what he was doing.

But luck was on his side after all. He finished, zipped up, closed the doors, and walked around to the other side of his truck just as the other driver passed him by. They gave each other a wave as the driver continued on his way. Zane got back in the truck and let out a sigh of relief.

Two hours went by with no activity when, finally, an SUV drove out of the ranch. Hubbard's hired hand Carrie was at the wheel. She stared at Zane and gave him a middle finger as she turned onto Sheep Creek Road, heading away from town.

A few minutes later, Zane spotted a dust cloud coming towards him. He soon saw the flashing red lights of a sheriff's vehicle. It stopped behind him, and a deputy stepped out and walked up to Zane's truck. Deputy Ambler tapped on the side window. Zane turned off the audiobook and rolled down the window.

"Mr. Grayson. Can you tell me what you're doing out here?"

Zane knew the routine. "Listening to this audiobook."

"Why are you doing it here?"

"As good as any other place," Zane replied, his voice thick with sarcasm.

Ambler continued, "We got a report that you're harassing Mr. Hubbard and his employees."

"Considering I haven't set foot on his property today, nor have I spoken to Hubbard or his employees, I can't say I've harassed them. One drove out a bit ago, flipped me the bird, and drove away."

"I recommend you be on your way, Mr. Grayson."

"Well, the way I see it, I have harassed no one. I'm not blocking traffic, nor am I on private property. I think I'll sit right here."

"So, you're refusing to comply with a peace officer?"

"Nope. I'm stating my constitutional rights. If you don't like that, I'll speak with your supervisor."

"No need to do that, Mr. Grayson," Ambler said. "Have a nice day."

Ambler got in his SUV, turned around, and headed back to town.

Zane got out and walked around the truck, stretching and getting the kinks out. Carrie returned and flipped him off again. He settled back in the truck and returned to Louis L'Amour.

When evening approached, Zane was hungry. He'd eaten all his sandwiches hours before. A few people had driven by, but other than Carrie, no one had gone in or out of the ranch. He called his mom to say he was on his way back home.

On the drive back, he wondered if he had been right to begin with. Sitting on the side of the road waiting for Hubbard may have been a waste of his time. He needed a better strategy. He longed for the days he wore a badge that would get him in the door and some answers.

Sitting at supper with Marcia, he said, "Tell me more about Wayne Hubbard."

"I already told you everything. He's from Loa. Moved here and opened his dude ranch."

Zane wondered where he was really from. He'd been told both Loa and Roosevelt. The newspaper article he'd found said he lived in Richfield. Loa and Richfield weren't that far apart, but Roosevelt was a different area of the state. Of the three, Roosevelt was the closest to Mathoni, and the other two were several hours away.

"Does he get many guests?" Zane asked.

"He must. Otherwise, he wouldn't stay in business."

"Have you talked to him much?"

"Just a little at church. I've run into him at the general store a few times. We didn't say more than hello. Zane, I know you suspect him of murdering Will. But after what happened when you tried to talk to him, be careful."

Zane hugged his mom. "I've dealt with far worse people. I'll be fine."

As the moon rose in the night sky, he smoked his usual cigar and sipped his usual bourbon and thought about Hubbard. Then he wondered how Tiffany was doing, sitting in jail. He called George Needham.

"She's scared, Zane. And I'm sure she's depressed," George said.

"What did her attorney say?"

"There's a bail hearing on Monday. He'll be here for that. But he said in a capital crime, it's unlikely there will be bail. What are we going to do? Where are you in finding the actual killer?"

Zane walked around the yard. "I have a few suspects. I haven't talked to them all yet, but I'm working on it."

George asked him about the hay hook. Zane didn't mince his words and told him it was someone at the ranch that day or planted afterwards.

"You need to solve this. We're worried Tiffany will go to prison—or worse." George choked up.

"I'll get to the bottom of it. I just need more time."

Chapter 20

MARCIA HOLLERED UPSTAIRS TO ZANE that she was leaving for church.

"Wait a minute, Mom," Zane hollered back.

She gasped when he came downstairs wearing a suit, tie, and newly polished shoes. "Oh Zane," she said. "I prayed last night that the spirit would touch you and you'd go to church with me today; but are you sure you feel up to it?"

"I am going to church just this once. And yes, I'm fine." Although he had a brief thought that something *was* actually wrong with him if he was going to church.

"Zane, I'm so happy you're joining me. You'll remember how much you used to like it growing up. Now let's get going so we're not late." She picked up the small bag that contained her Bible and other scriptures and walked out. Besides the Bible and *Book of Mormon*, Mormons have two other books of scripture. The first is the *Doctrine and Covenants*, which were revelations given primarily to church founder Joseph Smith. The other is *The Pearl of Great Price*, which contains what Mormons believe were revelations given to the Old Testament prophets Moses and Abraham, and also to modern-day Mormon prophets.

I used to have a scripture bag almost like that. I took it with me when I moved to California. What happened to it?

When they arrived at the church, Zane thought a bolt of lightning from heaven would hit him as he walked into the foyer. While technically he was still a member of the church, he hadn't practiced the tenets in decades, and he had broken many of the faith's commandments. Luckily for him, there was no lightning.

Zane sat in a chair in the foyer, a picture of Jesus on the wall above him. He had a perfect view of the entrance as people came in. He got up and down multiple times as ward members who remembered him from his youth, came over and shook his hand to welcome him home or thank him for coming back to take care of his mom, or asking how he was after the incident at Founder's Day. Bishop Brough was especially happy to see him. Others gave him a disgusted look, like he didn't belong there because he was now an outsider from a heathen state. Some had probably seen him drinking coffee at Lou-Lou's, making him a sinner on top of everything else. People he didn't know walked right past him. He assumed they were likely tourists as the locals welcomed them.

When Bruce Hubbard walked in, he went straight into the chapel. The same chapel where Will's funeral had been held. Zane followed and sat in a pew at the back next to Hubbard, who looked over and snarled. Zane expected him to find another seat, but the back rows were all filled. Hubbard took a hymnal out of the storage slot and looked for the first hymn.

Zane looked around for his mom and found her sitting several rows in front with her cousin Ruby. She turned to find where he was sitting and smiled when she spotted him.

The chapel was a simple room. The only things on the walls were a clock on one side and a list of hymn numbers for the day's meeting on the front wall—no crosses or altars are in a Mormon church and no stained glass except in a few older buildings. At the front of the room, the choir sat in three tiers of chairs, with an organ and piano in front of them. Off to their left, was a riser with a podium and seats for the bishopric and the ward members who would give talks. The priests, three young men ages sixteen to eighteen, sat just below the riser, facing the congregation. Their job was to bless the sacrament on a table covered with a white cloth. Twenty rows of pews ran to the back of the room, long rows that could seat about fifteen on one side and a short row seating about six on the other, with an aisle between them.

Bishop Brough and the two counselors in the Bishopric, the three men who ran the ward, sat behind the podium. The bishop soon stood and went to the podium, adjusted the microphone. The organist stopped playing. "Brothers and sisters," he said, "welcome this morning to Sacrament meeting." He then announced several items of interest to the ward members.

The bishop sat, the organ started again, and the chorister stood to lead the congregation in singing the hymn. Zane's mind wandered off, thinking about Tiffany sitting in jail. Wondering how she was doing.

Zane heard a chorus of amens. Nothing loud, like in many evangelical churches. Amen was reserved for ending a prayer and said by the congregation in a quiet, reverent manner. There were no hallelujahs either.

Zane looked up and realized that the opening prayer was over. He was as bored now as when he was a kid. The woman who had said the prayer left the podium and went to sit with her family.

Another hymn was sung by the congregation to prepare for the sacrament as the priests broke the bread—tearing slices of bread into small pieces to represent the body of Christ—and placing them onto trays. Just like the young men doing it now, Zane had also blessed the sacrament when he was sixteen. At the end of the hymn, the deacons, twelve- and thirteen-year-old boys, stood. A priest kneeled and blessed the bread, then the deacons dispersed throughout the chapel, offering the bread to all worthy members. Zane wondered how many times he'd walked up and down the aisle when he was a deacon.

Zane knew that many people taking the sacrament likely weren't worthy. The teachings were that you had to obey the commandments to take the sacrament. Most members felt that telling a little lie or breaking the law by driving over the speed limit were fine and still took a piece of bread. He declined to take a piece when the tray came down the pew to where he sat. He knew his "sins" were too great, and he just handed the tray to the next person, Wayne Hubbard, who took a piece of bread, put it in his mouth. Zane wondered if breaking the commandment *Love thy neighbor as thyself* then running them off at gunpoint disqualified someone from taking the sacrament.

The deacons soon returned to the front and handed back their trays. A priest kneeled and blessed the water, representing the blood of Christ. Deacons then distributed the small water cups to the congregation, returning to the front when done. They then went to sit with their families.

Over the next forty minutes, the choir sang hymns, ward members gave talks, and a prayer was offered to end the meeting. Organ music once again flowed through the chapel as people got up either to go to Sunday School classes or back home to tend to their farms.

Zane quickly leaned over and extended his hand. "Mr. Hubbard, I think we got off to a poor start the other day. I'd like to be friends. After all, I've moved back to Mathoni and would hate it if we were enemies."

Hubbard looked at Zane's outstretched hand, then looked up, right into Zane's eyes. "I think I was pretty clear. I have nothing more to say to you." With that, Wayne Hubbard stood and walked out.

Marcia came over to him. "Zane, I'm tired and need to go home."

They got out in time to see Hubbard get in his SUV and drive away, giving Zane the middle finger as he passed.

"Oh dear," Mom said, seeing Hubbard's gesture. "Did you go to church just to talk to Brother Hubbard?"

Zane said, "Yes. That is exactly why I went. It didn't go any better than when I went to his ranch."

"I'm still happy you went to church and took the sacrament. It should help your soul."

He'd been through this enough with her since his return. Zane couldn't bring himself to tell her he didn't take the sacrament. He chose his words carefully. "Thank you for your concern, but I can't say I'm ready to go back again, Mom."

"I'll keep praying for you."

But Zane knew he was back at the beginning of his investigation with no idea how to talk to Hubbard.

* * *

ZANE DIDN'T UNDERSTAND WHY HE missed his dad so much after going to church, but when he got back home, he went straight to the office and pulled one of his dad's journals from the bookcase.

Saturday, March 2, 1991

It was cold and snowing today, but what a blessing the day was. Mary Elizabeth turned eight this week, and today I baptized her at the stake center in Vernal. We were concerned about the travel because of the storm, but the Lord watched over us and we arrived safely.

What a marvelous feeling it is that she accepted the gospel and teachings of Jesus Christ. And tomorrow in Fast and Testimony meeting, she'll be confirmed as a member of the Church.

The ceremony was beautiful. It started at 1:00. The stake president, President Buttars, presided and conducted. The opening hymn was *"Families Can Be Together Forever"*. Glenn Wilson gave the invocation.

President Buttars then spoke about the importance of baptism. The cleansing of the soul and washing away of sins and being baptized was an important step in the Plan of Salvation.

There were three other children baptized, then it was Mary Elizabeth's turn. She looked so beautiful in her white baptismal dress. I went into the font first, then held her hand and helped her down the stairs. I looked out at the members there. Marcia looked so proud and happy. I gave the prayer and then immersed Mary Elizabeth.

After we'd dried off and changed into our Sunday best, we all met again and sang *"I Am a Child of God"*. Donald Friesh gave the benediction.

We had a family dinner at JB's. That was Mary Elizabeth's choice because she wanted pancakes. Then we drove home through the snow.

* * *

Zane closed the journal. *I remember that day. I was scared and thought we would slide off the road because of the snow. Dad loved the gospel and was so proud that day.*

Maybe Dad's love of the Gospel was the reason he was missing him so much at the moment. Church had brought that out. He could almost feel Dad sitting in his chair, paying bills, or reading scriptures. He sat at the desk and thought for some time, then went upstairs to change out of the suit.

COCINA DE TACOS, MATHONI'S ONLY Mexican restaurant, sat at the south end of town. A Latina girl, maybe fifteen or sixteen, greeted Zane and led him to a table and gave him a menu. He'd just had Sunday dinner, but thought it might help to place an order, so he got three tacos and a Coke. He also asked for the owner. Tomás Sanchez, the ranch hand fired by Will Massey, was the nephew of restaurant owner, Pablo Bravo.

A man, about 5'6" with a small mustache, soon appeared at his table. "I am Pablo Bravo, the owner. You wish to see me, Señor?" the man said.

Zane had learned some Spanish in California but was far from fluent. "Sí, Señor Bravo. My name is Zane Grayson. I am looking for Tomás Sanchez. I understand you are his tío."

"Why do you want Tomás? Are you policía?"

"No policía." Zane didn't want to let on why he was looking for Sanchez. He thought up a lie. "I heard he used to work on farms around here. I may have work for him."

"He is the hijo of mi hermana. He live in Vernal in green house."

The girl arrived with the tacos.

Pablo put his arm around the girl, pulling her to him. "This is my hija, Marisol," he said proudly. "We had her quinceañera last month. Say hola to Señor Grayson."

"Hola, Marisol," Zane said. "I'm Mr. Grayson. Happy quinceañera."

"It's nice to meet you, Mr. Grayson," she said. Pablo kissed her forehead and sent her back to work.

"I get you the address for mi hermana," Bravo said, then disappeared into the kitchen.

Zane bit into a taco and smiled. Having lived in California for thirty years, he'd had some very good and authentic Mexican food. He had doubted he'd find any in the area, especially in Mathoni. His assumption was wrong. The taco was as good as any in Santa Barbara.

He was just finishing up when Pablo returned and gave him a slip of paper. "Mi hermana live here but she no speak Inglés."

"Gracías, Pablo. The tacos are muy bueno." He paid his bill and left.

AS ZANE DROVE AWAY, HE realized he had another problem. He could go to Vernal and find Sanchez or keep watch on the Hubbard ranch. While he doubted surveillance on the ranch would yield any results, there was a sliver of hope that it would succeed. He didn't have any other ideas about how to talk to Hubbard. How could he be in two places at the same time?

An idea hit him. Bruce Colby had helped him once, although the results were less than ideal, maybe he could get Colby to help again. But it was Sunday afternoon. Colby wouldn't be in his office, and Zane didn't know where he lived. He U-turned and pulled up at Lou-Lou's. Louise would know.

A teenage server that Zane didn't know looked over at him from behind the counter. "Sit anywhere you want. I'll be right with you."

"Is Louise here?" he said.

"No, she's out of town. Her sister fell and is in the hospital in Craig. She went to visit."

Craig was a town on US 40 in Colorado, about a three-hour drive away.

"How about Lou?" Zane sat on a stool.

"He went with her. They'll be back for breakfast tomorrow. What can I get you?"

Zane got up to leave, then turned around and said, "Do you know the man who runs the insurance company next door?"

"Mr. Colby? Sure, I know him. He's in here all the time."

"Do you know where he lives?"

"Yeah, it's a white house on the corner of 200 East and 100 North. You can't miss it."

Zane drove the short distance to the location the girl had given him, only to find there was a white house on each corner. Only one had Bruce's new black Ford F150 pickup, a temporary vehicle license taped to the back window, parked in front. Mrs. Colby answered the knock. She had dark, short hair and wore an apron over her dress. Zane introduced himself, and she invited him in. Bruce was on the living room floor playing a board game with his kids.

"Can we speak for a minute, Bruce? In private," Zane said.

"Sure. Let's go outside." Bruce groaned as he got up. "Getting old isn't for the young at heart. It gets harder to get off the floor every year."

Zane laughed. "I feel that all the time."

"How are you after the beating you took on Founders' Day?"

"I have a lot of aches and pains, and bruises are forming an ugly picture all over, but I'm still here."

They talked next to a large pine tree in the front yard.

"What's up, Zane? And why this secrecy?"

"I could use your help again."

Bruce put his hands on his hips and bent backwards to stretch his back. "You're still on the case? I would have thought you'd quit once Tiffany was arrested."

"She didn't do it."

"The sheriff found the murder weapon in her closet," Bruce said as he continued stretching.

"Except she didn't put it there. There are too many things that don't add up."

Bruce looked at Zane. "Like what?"

"Rich got an anonymous tip that told them to look in her closet, and they happened to find the murder weapon in there over a week after the crime—a closet they supposedly searched the day of the murder? That sounds hokey in my book."

"Huh." Bruce rubbed the back of his neck. "That sounds odd. But I don't know if I should get involved. Last time I thought

Wayne would kill me."

"Hear me out," Zane pleaded. "There's a suspect on my list that used to work for Will that swore vengeance when he was fired. He's an eighteen, nineteen-year-old kid. It doesn't make sense that he'd murder Will over that. I need someone to track him down. You don't even have to question him, just find out for sure where he lives."

"Where is this kid?"

"He's in Vernal. You know Pablo Bravo?"

"The guy who owns the Mexican restaurant?"

"I was just over talking to him. He gave me the address of his sister in Vernal. The kid, Tomás Sanchez, is Pablo's nephew."

"And what if he is the killer?"

"I don't think he is. All I'm after is confirmation to take his name off my suspect list."

"But. What. If. He. Is." Bruce emphasized each word.

Zane thought about that. "Tell him I have farm work for him and give him my phone number. That's it. No mention of Will or the murder."

Bruce thought about that, then finally said, "Alright, I'll do it. What's the address?" But the hesitation in his voice told Zane that he still wasn't convinced. "I'm going to Vernal tomorrow anyway."

Zane gave him the address. "Thanks, Bruce."

Bruce headed back into the house. Zane headed for Wayne Hubbard's ranch.

But he was as unsuccessful as the day before. Two SUVs came in just after 5:00, both filled with people. Zane assumed it was a new group of guests. Other than that, there was no one going in or out of the ranch. It was dark when Zane returned home, exhausted from sitting in the heat all afternoon. He didn't even have his bourbon and cigar. He just went straight to bed.

Chapter 21

TWO WEEKS SINCE WILL'S MURDER and Zane's investigation had gone nowhere. Not knowing how to talk to his primary suspect, he decided to re-interview some people connected to the case. That took him back to the Massey ranch, where he needed to question Jacob again, especially after they found the murder weapon.

Jacob was loading salt licks into the bed of a pickup truck.

"I've been thinking about it. I remember hearing a door close and a car drive away," Jacob said.

"And you have no idea who was here?"

"None. I thought nothing of it at the time. Then, with the shock of Will's death, I forgot all about it. I wish I had checked it out. Will might still be alive today."

"From what I've heard, you couldn't have saved him."

Jacob looked down and kicked the dirt. "I know, but still—"

Zane thought about how he felt when he was under investigation for planting evidence. "You'll just get yourself depressed thinking that way, Jacob."

"Yeah, you may be right," Jacob said, looking at Zane. "And I would have had a job."

"What's that?"

"Mrs. Massey told me to sell all the cattle. She was planning to sell everything and build a house in town. But now? Mr. Needham is running things, and he doesn't want a cattle ranch either." Jacob shrugged. "There's no reason to keep me around."

"Sorry to hear that. I was told the cattle and the guest house were Will's projects."

"Mrs. Massey was fine with the cattle, at least when Will was alive. Now, with her going to prison, who would want it?"

"She's a long way from going to prison," Zane said.

"Either way, I won't be needed." He looked off into the distance, sadness in his eyes.

"The sheriff found what he thinks is the murder weapon in a closet in the house."

"I heard that," Jacob said. "I've been thinking about how someone could get into the house. We have a good security system."

"Who knows the code to turn it off?"

"As far as I know, just me and everyone in the family. However, it didn't get turned on after the sheriff finished the day Will died. I turned it on the next day."

Zane wondered whether that had happened before or after he had inspected the crime scene. "What time did you set the alarm?"

"I was busy with the herd in the morning. It was late afternoon before I checked it."

I was here in the morning, and the house was locked. How did someone get in?

"I don't see any cameras," Zane said.

"That's because there aren't any. Mr. Massey thought the alarms would be enough, and he wanted to keep his guests' identities private, if you know what I mean."

"Seems odd to me not to have cameras at a place like this, but I understand the privacy issues." Zane moved on to another topic. "You ever hear the name Sal Giovanni?"

Jacob shook his head. "No, who is he?"

"An attorney in Sandy. He's listed by the state as the corporate agent for Mathoni Hospitality."

"That's strange. I've never heard of . . . what's his name again?"

"Sal Giovanni."

"Will's attorney is Delbert McConkie. His office is downtown Salt Lake City, right by Temple Square."

"That's interesting. I know little about the connection between Will and Giovanni, but I'll figure it out. Tell me about McConkie."

"As far as I knew, he handled all the legal stuff for the guest house, including the rezoning request. Will and I met with him several times. This Giovanni guy is new to me."

"This is getting more twisted. Why have two attorneys from different firms involved in the guest house?"

"I don't know," Jacob said. "But I agree; it seems strange. Maybe Will started working with Giovanni, then switched law firms, and the agent information hasn't been updated yet?"

"That could be. I'll follow up on it." An idea popped into Zane's head. "Can you help me with an experiment right now?"

"What kind of experiment?"

"Show me where you were working at the time of Will's murder."

Jacob led Zane behind the barn to a storage area. Several ATVs were parked there.

"Now, go out front and start my truck." He gave his keys to Jacob. "I want to find out how loud an engine would be back here."

A couple of minutes later, the truck roared to life.

He walked back to Jacob.

"I could hear it plain as day. Thanks, Jacob."

"TIFFANY'S NOT DOING GREAT," GEORGE told Zane when he stopped at the Needham home. "Her arraignment is tomorrow at 10:00. Her attorney thinks he can get the charges thrown out."

"That's the good news I was expecting. Now for the bad news. I'm no closer to solving this. Wayne Hubbard is acting strangely. I haven't been able to talk to him about Will's death."

"You've got nothing from him at all?" George said.

"He had no love for Will and told me he wanted to pin a medal on the person who did it."

George gasped. "I know he felt Will's guest house would hurt his business, but I didn't know he hated Will that much. Where exactly are you on your investigation?"

"I'm re-interviewing people connected to it. I was just talking to Jacob. He remembered hearing a car leave that morning. That means someone was there. Have you ever heard the names Sal Giovanni or Delbert McConkie?"

"Yes, I have. McConkie is the attorney working on the guest house. I met him once or twice," George said. "I've never heard of the other one. Who is he?"

Zane said, "Another attorney whose name came up. Jacob didn't know him either. I'm still working on figuring out who all the players are. Sometimes cases are clear-cut. Other times, there are twists and turns that I can't explain. Anyway, I think it's likely that the judge will dismiss the charges. The botched searches and the improper delivery of the search warrant are really damning to the prosecution. Plus, the anonymous call that alerted the sheriff to the murder weapon is fishy."

THAT EVENING, THERE WAS A knock at the door. Zane answered it to find Bruce Colby. Zane stepped onto the porch and closed the door behind him.

"Bruce, I didn't expect you to come by. Are you all right?"

"I'm fine. There were no threats this time. I did what you asked."

"And?"

"I met with my brother down in Vernal. We get together about once a week. We talk business, family, everything. He runs the Vernal office, and I'm up here in Mathoni. We had lunch on his patio while his three rugrats chased each other around the yard.

"Anyway, afterwards I drove down to the address you gave me. Did you know house was green, and I mean bright, lime green? I've seen nothing like it. Stuck out like a beacon. There were a couple of old bicycles in the yard and an old beat-up Chevy in the driveway."

Zane listened carefully, but wished Bruce would get to the end.

"I knocked on the door. When no one answered, I knocked again. Finally, a woman opened the door, but she didn't speak any English, just like you told me."

"That must have been Pablo Bravo's sister," Zane said.

"Yes, that's what I found out. She called her daughter over to translate. I think her name was Emilia. She must have been twelve or thirteen. I asked about Tomás. The aunt wondered how I got Tomás' name. I told her I knew he used to work for a man in Mathoni. She seemed suspicious of me. I wondered if they're here illegally, and she thought I was looking for him to send him back. In the end, she said he already has a job."

"Did they say where?"

"Well, I figured if you wanted to talk to him, you should know where he's working. So, I asked them. The woman shook her head and said something I didn't understand. She and Emilia got into an argument. I felt awkward standing there on the front porch while they argued and turned to leave."

Zane said, "That means we're no closer to finding him."

"Actually, we are. I was half-way down the sidewalk when Emilia called out to me. She told me he's working construction up by Flaming Gorge in Manila."

Zane chuckled. "That guy is a jack of all trades. Of all places, why the hell would someone build in Manila?"

"A summer cabin maybe? I never found out if Emilia's mother wanted me to know that or not. I was happy to help since I was in Vernal anyway, but I don't know if I'm cut out for the detective business. I feel much better sitting in my office, selling insurance."

"I appreciate the help, Bruce. I'll take it from here."

ZANE OPENED HIS LAPTOP TO research Brian Christian. The Internet proved useful with lots of information about the man. He grew up in Provo. His mother was a schoolteacher, and his father was a linguistics professor at BYU. He and his wife, Janis, had eight children. He was currently the chief technical officer at Verling Technologies in Palo Alto, CA.

The company website included pictures of the executives. Christian had gray hair, cut short on the sides and long on top. Zane called it 'hipster cut.' He had a neatly trimmed beard, also gray, and black, rectangular glasses.

Zane typed in some search terms to get more information about the company and found himself in a technical jargon quicksand. However, he understood Verling had something to do with computer security. The company was privately held and had received several rounds of venture capital funding.

He dug deeper and paid for several search tools that got him a home address and phone number in the Portola Valley, then mapped it and found a satellite image that showed a large house, swimming pool, and lots of land around it. He couldn't imagine Christian made the money that Will Massey had, but it appeared the CTO of a Silicon Valley tech company was well paid.

Zane did more web sleuthing. Christian's home was valued at $12 million. He wasn't just making good money; he was making *very* good money.

He turned to researching Janis. She worked with several charities in the area, and a news article mentioned a sizable donation in her name for a women's health center at a local hospital.

It was always better to interview suspects in person than over the phone, but jumping on a plane made little sense. He made a note to call Christian after Tiffany's arraignment and hopefully make an appointment to visit in person.

ZANE WAS FINISHING HIS NIGHTLY cigar when George Needham called.

"Did Jacob say anything to you about leaving town?" George asked.

"He didn't mention it. He said that Tiffany had told him to sell all the cattle. Could he be out of town to do that?"

"I've been calling him all afternoon. It just goes to voicemail." George sounded more annoyed than anything else.

Is he on the run?

"Could he be back up in the hills with no cell service?" Zane stood and walked down the lane, toward the highway.

"There are some areas of the property that don't have service, but he wouldn't be out there all afternoon and evening," George said.

"Is it unusual for him not to answer?"

"I don't know. I don't normally call him, but with Tiffany in jail, I had to take over running the ranch."

"His ATV might have broken down or something like that."

"You're probably right. If I don't hear from him by morning, I'm calling the sheriff."

"That's a good idea. Search and Rescue can track him down."

"Thanks, Zane. Good night."

"Night, George." Zane went up to bed. But he couldn't sleep. His suspicions about Brian Christian, Jacob's apparent disappearance, and Tiffany's arraignment floated around his brain. He hoped he could get some time with her attorney after the hearing.

Chapter 22

CLOUDS HAD MOVED IN AND kept it dark at the Red Cloud Loop parking lot off US Highway 191 between Mathoni and Vernal. It was 12:30 am and Jacob Faust was late.

"I'll wait another fifteen minutes."

Ten minutes later, headlights appeared as a pickup truck pulled into the lot and stopped, then flashed its lights.

When the other car's lights flashed, Jacob got out and walked toward them. He'd gone about twenty feet when a door opened on the other vehicle, and the driver stepped out, leaving the door open. No light appeared, which meant the dome light was off.

Jacob stopped. "Do you have the money I asked for to keep quiet about your killing Will?"

The driver leaned into the car to retrieve something, then stood again and threw a duffel bag toward the Massey ranch foreman. It landed with a thud at Jacob's feet.

He crouched and unzipped it, reached inside, then looked back toward the other vehicle.

"What the hell is this?"

"It's your payment."

"All you gave me was blank paper."

"You're right. I have something for you, but it isn't money."

A gunshot shattered the quiet darkness. Jacob lay sprawled backward on the pavement.

The assailant walked over to Jacob, aimed at Jacob's head, and pulled the trigger again.

"Just two more loose ends to tie up." The assailant picked up the duffel bag and drove away.

Chapter 23

ZANE COOKED BREAKFAST TUESDAY MORNING, sunshine streaming through the window, the radio tuned to a Vernal station. He paused to pay attention to a news story.

"The Uintah County Sheriff's Office has confirmed that they are on the scene of a homicide on Forest Service land near the turnoff to Red Cloud Loop from US 191 north of Vernal. Details are limited, but early reports this morning are that the victim is a man in his early to mid-forties. A Sheriff's Department spokesperson confirms the FBI is assisting in the investigation but refused to provide any information on a victim, pending notification of next of kin. KVUR will have more information on this developing story as we receive it.

In other news, the Governor has signed into law a bill passed by the special session of the Legislature . . ."

Zane turned off the radio and was thinking about the news story when Levi came in. "This was taped to your front door." He handed over an envelope. 'Zane' was handwritten with a black marker on the outside.

Zane opened it to find a single sheet, printed on a laser printer. He read it out loud. "This is your last warning. Stop investigating." He showed it to Levi.

"Are you going to quit looking for this unknown killer?" Levi said.

"An anonymous letter won't stop me. I'll keep doing what I'm doing."

"You're not worried that Will's killer might get you too?"

"I've had threats before. They didn't stop me then. They won't now. Someone's worried that I'm on the right trail. The problem is, I'm not on any trail. I don't know who did it. By the way, did you hear the news this morning?"

"Nah. I don't pay no attention to news."

"There was a murder up on Highway 191. The news said it was a man in his early forties but gave no name."

Levi sat at the table as Zane dished up bacon and eggs. "Another killing? You think it's connected to Will Massey?"

"There's nothing to say it is. Then again, nothing to say it isn't. Right now, let's eat. I'm starved." He'd took a bite when his phone rang.

"Good morning, George," Zane said after pressing the answer button. "Yeah, I heard that . . . Take a deep breath. There's nothing to say it's him . . . Yes, I'll be at the arraignment . . . Okay, see you then." He hung up.

"That dead body I told you about? Jacob Faust's been missing since yesterday. George Needham has been trying to reach him since yesterday afternoon. He thinks the dead man is the missing ranch foreman. It gets worse. It's possible I was the last person to see Jacob alive."

EVERY TV STATION IN SALT Lake was at the Smith County Courthouse to cover Tiffany's arraignment. It was just the type of story to bring in viewers and boost ratings—the small-town murder of a wealthy man and his wife arrested for killing him.

Zane had to maneuver around four TV news vans to get inside and eventually sat next to George and Betty in the gallery in the courtroom. "Any word from Jacob?" he asked.

"None. I'm worried that dead man I heard about on the radio is him," George said.

"Nothing to do but wait it out. How are the grandkids?"

"They seem fine. I talked to them last night. Will's parents are keeping them busy."

A deputy soon led Tiffany into the courtroom. She wore in an orange prisoner uniform with 'SCSO' printed across the back. Betty gasped when she saw her daughter shuffling in wearing shackles and handcuffs.

Tiffany looked around and gave a weak smile when she saw her parents and Zane, then sat next to her lawyers.

The bailiff called the court to order. Everyone stood when Judge Nelson Snow came in. Marcia's cousin had been the judge since Zane was a kid. He was a large man, bald on top with white, neatly trimmed hair around the sides. He wore a pair of wire-rimmed half-moon glasses perched on the end of his nose. The collar of a white button-down dress shirt and dark tie peeked out of the top of his judge's robe.

Judge Snow banged his gavel, bringing the room to order, and the clerk then read the charges of first-degree homicide and interfering in a police investigation. Zane knew that could mean a life sentence or worse, as Utah was a death penalty state.

"I assume," Judge Snow said, "that the state has an attorney here."

The District Attorney announced himself, "Courtland Skonnard for the prosecution."

"David Miller for the defense, Your Honor."

The judge asked, "How do you plead, Mrs. Massey?"

"Not guilty," Tiffany said.

"Your Honor," Miller said, "the warrant used to search the Massey residence was improperly served. The sheriff's department failed to provide Mrs. Massey with a copy. We request that the search be declared invalid, and any evidence seized ruled inadmissible."

"Mr. Prosecutor," Judge Snow said. "Do you have anything to say on this matter?"

"Your Honor, the state contends that a copy of the warrant was left on the kitchen counter; therefore, the search was legal."

George leaned over to Zane. "That's poppycock. I never saw one."

"Mr. Miller?" Judge Snow said, looking at the defense table.

"Mrs. Massey, the only living legal homeowner, never saw the warrant, and one was not on the counter at the time of her arrest. Her father, who was at the home at the time, has also sworn in an affidavit that he didn't see a warrant either. The defense contends that the search was illegal, and any items seized are poisoned fruit and should be excluded."

"Thank you, gentlemen," Snow said. "I will not rule on the motion at this time. For now, the evidence stays in play. I assume, Mr. Miller, that you want to make another motion regarding bail."

"Yes, Your Honor," Miller said, "Mrs. Massey has deep roots and family in the community. She is not a flight risk and is requesting bail."

Judge Snow said, "Mr. Skonnard."

"Thank you, Judge Snow. The prosecution contends that Mrs. Massey did plan the murder of her husband. The crime was vicious and committed near her children. In fact, the children saw their father lying in a pool of his own blood. The defendant also has sufficient funds to flee the jurisdiction and even the country. Because of the nature of the crime and the fact that the charges are for a capital offense, the state requests that bail be denied."

"Bail is set at one million dollars cash," Judge Snow said. "I assume Mrs. Massey will post bail. If she does, the defendant will be required to surrender her passport and wear an ankle monitor. She will be restricted to the Mathoni area, with one exception that I'll get to in a moment."

"We understand, Your Honor," her attorney said. "Bail will be posted."

"Now, I have another item," Judge Snow said. "I've known the defendant since she was a baby. I am recusing myself from further proceedings in this case. It will be remanded to the Eighth District Court in Vernal. A preliminary hearing will be scheduled there by the court . Mr. Miller, you can bring up your motion on the warrant with the Eighth District." He pounded his gavel. "We are adjourned."

Two deputies stepped forward to take Tiffany out of the courtroom.

"I'll see you in a few minutes," her attorney said to her. He then turned to the family.

George Needham introduced Zane to the attorneys. David Miller was a tall man in his late fifties. The lights reflected off the top of his bald head, and Zane wondered how long it took him to polish it every morning. Miller had his own law firm in Salt Lake City that specialized in felony cases, particularly homicide. His assistant council, Hillary Pace, was average height, but her heels made her taller, and she had pulled her dark hair into a bun.

"Mr. Grayson," Pace said, holding out her hand to shake Zane's. "I understand you're retired law enforcement and were hired to look into the case."

Zane shook her hand. "That's not correct, Ms. Pace. I'm working for myself. Sheriff Richman told me I'm a suspect, and I'm merely trying to clear my name."

"So, you aren't trying to find evidence for my client?"

"If I do happen to locate any evidence that clears Tiffany, I'll contact you."

"Be careful, Mr. Grayson. You're not a licensed investigator in this state, and this is an active case. I'd hate for anything you find to be excluded and harm our client's case."

"I'll keep that in mind, Counselor."

She looked at him with disdain. "See that you do. Now, I need to work on getting my client released. It's going to take some time to post bail."

Zane spoke up. "Mr. Miller, I'd like to speak with you, if I may."

"I need to see Tiffany first, Mr. Grayson. If you'll wait in the hall, I'll be with you when I'm done with her."

Zane looked through the hall window at the media assembled outside. They tried to get comments from people leaving the courthouse. Some people pushed the microphones away. Others stopped, hoping to get their pictures on TV.

Sitting on a bench, Zane wondered how Tiffany was holding up. She didn't look great in court, but at least she'd brushed her hair, no doubt at the insistence of her attorneys.

An hour later, Miller showed up. He appeared rushed but sat next to Zane. "Mr. Grayson, you wanted to talk to me?"

"I thought I might have some information to help."

"You just told me you aren't investigating Tiffany's case."

"As I said, I'm investigating my case and will pass on anything I find that may help Tiffany. First, how is she?"

"I told her our chances are good. Getting bail seemed to improve her spirits."

"That's good to hear. Now, this is what I've learned." Zane outlined his investigation, covering people he felt were innocent and his suspicions about Lavell Bateman and Wayne Hubbard.

"I agree about Mr. Hubbard. I'll get one of my investigators to talk to him. Unlike you, I have subpoena power, if needed. I have a long drive back to Salt Lake and need to get on the road." Miller stood to leave.

"Thank you, Mr. Miller, just one more question."

"What is that, Mr. Grayson?"

"Truthfully, how do you see Tiffany's chances?"

"It would really help if the court suppressed that warrant and all the evidence from the search. Otherwise, I'll need to convince a jury that anyone could have planted the evidence found after the initial search. Thank you for your information." Miller turned and walked down the hall to the exit.

Miller's statement echoed Zane's own thoughts. If this had been his case, he too would have questioned the validity of the hay hook found in Tiffany's closet. He also would have properly served the warrant.

WHEN ZANE GOT TO HIS truck, Deputy Ambler was waiting for him. "The Sheriff wants to talk to you," Ambler said.

"I'm busy at the moment, Deputy," Zane said.

"My orders were to bring you in to talk to him. He specifically said to put you in handcuffs if needed."

What the hell does Richie want now?

Sheriff Richman wasn't alone in his office. The other man was introduced as Detective Sharp of the Uintah County Sheriff's office.

Zane knew this was about the dead man found on the highway to Vernal. A dead man that was likely Jacob.

Sharp turned on an audio recorder. He stated his name and gave the names of the others in the room, as well as the date and time. Then he said, "Mr. Grayson, I understand your mother is ill."

Build rapport. That's how I would do it. "Yes, she is."

"I'm sorry to hear that. I hope she's recovering," Sharp said.

"Thank you for your concern. She is responding well to treatment."

Sharp continued, "And her illness led to your return from California to Mathoni?"

"That's correct."

"What did you do for a living in California?"

"I was a detective with the Santa Barbara Police Department."

"And, you resigned your position?"

Zane had grown weary of hashing out his life history. "Can you just get to the point?"

"Mr. Grayson is familiar with all your interview tactics, detective," Richman said. "Move it along."

"Very well. Sheriff Richman tells me you've been poking around the Will Massey murder."

"Last I checked, Will's murder took place in Smith County."

"Have you ever talked to Jacob Faust?"

"Again, not your jurisdiction."

Richman spoke up. "But it is mine. Answer the question."

"I have better things to do than sit here. So here's everything. Yes, I have talked to Jacob. The last time was yesterday morning. Because I'm sitting here right now and we have a detective from a neighboring county, I have to assume that your murder victim that's all over the news today is Jacob. And no, I didn't kill him just as I had nothing to do with Will Massey's death. Unless I'm under arrest, we're done here."

Zane walked out, hoping he never saw Detective Sharp again. But more importantly, he wondered about the connection between the two murders.

ZANE SAT OUTSIDE HUBBARD'S RANCH. Solving a murder without a badge, without warrants, and without subpoenas was harder than he expected. Every turn was met with another turn or a brick wall or both. Now he had not one, but two murders to solve.

Why was Jacob out on the highway? To meet someone? Perhaps to meet with the killer? He ran through the scenarios. Jacob was blackmailing the murderer because he had actually seen something the morning Will died. Or, the murderer thought Jacob saw him and set up the meeting to get rid of him. A third scenario was Jacob, and the murderer were in on it together, and things went south between them.

It could also all be reversed. Thinking about someone entering the Massey residence and planting the murder weapon, maybe Jacob was the murderer after all and he was the one making a payoff.

Another possibility was Jacob getting killed was a coincidence, but that was never a good theory and he didn't believe in it.

He moved on to what he knew. Tiffany did not kill Jacob. She was still in jail, waiting for her bail to be posted. He didn't kill either man. His beating and the threatening note proved that the killer thought he knew something.

There were also loose ends regarding Brian Christian. He looked through his notes and found Christian's business number, then picked up his phone and dialed. He was surprised when he was put through.

"Mr. Christian. My name is Zane Grayson. Do you have a few minutes you can answer some questions for me regarding Will Massey?"

"Are you a reporter?" Christian's voice was deep and authoritative.

"No, I'm not. I don't know if you heard, but Will is dead."

No response.

"Mr. Christian?"

"Sorry. What? How?" Christian sounded surprised.

"He was murdered."

Silence again on the other end of the call.

"Mr. Christian? Are you there?"

"Yes, I'm here. I hadn't heard. Who did you say you are again?"

"Zane Grayson. I was a childhood friend of Tiffany's and now a former cop. I'm looking into his murder."

"How are Tiffany and the kids?"

"They're not doing well."

"Do the police have a suspect?"

"Based on very shaky evidence, Tiffany was charged with his murder. She's currently in jail awaiting bail. I understand her kids are in Sacramento with Will's parents."

"Oh no," Christian said. "Then I can tell you, and this will sound bad, but I have nothing but hatred toward Will. I haven't seen him for years. Tiffany, however, is different. Is there anything I can do to help her?"

"I'd like to talk to you more in person, if that's possible. I need some background on Will from when you met in college until you left the company."

"Just a moment." Zane heard Christian typing on his keyboard. "I have an hour tomorrow morning at 9:30."

"I'm in Utah. I don't think I can make that."

"Can you be here Friday at 10:00 am?"

"Yes, I can. Thank you, Mr. Christian." Zane ended the call and then looked for flights to San Jose.

ZANE HAD BEEN SITTING IN front of the Flying H Ranch for a couple of hours when a dust cloud coming from the ranch road caught his attention. One of Hubbard's large SUVs stopped at the entrance. He couldn't see inside the car because of the sun reflecting off the windshield and the tint on the side windows. The driver rolled down the window and looked right at Zane. It was Wayne Hubbard. He did a finger gun, pointed it at Zane, then drove off toward town.

He followed and wasn't discreet because Hubbard knew he was there. When the SUV got to the highway, instead of continuing into town, Hubbard turned away from Mathoni. He stuck to the SUV all the way to Vernal.

The Vernal airport was small, with only a handful of scheduled flights a week. Zane could park and jog to the terminal door. He watched as Hubbard and three men got out of the SUV. Hubbard opened the tailgate and took out several suitcases and set them on the ground. Zane wondered if now he had a chance to finally talk to him. Surely, he wouldn't get the brush-off in front of customers.

Zane casually walked up to them. "Wayne? How have you been?"

Hubbard looked up, surprised to see Zane standing on the curb. He continued unloading the luggage without saying a word.

"Wayne, man. It's me—Zane. You aren't even going to say hello?"

The three men looked at Hubbard. They clearly expected him to acknowledge Zane.

Hubbard looked at his customers and then back to Zane. "Let me take care of these gentlemen, and then I'll be right with you." His friendly tone surprised Zane.

"Yeah, sure," Zane said.

Wayne loaded the luggage onto a cart and disappeared with the other men into the terminal. Zane leaned against the SUV.

When Hubbard returned, he walked past, not even looking up. Zane went the other way around the vehicle and blocked the driver's door. Hubbard stared Zane down.

"I've been clear that I have nothing to say to you," Hubbard said, his friendly tone gone. "Now get out of my way. I have important things to do."

"I just need to clear up a few questions."

"The only thing you need to hear from me is a restraining order. Leave me the hell alone or I'll get one."

"You said you liked Mrs. Massey," Zane said. "Well, I'm trying to get her out of jail, and I need your help."

Hubbard sighed. "I guess when you put it that way. Be at the ranch tomorrow at 10:00. I'll talk then."

Zane stuck out his hand. "Friends then?"

"We'll see tomorrow," Hubbard said without shaking hands. Zane stepped aside and watched Hubbard drive away.

Success at last. It was a small win, but Zane took it. He realized that if he removed Hubbard from his suspect list, he'd have only a couple of iffy suspects. He wasn't sure if he wanted to know whether Hubbard was innocent or guilty. After the first visit to the ranch, he was sure he'd let people know where he'd be tomorrow morning.

Chapter 24

ZANE WAS IN A GOOD mood on Wednesday morning when he got to the Flying H Ranch to talk to Wayne Hubbard. It was a beautiful day with a light breeze, and he was finally going to get some answers from his primary suspect.

The place seemed quiet. Zane figured they were between guests. When he tried the door to the main building, he found it locked.

He wandered over to the barn, where he found one of the ranch hands cleaning out a stall with a pitchfork. There were five horses in the other stalls. Straw bales were stacked on one side. He recognized the hand as one of the henchmen from when he was run off at gunpoint but didn't know if it was Deke or Clay.

"Is Mr. Hubbard around?" Zane said. "I have an appointment."

The henchman stopped work and leaned against the handle of the pitchfork. "He ain't here."

"I have an appointment."

"Yeah." He stretched it out, so it was more like 'yeeeeah.' "'Bout that. Mr. Hubbard wanted me to tell you he had changed his mind. He ain't gonna talk to ya."

Zane clenched his jaw and wondered if Hubbard had meant to lie when he set up this meeting or if he'd stewed on it since then and decided against it. "Will you give him a message?"

"Ahhh, yup. What do you want him to know?"

"Just ask him to call Zane Grayson."

"I'll tell him. I can't promise he'll do it. Now that yer uninvited, you best git unless you want to get thrown off the property again."

After he was forced off the ranch the last time he was there, Zane thought it best to comply. He tipped his hat and got on his way. When he got to the end of the drive, he stopped and pounded his fists against the steering wheel. "FUCK!" he yelled into the wind.

ZANE'S IRRITATION GREW AS HE drove home. There was a reason Hubbard kept dodging a meeting, and the only one he could come up with was that Hubbard was guilty. By the time he got to the farm, his mood was surly. Marcia was loading the washing machine when he came through the door, letting it slam shut.

"You're home early. What happened with Wayne?"

"He changed his mind."

"Oh, Zane. I'm sorry. I know you were looking forward to getting his story."

He went to the kitchen, took a glass from the cupboard, and then slammed the cabinet door shut, then opened another cupboard, took out a bottle of bourbon. He slammed the door too before pouring himself a drink.

"A little early, isn't it?" Marcia said.

"Not now. I'm not in the mood," he barked.

She gasped.

He threw back the drink.

"Zane."

"What?" he snapped.

"I just wanted to tell you I'm going to the temple in Vernal on Friday."

"I suppose you want me to take you?" he growled. The last

thing he wanted was to run a taxi service to take his mom to Vernal so she could attend one of her church's most sacred meetings. Only members "in good standing" and with a recommend signed by both the Bishop and Stake President were allowed inside the temple.

"Zane Lorenzo Grayson." When she used his full name, he knew he was in trouble. "That's enough. You will not act this way, and you will not talk back to me."

He collapsed into a chair. "I'm sorry, Mom, really. I'm frustrated."

"I know, but you still shouldn't take it out on me."

"You're right. I'm sorry. I need to follow up on a lead and will be in California on Friday and have a flight booked for tomorrow."

"Ruby is driving. Now what's this lead in California?"

He tried to sound chipper. "It will be good for you to get out." He told her about Brian Christian and his connection to Will.

"I understand why you need to talk to him."

He put the bourbon bottle back in the cupboard and picked up his keys. "I need to go to Manila. I'll be back for supper."

"Um, Zane? I don't think you should go. You've been drinking, and the roads will be busy this time of year."

"Then I'll have some lunch first." He knew one drink would not make him drunk, but he didn't want to argue with her again.

ZANE COULDN'T FIGURE OUT WHY someone would build anything in Manila. His dad had joked that one side of the sign said *Welcome to Manila* and the other side said *Come back soon*. Yet, it was the county seat of Daggett County, the least populous in the state. The town of Mathoni had more people than all of Daggett county.

After lunch, Zane headed north from Mathoni to Dutch John, then crossed Flaming Gorge Dam and weaved around the west side of Flaming Gorge Reservoir to Manila. He figured there couldn't be much construction going on and asked around to find the site where Tomás Sanchez was working, only to learn that several new summer cabins were under construction.

The first two were easy to find, but Sanchez was not at either of them. The third gave Zane trouble. He had to double back more than once before getting on the correct road to find the construction site. This time he got lucky.

Sanchez was in his early twenties; his muscles stretched his t-shirt across his chest. He spoke very little English. Zane hoped his rudimentary Spanish skills would be enough.

"You worked for Mr. Massey?" Zane asked.

"Si, Señor. I fired."

"You know he's dead?"

A blank stare was the reply.

"Señor Massey es muerto."

Sanchez's eyes went wide. "¡Yo no lo mate!"

"Yo no policía," Zane said. Sanchez relaxed a bit.

Zane laid out the details of the murder. At least he hoped Sanchez understood. "Where were you the day Mr. Massey was killed?"

"I in Vernal."

"With your familia?"

"Si Señor, con mi familia."

"Where do you live now?"

"No intiendo."

"¿Donde vive ahora?"

"Manila. Con el jefe." He pronounced it like a Spanish word, mah-NEE-la instead of the English pronunciation that rhymes with vanilla.

Zane cringed, thinking what it would have been like to live with his boss when he was a cop.

"Have you been to the Massey Ranch since you were fired?"

Another blank stare.

Zane sighed. This was getting nowhere. "Gracias, Señor Sanchez." Convinced Sanchez was not tied in with the murders, he knew it was time to return to Mathoni.

As he was leaving Manila, Zane got a call from George Needham. Tiffany was home and she wanted to see him.

THE SKY WAS RED AND orange, and shadows from the evening sun stretched across the hills. Zane and Tiffany sat at the kitchen table and her parent's house. She was calm and collected compared to the withdrawn and non-responsive person she was before her arrest. She had showered and wore clean clothes, her hair pulled back in a ponytail, but also had a monitor strapped to her ankle so the Sheriff could track everywhere she went.

"How are you after your Founders' Day attack?" she asked.

"The bruises are a lovely black, blue, green, and yellow. My body looks like it was tie-dyed. I'm doing better every day. What about you? How are you doing?"

"Jail was awful. It was noisy and smelled so bad. The bed was lumpy, and I didn't sleep well. Except for a few minutes each day when they let me out to walk around, I never saw the sun. I lost all track of time and cried, a lot. I miss my kids and Will. Eventually, I accepted that it may be like that for the rest of my life."

"Don't think that way. I read up on your lawyer. He's very good. I think the judge will throw out the search warrant, which means the hay hook will be inadmissible. The state won't have a case. You'll get set free."

"Speaking of the hay hook," Tiffany said, "how did it end up in my linen closet?"

"I've wondered the same thing. It had to have been someone who had access to the house. Either after the Sheriff wrapped up the initial investigation the day Will died or the day of the funeral. Other than me, who else was here?"

Tiffany thought for a moment. "There was me and the kids, the Sheriff and deputies, Jacob, and the other ranch hands—hang on—Jacob? He did it?"

"I've talked to Jacob. He had an opportunity, but I don't think he had a motive, unless he didn't tell me the truth. My guess is, whoever murdered him is the actual killer. How were things between him and Will?

"They were great. No problems."

"So, let's assume Jacob wasn't the murderer. Who else was here?"

"Mom and Dad, but no way they would have done it."

"I agree. When I stopped here the next morning, the house

locked."

"From what I remember, no one else was here, but I was not very coherent. Maybe my dad knows."

"Ask him about it."

"If the judge throws out the search warrant, can the sheriff still keep after me?"

"That depends on the judge. If he dismisses the charges with prejudice, it means they can't refile. My gut tells me your attorney will request that."

"What about this?" She lifted her leg to show the monitor. "Except for going to court in Vernal, I'm limited to the Mathoni area," she explained.

"When they release you, they'll have to remove that too," Zane pointed to her ankle. "Right now, I'm just happy you're back home. Are your kids still in Sacramento?"

"Yes, I talked to them earlier. They're all worried, but Will's parents have kept them busy. Larry and Sarah took them to San Francisco for a Giants game a couple of days ago. We used to take them all the time when we lived out there. They'd missed it and had a great time."

"Sounds like their grandparents are doing everything they can to keep their minds off things. What did you want to see me about?"

"I had lots of time to think in jail. I don't know why he didn't occur to me before."

Zane leaned forward, his arms on the table, fully concentrating on what Tiffany was saying. "Who didn't occur to you?"

"Will's old business partner."

"Brian Christian," Zane said. "I know about him. I phoned him yesterday, and I'm flying to San Jose tomorrow to meet with him on Friday."

She looked at him, her eyes wide. "Why didn't you tell me?"

"I haven't had a chance. I was going to talk to you about him days ago, but then I was attacked and you were arrested."

"What did he say?"

Zane wondered how much he should tell her and decided the truth would be best. "He hated Will but wanted to help you. What can you tell me about him?"

She told Zane everything he had discovered online; how Will met Christian at BYU and became fast friends. Each was best man at the other's wedding. They had kids of about the same age. They did everything with Brian and Janis. After graduation, Will and Brian went into business together, starting Timpanogos Security and developing their computer security software. They moved the company from Lehi, Utah, to Silicon Valley to be closer to funding sources.

"Then, Janis got sick, and Brian wanted out of the company to take care of her and their kids. I don't know exactly what happened between Will and Brian," she said, "but they had a nasty falling out over it. After traveling the world with them, we just stopped seeing them altogether."

Zane said, "Do you think Brian may have finally taken revenge?"

"I don't know. It doesn't sound like Brian. Maybe?" she said. "But after being so close and then to cut off every connection with them? I tried to call Janis, but she never answered my calls or returned messages. Doesn't that seem strange?"

"It seems that there was bad blood between them. Did he get any money from the sale of the company to Microsoft?"

She shook her head. "I don't think so."

"Which means, he missed out on hundreds of millions? Just how much did you get?"

"Close to nine hundred million." She couldn't look at Zane, as if she was embarrassed. "It was mostly stock."

"So, assuming Brian would get half of that, it's still a hell of a lot," Zane said as if the number was nothing. "If his hatred of Will has festered after all those years, I can see how that would eventually drive him to murder. I hope to know more after our meeting."

"Be careful. If Brian is who you're looking for and he comes after you, I don't know what I'd do if he hurt you. Or worse."

"I appreciate your concern, Tiff, but I'll be fine." He told her about the rest of the investigation, the struggle to talk to Wayne Hubbard, clearing Sanchez, and his suspicions that the same person killed both Will and Jacob.

"I still can't believe Jacob is dead too," she said. "I have to get out of this house. There's nothing but death here. As far as I'm concerned, it can sit empty. I packed a suitcase and am staying with my parents. Daddy will supervise the ranch hands until the herd is sold."

"I think it's a good idea to stay with your parents. Their support will help you. The kids too, when they come back." He stood to leave. "It's late. I need to go."

"Wait, Zane. One more thing."

He sat again.

"That day that I kissed you. I shouldn't have. It's just—after we ran into each other that first day, I kept thinking about you. Then Will died, and you were there."

"It's fine, Tiff. It never happened."

Chapter 25

THE SUN WAS NOT YET peeking over the eastern horizon as Zane headed out. He figured as long as he needed to go to Salt Lake City for his evening flight to California, he could go early and get some information on Will's attorney, Sal Giovanni.

He stopped in Vernal long enough to get breakfast at McDonald's. His mind was still on his mom back home. She'd told him to go, that it was green week and she'd be fine, but she also agreed to check-in every day with Ruby. That eased Zane's concerns.

Three hours later he was in Sandy, a city fifteen miles south of Salt Lake City. Giovanni & Chesterton was on the fourth floor of an office building near city hall. He had an appointment with Maxwell Chesterton. Zane expected that the most he'd get from the lawyer would be "privileged information," but he had to try.

Chesterton was about sixty years old, a short, stout man with a comb over and a suit that looked like it came from the popular local menswear shop, Mr. Mac, best known for inexpensive, long-lasting suits for Mormon missionaries.

"I have to tell you, Mr. Grayson," he said as he swiveled back and forth in his leather desk chair, "that I do not know what happened to Sal. He had planned a two-week vacation in the

Caribbean, but he never got there."

"Yes, I understand he went missing. I'm here about one of your clients, William Massey."

"I never met him. Sal handled everything for Mr. Massey."

"You probably know that someone murdered Will."

"I watch the news," Chesterton said derisively. "I understand they arrested his wife."

"She's currently out on bail. The state lists Mr. Giovanni as the corporate agent. I'm curious about what work was being done for him."

"You know I can't tell you that. Attorney-client confidentiality."

"Alright. Can you tell me why Will hired a criminal law firm for business purposes?"

"You'd have to ask Mr. Massey."

"Which I can't do."

Chesterton grinned like the Cheshire Cat.

"When did you last see Mr. Giovanni?"

"We both left the office about 5:00 p.m. the evening before he disappeared."

"And you went home?"

"Yes, I was at home, and for the record, my wife and granddaughter were with me all evening."

Zane shifted in the chair. "Let's take a different approach. Does Mr. Giovanni have any family?"

"None in the area. He has an extensive family back east in New York."

"Utah is a long way from there. What brought him to Salt Lake City?"

Chesterton picked up the pitcher of ice water from the desk and poured himself a glass without offering one to Zane. He took a sip, then said, "He loves to ski."

"That makes sense. If he doesn't have family, is he seeing anyone?"

"Yes, but I don't think I should tell you who it is. The police have already upset her enough."

"Was she planning to go to the Caribbean with Mr. Giovanni?"

"Yes, she was."

"So, she's still in town?"

"She was when I last talked to her a couple of days ago." He took another drink of water.

"What kind of car does he drive?"

"He has a black 2025 Mercedes-Benz E-Class. It has also disappeared."

"Doesn't it seem odd to you that Mr. Giovanni's disappearance coincides with Will's murder? Because it looks suspicious to me."

"Are you saying that Sal had something to do with Mr. Massey's death?"

"That's exactly what it looks like."

"Sal and I have represented some nasty people. When you're in criminal law, you have to. Some clients get acquitted. Others end up at the Utah State Prison. We both know what it looks like being on the wrong side of the law. Neither of us would cross the line. Now, I have a brief to finish. My secretary will show you out."

Zane sat in his truck thinking about Chesterton. Something didn't feel right with the man, but he couldn't put his finger on exactly what it was. He wanted to talk to Giovanni's girlfriend. Maybe Tiffany's lawyer could help. He took his phone out of his pocket and made a call.

"I'm sorry, but Mr. Miller is in court today. Could I direct you to another attorney?" the receptionist said.

"Maybe Ms. Pace can help me?"

"She is also unavailable."

Zane thought quickly. "I need to talk to someone about the Tiffany Massey case. Perhaps Mr. Miller's investigator would be best."

"One moment, I'll see if he's in."

It took about a minute before a man came on the line. "Roy Hinkle."

"Mr. Hinkle. This is Zane Grayson."

"I know who you are. What can I do for you?"

"I just talked to Sal Giovanni's partner . . ."

He heard paper rustling. "That would be Max Chesterton?"

"Yes, that's him. He told me that Giovanni has a girlfriend but wouldn't give me a name. You don't know who it is, do you?"

"We've been looking into Mr. Giovanni, so of course I know. It's Ariel Sanders."

Zane wrote the name on his notepad. "Do you have an address for her?"

He heard Hinkle shuffle more paper.

"She has a condo in Park City that Giovanni pays for."

"That doesn't surprise me," Zane said.

Hinkle gave him the address.

"Thank you, Mr. Hinkle." He pressed the disconnect button on the phone and headed to Park City.

ORIGINALLY A MINING TOWN, MOSTLY silver, Park City was now known for its skiing. Since it was only thirty minutes from Salt Lake International Airport, it was easy for people to fly in and spend time on the slopes. In mid-June, there were no skiers and no snow. It was also home to the wealthy, including several Hollywood stars.

Zane had driven past Park City on his way to Salt Lake City. He headed back towards home but took the exit off Interstate-80 at Kimball Junction and was soon parking near Ariel's building on historic Park City Main Street and took an elevator to the third floor and rang the doorbell.

He wasn't sure what to expect from Ariel. The blonde bombshell who appeared on the other side of the door surprised him. She was in her mid-twenties—half Sal's age—and her skimpy dress showed lots of leg and cleavage. She clearly wasn't wearing a bra to support what he assumed were surgically enhanced breasts. He could see why Sal paid for her condo and wondered how much he paid for her. He'd seen oversexed women in California. They all had money or pretended they did. After interviewing several of them, he decided that their IQ got lower as their breasts got bigger. Zane wasn't looking forward to this interview.

"Ariel Sanders?"

"Who the fuck are you?"

Not the greeting Zane expected. "My name is Zane Grayson. I'm looking for Sal."

"My Sal? Do you know where he is?"

"No, I don't, but it's important I talk to him."

She invited him in. They sat in the living room. It was bright with floor to ceiling windows that looked out onto the ski area. The furniture was white leather, and the art on the walls was original. In the light, Zane could see the dark roots of her hair. Bottle blonde didn't surprise him.

"Can you really find my Sal?"

"I can't make any promises, but I hope to locate him. When did you last see him?"

"The night before he disappeared. He came here straight from his office."

Zane took notes and asked, "Did he spend the night?"

"Oh, yes." She stretched out the sentence. "We had dinner delivered. Then we went to bed. God, he was amazing that night. We screwed for hours. Sal is an unbelievable lover."

"What time did he leave?"

"Around 8:00 in the morning. He was going to his place to get his luggage and then come back to get me. Then off to the airport. We were going to the Caribbean for two weeks. He'd rented a yacht. It would just be me and him and the crew. He never came back." Ariel sniffled.

Zane could tell she was close to tears. "Did you call him?"

"I called and texted, over and over. I got his fucking voicemail, ya know? I miss my Sal."

"And he said nothing about not returning?"

"Fuck no. I told him about the new bikinis I bought for the trip. He couldn't wait to see me in them. Come to think of it, maybe that's why he was so horny that night. Everything you hear about Italian men tells you all you need to know about Sal's sexual skills." She wiped the tears from her eyes.

"Do you know if his luggage was still at his house?"

"The cops said it was, so I guess so."

"How did you meet him?"

"At the ski lodge in January. He'd finished skiing, and I was at the bar. He bought me a drink, Sex on the Beach." She winked. "I had on this pink ski parka that was unzipped down to here." She pointed just south of her cleavage. "And tight ski pants that really showed off my ass."

"So, you finished skiing before him?"

She shook her head. "Oh no, I don't ski. I was there to find a sexy man for the night. Boy, did I."

"Do you have any idea where Sal could be?"

"Like I told the cops, he wouldn't just run off. Sal and I are in love. Just between you and me, I thought he was going to propose while we were on that yacht. Can you imagine? Me! Mrs. Sal Giovanni." She waved her hand in front of her face as if trying to cool herself.

"I can see why you'd think that," Zane said.

"Have you talked to his family in New York?"

"They called me. You'd think the world ended the way they acted. Called me a gold-digging whore. When we met, I wasn't looking for love. I was just after a good fuck for the night." She shrugged. "But after we spent some time with each other, it was like we were meant to be together."

"So, they didn't know where Sal is?"

"The fuckers blamed me for his disappearance."

It was clear that Ariel did not know where Sal was. If she did, Zane was sure they'd be in bed. "Thank you for your time. I need to get to the airport for a flight."

"If you find him, tell him to hurry back. It's no fun being in bed alone."

As soon as Zane was in the hallway and she'd shut the door, he shook all over, trying to get the ick off. He doubted Sal had murdered Will, and his gut told him something bad had happened to Sal Giovanni.

ZANE DROVE HIS RENTAL CAR through Silicon Valley. He'd been here before. In college, UC Irvine came to play San Jose State, but he paid little attention to the area as a bus hauled the team around. Urban sprawl was the best way he could describe the valley. There was also a lack of tall buildings, but it seemed like thousands of three- or four-story office buildings lined street after street. Taller ones popped up now and then, but mostly the shorter offices.

His route took him in all four directions, sometimes heading north, then west, back north, and then even south, from one freeway to another. His hotel was on a road named El Camino Real in Palo Alto. He was finally driving north on the famous road. More of the same three-story offices, strip malls, gas stations, stores, and fast-food restaurants lined the street. Other than a sign announcing he was in a different city, he couldn't tell when he left one city and entered another. When his phone notified him he had arrived at his destination, he looked around. He was at a small strip-mall with no hotel in sight. He double-checked the street number for the hotel. It matched a beauty salon in the strip mall.

Confused, he went into the beauty salon. "I'm looking for a hotel that is supposed to be at this address," he told the woman at the check-in desk.

"I don't know about a hotel, but El Camino Real is difficult. The building numbers start over in every city. This is Sunnyvale."

"I'm looking for Palo Alto."

"Keep going north. You'll hit it."

Back in his rental car, Zane entered the name of the hotel into the map phone app instead of the address. He pulled out into the stop-and-go traffic, heading in the direction the beautician had indicated.

He arrived at the hotel later than expected and checked in. Once in his room, he called home. His mom was doing fine, but she'd been hearing gossip in town about Tiffany. Seems people had already decided she was guilty.

"I've heard the same thing," Zane said. "It doesn't surprise me it's ramping up after her arrest. It's a good thing the trial is being moved to Vernal. I doubt she would get a fair trial in Mathoni."

Chapter 26

VERLING TECHNOLOGIES WAS IN A nondescript three-story office building that looked similar to all the other nondescript three-story office buildings in Silicon Valley. Once inside, Zane looked around the large lobby and saw that it extended the full three floors. He stepped up to the welcome desk, where a uniformed guard sat.

"I'm here to see Brian Christian," he told the guard. His nametag informed Zane that his name was Broderick.

"Your name, sir?"

"Zane Grayson."

The guard tapped on the keyboard in front of him. "Are you sure you have an appointment with Mr. Christian?"

"Yes, I made it directly with him."

"One moment, sir." The guard picked up the handset of a desk phone and made a call. After he hung up, he said, "Mr. Christian's assistant is on her way down. Sign in here." He indicated an electronic signature pad on the desk.

"Now, look at this camera, please." Broderick clicked his mouse and then handed Zane a visitor badge with his name and picture printed on it.

Zane pulled off the paper backing and stuck the name tag to his shirt.

"Please make sure you sign out when you leave."

A few minutes later, the elevator dinged, the doors opened, and a twentyish brunette stepped out. She extended her hand. "Mr. Grayson? I'm Cindy, Mr. Christian's personal assistant. Come with me and I'll take you up."

They entered the elevator, and Cindy pressed three. Zane grinned because he'd guessed right that Christian's office was on the third floor. Cindy used her employee badge to open a set of glass doors that led him through heavy, wooden doors at the end of a hall.

They were in an outer office waiting room. A sofa and chairs sat at one end next to a side table with several magazines on it. A desk was at the other end. Zane assumed it was Cindy's. Next to her desk was another set of wooden doors with 'Private' painted on them.

Christian's office was large and furnished with leather chairs, a sofa, and a glass desk. Brian Christian stood, walked from behind it, and extended his hand. Zane shook it.

Christian wore a white, long-sleeved, button-down dress shirt and a red silk tie with silver polka-dots. A charcoal gray jacket that matched his trousers hung over the back of his executive desk chair.

Christian looked at his assistant. "Tell Vihaan that I'm ready for him."

"Mr. Grayson," Cindy said, "can I get you anything, coffee, soda or water?"

"Water would be great."

Cindy left.

"Please, sit, Mr. Grayson." Christian held out his hand, directing Zane to sit on the sofa.

"Thank you. I felt it was important to ask you some questions in person."

"That's obvious, as you've come all the way from Utah."

The door opened, and a middle-aged, chubby Indian man, also dressed immaculately in a dark blue suit with a red and blue striped tie, came in.

Christian said, "I asked Vihaan Singh, our corporate counsel, to join us. I've already updated him on our conversation earlier in the week."

Zane didn't expect a lawyer to be present and wondered what Christian had to hide. "Very well, Mr. Christian."

"Please, call me Brian."

Zane had played this game before when he was a cop. A suspect wanted to seem open and friendly. It didn't mean he was guilty, but more often than not, it turned out that way.

Cindy returned with a pitcher of water and three glasses. She set it all on a table in front of the sofa, poured a glass for each person, then left.

Zane took a drink and put his cell phone on the table. "Do you mind if I record this? It's easier than taking notes."

Christian looked at Vihaan, who nodded and said, "I'm fine with being recorded."

Zane tapped the record button.

"Mr. Grayson," Vihaan said, his heavy accent coming through, "we will do the same." He placed his phone in front of the group and hit record. "First, I want to make it clear that Mr. Christian was kind enough to allow your visit with him because he has nothing to hide. He is speaking with you voluntarily."

"I understand, Mr. Christian," Zane said again.

Christian waggled his finger back and forth. "It's Brian. Before we start, please tell me how Tiffany and the kids are doing."

Zane noted how all the employees called him Mr. Christian, but he was asked to call him Brian. Another indicator that he was trying to seem friendly.

"She was shaken at first. The sheriff found . . ."

"Just a moment. You told me you're with the Sheriff's office," Christian said.

Vihaan looked up, concern on his face.

"That's not quite accurate. What I said is I'm investigating Will's murder."

"So, you're a private investigator?" Vihaan asked. "Who are you working for?"

Zane explained his background, and that the sheriff still looked at him as a suspect. What he was doing was clearing himself, and then continued. "As I was saying, the sheriff found what I believe is sketchy evidence and arrested Tiffany. When she got out on bail, she'd come to grips with her situation. When I asked her again if Will had—" He didn't want to say enemies. "—anything in his past that even smelled of an issue against him, it would be helpful, she gave me your name." He didn't lie. Tiffany had told him, but not until after he'd found the connection to Christian.

Even though he was recording the conversation, Vihaan took notes on what Zane told them and then said, "So, you believe Mr. Christian committed the murder?"

"I'm doing what any good investigator would do. Follow the evidence and clear names from a possible suspect list. I'm here to do just that. Brian, could tell me how you met William Massey?"

Christian looked at Vihaan, who nodded.

"We were in college at BYU in a *Book of Mormon* class, our freshman year, talking before the professor came in. Found out we were both studying Computer Science."

Zane waited for Christian to continue. When he didn't, Zane asked, "And you became friends?"

Christian answered without waiting for Vihaan. "We became close friends. Beginning our sophomore year, we were roommates for a couple of years. Later, I was best man at his wedding, and he at mine. After graduation, we started a business together."

"What happened with that?"

Vihaan nodded, then Christian said, "We were very successful, eventually moving the company from Silicon Slopes to Silicon Valley."

Zane interrupted. "Silicon Slopes?"

"That's what they call the tech corridor in Utah."

"I guess it shows I was here in California for a long time. I'd never heard the term Silicon Slopes before. Please, continue."

"Our families vacationed with each other. We went to Europe, Australia, and elsewhere." He stood and walked to the credenza behind his desk, then returned with a picture in a gold frame. He handed it to Zane.

Taking it, Zane saw a much younger Brian Christian with his wife and two young children, the Sydney Opera House in the background.

Christian sat and continued. "With the success and money, Will changed. Our families saw less and less of each other. One day I realized we never saw each other outside of work. At the office, we argued over small things. After a couple of years of this, he offered to buy me out. I'd had enough of the rancor he brought to work and agreed."

Christian's story differed from the one Tiffany had told him yesterday.

"How much did he pay you?" Zane said.

"I'm afraid I can't answer that because of a non-disclosure agreement."

"Alright. In general, would you say it was fair?"

Christian sighed. "It was less than my share was worth, but by that time, I wanted out."

"Your wife wasn't ill?"

"She had a health scare about the same time that turned out to be minor. They took care of it, and she's fine now.

"And then what happened?"

"I moved on. I'm the chief technology officer here now. I'm happy."

"How did you feel about Will selling the company you helped build?

Vihaan spoke up. "Don't answer that."

Christian replied anyway. "What do you mean?"

"Were you happy for him? Or upset that you missed out on a big payday?"

"How do you think I felt?"

"I don't know. That's why I'm asking."

"At first? I . . ."

Vihaan leaned over and whispered in Christian's ear. Christian looked over at Zane and then waved off Vihaan. "At first, I was upset. Yes, I missed out. The more I thought about it, the less I cared. As I said, I'm happy where I am."

"Did you speak to him after the sale?"

"The last time I spoke to him was the day I signed the paperwork to sell him my share of Timpanogos Security."

"You don't think it strange that after such a close friendship, all contact suddenly stopped?"

"Like I said, he changed. It wasn't sudden. At first, it was the power, then the money. It became more difficult being around him."

"Difficult how?"

"He became demanding. Often barking out the simplest requests as if they were orders and acting as if he were better than everyone else. Our relationship deteriorated. After having traveled extensively with each other, we didn't even get together for dinner."

"What about Tiffany?" Zane asked.

"I don't know how she put up with him. Oh, she drove a nicer car and wore better clothes, but she never changed personally from our college days. My wife talks about her from time to time, and I've suggested more than once that she pick up the phone and call her, but she never has."

Zane said, "And you never did that?"

"My wife was closer to her than I was."

"When we spoke on the phone, you said you hated Will. Maybe it was enough for you to take revenge?"

"Sounds like we're done here," Vihaan said.

Christian said, "You never told me how the children are doing."

"I have seen little of them. They're staying with Will's parents in Sacramento for now. Tiffany said something about their going to a Giants game."

"Please tell her she's in our thoughts and prayers."

"I'll pass that along. I have one more question, if I may."

"Very well, ask your question," Vihaan said.

"Mr. Christian . . ."

"Brian."

"Brian, where were you on the day Will Massey was murdered?"

"Don't answer that," Vihaan said.

Christian waved him off again. "I take a break every June. Go off-grid at my cabin for a week. Clears my mind and relaxes me. I spend a lot of time hiking and mountain biking, you know, getting back to nature. I always come back refreshed and with a clear mind."

"Where exactly is this cabin?"

"You had your one question, Mr. Grayson," Vihaan said.

"I have no concerns about answering this. It's at Sundance, near Provo."

Zane knew where Sundance was, and he saw an opening. An opportunity for Christian to go to Mathoni and murder Will Massey. The small ski town was only a few hours from Mathoni. Before he could say anything, Christian continued.

"No, I did not see Will, and no, I did not kill him."

"Can your family confirm you were there?"

"They knew I went to the cabin, but I spent the time alone, decompressing from . . . everything." He waved his hand through the air. "And before you ask your next question, no one actually saw me there. Again, I did not see Will, and I did not kill him."

"And what about earlier this week, Monday and Tuesday?"

"What does that have to do with Mr. Massey's death?" Vihaan said.

Zane watched Christian as he answered. "Jacob Faust, his ranch foreman, was murdered late Monday night or early Tuesday morning this week, too."

"It seems like you're fishing, Mr. Grayson," Vihaan said. "We're not going to answer."

"Are you sad Will died?"

"I feel sorry for Tiffany and the kids, but there will be no tears lost for Will." Christian stood. "Now, I've given you the truth and have pressing matters to get to." He walked to the desk and pressed a button. "Cindy, please show Mr. Grayson to the lobby."

Cindy quickly appeared. "This way, Mr. Grayson."

"Before you leave, one more thing," Christian said. "Don't contact me in the future. I've told you everything I know. I won't make time for you again."

Zane followed Cindy to the lobby. He returned his visitor badge and left. On the way back to the hotel, he thought about everything Brian Christian had told him. There was nothing to clear him. In fact, based on what Tiffany had told him, the man had lied about why Will had bought him out. If he really was in Utah, he had an excellent opportunity to commit a murder.

Later that night, he called his mom. She was doing fine. Then he phoned Tiffany to update her on what he'd learned.

"I'm glad you called, Zane. I found something and need you to look at it. I don't want to tell you over the phone. Come see me as soon as you can."

Chapter 27

A TWO-HOUR FLIGHT DELAY PUSHED back Zane's return. He was eager to learn what Tiffany had found that she wouldn't tell him about over the phone the night before, but first, he stopped to check on his mom. She had two women from the church visiting with her, and that had her in good spirits. He dropped his luggage in his bedroom and then drove to the Needham home.

Tiffany wanted to hear about his trip and whether he had learned anything from Brian Christian. They sat in George's old office while Zane updated her.

"Brian wanted me to pass on a message."

Tiffany couldn't sit still and kept playing with her necklace.

"He said you and the kids are in his prayers and that his wife talks about you, but has never called."

"I haven't talked to Janis in so long. Maybe I should call her."

"I don't know exactly what happened between Will and him, but he's very bitter. His story about what happened between them wasn't the same as yours."

"What? I swear to you that Janis got sick."

"He confirmed that, but he said it was minor. His issues were with Will. He told me Will grew more and more demanding and became somewhat of a tyrant to the point they couldn't work together. That's when he asked to be bought out."

Tiffany walked to the window and looked out. "That doesn't sound right. Will was never like that."

"I can only report what he said. Maybe Will was different at the office."

Tiffany got up and looked out the window. "Brian must have been really upset. I guess that makes him a good suspect?"

"Especially because he was in Utah the day Will died."

"What?" She turned to look at Zane. "He told you that?"

"He said he has a cabin at Sundance and claims he was there alone all week. No one saw him. I think I can find his cabin from tax records. If I can, I'll go down and talk to the neighbors."

"Then we'll know. I feel so relieved."

"I hate to burst your bubble, but just because he was in Sundance doesn't mean he was here in Mathoni. It also doesn't mean he wasn't."

"Yes, you're right. Now how about we look at what I found? We'll have to go up to the house. I didn't want to take it out in case it's evidence of some kind."

When they arrived at Tiffany's house, they headed to what had been Will's office. Tiffany sat behind the desk and opened a drawer. "I was going through Will's desk. I took stuff out of this bottom drawer and found a false bottom. This was inside." She took out a large book and placed it on top of the desk.

"That looks like an old accounting ledger," Zane said. "I didn't think anyone used them anymore with computers to run a business."

"That's what I thought. I can't make head nor tail of it. You know I was never very good at math."

"Oh, the hours I spent tutoring you, and it never stuck. Let me look at that book."

She grinned. "As I recall, we did more than tutoring."

Zane thumbed through the pages, working to understand the debits and credits. "It definitely appears to be an accounting ledger, but I can't figure out the names; they're just letters and numbers. Look here." Zane turned the ledger so Tiffany could read it from where she sat on the other side of the desk. "This looks like a $10,000 payment to 100BC. There's another $2,000 to 84ZBV." He turned back a page. "And this one looks like a payment to CCBT8000 for $100,000."

"A hundred thousand?"

"Well, it's just a guess. Was he working on anything other than the guest house?"

"Nothing he talked to me about. How do we figure out who these people are?'

"More importantly, why did he keep a secret set of books, and how did the sheriff's deputies not find this in their search?"

Zane launched the calculator app on his phone, went back to the first page of the book. He added and subtracted numbers to come up with a total amount.

"Only the first ten pages are used. Looks like more than a million dollars."

"I know that sounds like a lot of money, but it was a drop in the bucket for us."

Zane said, "Well, the numbers in this ledger are a small fraction of that, and that's still more than I can comprehend. Let's see if we can trace this a different way. Do you have a pad of paper and a pencil?"

Tiffany opened a cabinet and brought Zane a legal pad and several pencils.

At the top of one page, Zane wrote 'BC100' then he wrote '+10,000'. On the next page he put 'SLSG4' and then '+2,000'. He worked his way through the ledger, writing additional numbers on the pages. He started a new page for each code. Some numbers increased totals; others reduced them. At the end, totaled up the amounts for each code name.

Tiffany asked, "So what does this tell us now?"

"I'm not sure, but as an example, whoever or whatever 17BOASC is, got paid $75,000 as did BC100." Zane pointed at each of the figures as he mentioned them. "Neither showed amounts going out. This one was 200K. The way I figure it, it looks like there's a grand total of 1.73 million."

"But we don't know who these people are."

"Or even if they are people. They could be people, companies, bank accounts, or investments, maybe a combination of those. We have no way of knowing."

Tiffany leaned back in the chair and rubbed her eyes. "What you're saying is Will was into something illegal."

"I suspect that is the case. Sorry, Tiffany."

"How does this help me?"

"It could point the finger at whoever or whatever these code names are. Any idea what these codes mean?" Zane asked.

"Initials? I don't understand the numbers with them."

"Neither do I, but I'm going to find out. You should call your attorney. Tell him what we found. In the meantime, I'll take pictures of each of these ledger pages."

Tiffany went to the other room and called David Miller. Zane took out his cell phone and took pictures of the used pages.

When she came back in she said, "Mr. Miller said to call the sheriff. So, I did."

It was after 11:00 p.m. before Rich Richman showed up. He donned blue latex gloves and went over the pages in the ledger.

"Tell me again where you found this, Mrs. Massey," Richman said.

Tiffany went through the story of sorting out the office and how she found it.

"And why didn't you call us right away? Why call Mr. Grayson first?"

"I didn't know for sure what it was or if it was important or not. I was never good at numbers. I knew Zane would figure it out."

"And you handled this book, Mr. Grayson?"

He nodded. "Yes, I did."

"And then you told her to call me?"

"I told Tiffany to call her attorney. He said I should call you."

"And what do you think this is, Mr. Grayson?"

"I think that's what you need to figure out."

"Smith County doesn't have the expertise to decode any of this, nor track what could be a financial crime. I'll need to get this to the state crime lab in Salt Lake. There are problems here. For example, there is no way of knowing if Mr. Massey really did this or if you two created it to point to a different suspect."

"What?" Tiffany screamed. "We did nothing like that. Zane, help me here."

"Seems to me, Sheriff, and I use that title loosely, that the problem is with you. Your team missed potential evidence. Again." Zane turned to Tiffany. "My advice, is say nothing more until your attorney is present."

"But he's accusing us, Zane."

"Yup, and the truth will come out."

Tiffany looked at the sheriff. "No, I'm not going to just give you something that you're going to use against me. No way."

"Alright then. I'll go down to Judge Snow's house and get a warrant."

"Let him take it, Tiffany," Zane said.

"No, I won't. He's listening to his preconceived ideas instead of logic."

"He's going to get it anyway. Just let him take it," Zane said. "Don't worry, your attorney will do his own investigation of it and find out we're telling the truth. I'm positive that Will's fingerprints will be all over it."

"No way. I'm not giving him anything willingly. Go wake up the judge and get your warrant." Her voice was thick with disgust.

Richman pressed the button on the microphone hanging from his shoulder. "Dispatch."

"Go ahead, Sheriff."

"I need a deputy up here at the Massey home to keep an eye on fresh evidence while I go get a warrant."

"Alright, Sheriff. I'll send someone over."

"10-4, dispatch."

"Can he do that, Zane? Can he have someone sit here while he goes down to see Judge Snow?"

"Yup, he can."

Richman then took out his cell phone, poked at the screen, and put it up to his ear. After a moment, he said, "Judge Snow, this is Sheriff Richman . . . Yes, Judge, I know it's late . . . I'll be on my way to get a warrant for some additional evidence in the Massey murder . . . No, I'm afraid it can't wait . . . Thank you, Judge. I'll be there as soon as I can."

An hour later, Sheriff Richman was back with his warrant, and he walked out with the ledger.

After Richman and the deputy left, Zane said, "We're in a good place here, Tiffany. First, the ledger does point to something. It may not be anything illegal, but it smells bad. Remember that the state must prove beyond a reasonable doubt that you're guilty. We've just given them reasonable doubt.

"Second, your attorney will bring up that the Sheriff missed important evidence in his search more than once, and play that as sloppy work. Between the ledger and the hay hook, he'll point out they could have bungled the rest of the case. They could have missed other evidence that clears you."

"I hope you're right, Zane."

"I know I am."

ZANE RETURNED HOME IN THE early morning hours. Mom's room was dark and Zane knew she was asleep. The travel had made for a long, exhausting day, and meeting with Tiffany had stretched it further, but he was too interested in the codes to sleep. He pulled out the papers where he'd written the amounts and zeroed in on the line with the largest amount, 'WMICI23' was one million dollars, but there were lots of amounts that went out of it. That bothered him and he rolled ideas around. *Maybe this is money that was used to pay all the others. But where did it come from? A bank? But a transaction that size would be reported to the Feds. If so, how much is unaccounted for?*

He opened the calculator app on his phone and punched in 1,000,000 then subtracted the other amounts. If that million was the original amount, that still left a large amount unaccounted for. He wondered where the leftover money was. A safe deposit box? A bank account we don't know about? A company?

Zane kept working on decoding until exhaustion finally overtook him, and he went to bed.

Chapter 28

ZANE SAT AT THE KITCHEN table with his morning coffee and returned to decoding the ledger. He stared at the codes for some time. The dollar figures were simple to understand. It was the codes next to them that had him guessing.

He wrote them all down alphabetically along with their totals.

    BC100 - 75000
    100BC - 50000
    17BOASC - 75000
    67BOASC - 10000
    CCBT8000 - 10000
    SLSG4 - 10000
    WMICI23 - 1000000
    84ZBM - 150000
    84ZBV - 150000
    84ZBS - 200000

Zane had many questions about this list. What was the difference between BC100 and 100BC? And 17BOASC and 67BOASC? And 84ZBM, 84ZBV, and 84ZBS? What do the numbers in the codes mean?

Next, he wrote them down in the order of the numbers in the codes, then he listed them in dollar amount order, followed by listing them in reverse order each way. Nothing he did got him any closer to solving the riddle of what they meant.

Zane rubbed his eyes. He'd stared at the codes for too long. He popped another pod into the coffeemaker. As he waited for the cup to fill, he stretched and groaned as some muscles were still sore from his assault at Founder's Day. When the coffee maker finished, he added cream and sugar to the cup and then took a sip, followed by a satisfied sigh.

Back at the table, he looked at the codes again and then smacked his hand against his forehead. "How could I be so dumb?" he said. "WMICI23 is William Massey ICI23." That bit of progress encouraged him.

He looked at the codes trying to work out other names. Could BC be Brian Christian? Did Will, after years, finally feel sorry he'd left Christian out of the big payoff and gave him some of the money, even if it was a tiny percentage of the total? He wrote Brian Christian's name next to the two BC entries.

The only other codes that seemed related were the ZB entries, but he didn't understand how three people with different last names could have the same first and middle names, especially a name that started with Z.

Maybe it was three payments to the same person? But he still did not know who ZB could be nor what the third letter meant.

Marcia walked in. "I'm home from church."

"What do you mean you're home? I didn't know you'd left."

"I told you I was going to church when I left over two hours ago. What on earth has all your attention?"

He told her about the codes and numbers. Marcia took one look at them and said, "What if ZB stands for Zions Bank?"

"Damn, you may be right."

"Zane, what have I said about language?"

"Yeah, sorry. I've been staring at this for hours with little progress."

He wrote Zions Bank, then just the word Bank next to all the codes with a B, including the ones he thought were Brian Christian.

Now he had to figure out the third letter of the Zions Bank entries. Maybe M was Mathoni and V was Vernal? Could S be Salt Lake City? Giovanni's office was in Sandy—maybe that S was not Salt Lake but Sandy.

Zane slid the chair back from the table. He had to get away from the codes for a while, let his mind rest. He gathered his papers and took them to the office, then helped Marcia with Sunday dinner.

THAT AFTERNOON, ZANE SET OUT to get information on Brian Christian's cabin. He knew the cabin was in Sundance, a ski resort near Provo. Actor Robert Redford back established Sundance in the 1960s. He filmed the movie *Jeremiah Johnson* near there and wanted to keep the area pristine. He bought a lot of the land so it could never be developed. That purchase included a ski area that he renamed Sundance after his role in the movie *Butch Cassidy and the Sundance Kid*. Today, besides being a ski resort, it had many vacation homes and others where people lived year-round.

Zane did an online search of property records in Utah County. It was simple to enter Christian's name into the search box on the county website. The search came back with over two dozen hits. Either Christian owned several properties or more than one Brian Christian owned property in the county.

He looked only at those properties in Sundance. There were five listed. It was likely Christian owned more than one. Now that he had addresses, he mapped them and found they were all near each other. He didn't need to know which one Christian was at only that he was there, but Zane printed each address so he could check them all. Next, he printed a picture of Christian from the Verling Technologies website. Now it was time to canvass the area.

The trip to Sundance took three hours and twenty minutes. It looked as if Christian could have driven from his cabin, to Mathoni, killed Will Massey, then driven back.

Zane easily found each property listed with Christian as the owner and photographed each one with his phone camera. He knocked on the neighbors' doors. There were no answers at the first three. At the fourth house, a man in his forties, well dressed with neatly cut blond hair, opened the door.

He didn't want to let on why he was poking around Christian's property, so he lied. "Hello. I'm trying to find this man, Brian Christian." Zane held up the picture he had printed out. "I understand he has a place around here."

"What did this guy do?" the man asked.

"Nothing. We've been out of contact for years, and I'm trying to reconnect."

The man looked closer at the picture.

"Nope, I've never seen him."

The next five houses yielded the same result. The residents hadn't seen him. Then he got lucky.

"I know him. That's Brian. Yeah, he was here," a man across the road from one of Christian's cabins said.

"When was this?"

The man scratched his head. "Maybe a couple of weeks ago."

"Are you sure about the dates?" Zane asked.

"Oh yeah. The wife and I had him around for dinner one night. I grilled burgers out on the patio."

Christian told me no one had seen him.

"That's his place over there?" Zane pointed toward the home.

"Yup. Right across the street. The one on the corner."

The fourth house on Zane's list. "Did he come and go or just stay put?

"He'd go out hiking or cycling. Sometimes, run down to the valley to the store. Now that you ask, there was one day he left early and came back late. I thought nothing of it. He had his bike on the carrier, you know, on top of his car. I figured he wanted to hit a different trail. Is Brian in some kind of trouble?"

"I'm a friend of a family that he was close to. They're trying to reconnect after several years," Zane lied again.

"So, they sent you? Why not try his home in Silicon Valley?"

"I don't know. They don't live here, and I'm close by. They asked me to see if he was around. I tried knocking, but didn't get an answer, so wanted to check that I got the right place. You've been a great help. Thanks."

Zane walked across Timphaven Road to Christian's cabin. The lot was heavily wooded with pine, maples, and quaking aspen. The cabin itself was huge, all wood construction with vaulted ceilings. He went around back to a deck and looked through the sliding glass door. Inside the cabin, he saw furniture covered with sheets. At one end of the deck was a built-in grill near a round picnic table. Wooden patio furniture, missing the cushions, was on the deck near the table. He also found a hot tub, protected by a thick cover. He saw the appeal of coming here to get away. The area was peaceful and relaxing.

Zane headed back to the front of the cabin, a big grin on his face. That changed when he saw two SUVs, emblazoned with "Utah County Sheriff" parked behind his truck. One deputy had his hands around his face to shade his eyes as he looked through the driver-side window of Zane's truck. Zane hollered out, "Can I help you, deputy?"

The deputy at his truck stepped back and put his hand on his pistol. "Is this your vehicle, sir?"

"Yes, it is. What's the problem?".

"Can you step over here?"

Zane walked down the driveway, his hands in plain sight, to where the deputies were waiting.

"We've had several reports of a prowler in the area in the past few days. When a call came in about a suspicious person looking around, we were called out. Can you tell me what you're doing here?"

"Looking for information about the owner of this cabin."

"What kind of information?"

Zane saw the blond neighbor across the street looking out his front window. He knew who had called the sheriff. "My name is Zane Grayson. I'm looking into a murder up in Mathoni, and the owner of this and other properties in the area is on my suspect list."

"Are you law enforcement?"

"Retired." Zane looked over at the other officer. He'd

unsnapped the strap over his service weapon, and his hand rested on the pistol butt.

"You're a private investigator?"

"No deputy. I'm just working to clear myself."

"Turn around, slowly."

"I'm not armed." Zane lifted his hands up and turned around as instructed so the deputy could see he was telling the truth.

"Show me some identification."

Zane removed his wallet from his back pocket, took out his driver's license, and handed it to the deputy.

"California." The other deputy came over and took Zane's ID, then stepped back and talked into the microphone on his shoulder.

"Why is a retired cop from California involved in a murder in a small town like Mathoni?"

"I grew up there and just moved back. I haven't had a chance yet to get my Utah driver's license."

"How is the homeowner involved?"

"Former business partner of the vic. There was bad blood between them."

"You thought you'd just drive down here and what? Confront him?"

"I already talked to him last week in his office in Silicon Valley. He told me he was here, at this home, at the time of the murder. I'm ascertaining whether he could have driven from here to Mathoni, killed the man, then driven back here. I confirmed he could."

The other deputy returned. "They're working to check out his story. In the meantime, the sergeant says to bring him in."

"What?" Zane said.

Both the deputies looked at him and shrugged.

"Zane Grayson," the deputy said, "you're under arrest."

ZANE SAT IN THE BACK of the sheriff's vehicle, his head hanging down. The deputy read his rights and cuffed his hands behind his back. He'd always been the arrester, never the arrestee. Sure, he'd been cuffed before. While at the Police Academy, they'd run through many arrest scenarios, taking turns at being the cop or the perpetrator. To actually be the criminal was an unfamiliar experience—one he didn't like.

Both deputies were talking outside the vehicle, far enough away that he couldn't hear them. He watched as the neighbor across the street came out and talked to them. Probably telling them they did a good job getting the bad guy.

He debated the advantages and disadvantages of remaining quiet or cooperating. Both had reasons for and against them. He'd used comments from criminals in putting together cases. He'd also seen plenty of defense attorneys keep their clients quiet and then get them off. In the end, he cooperated. He'd not damaged any property. All he'd done was look in a window. And trespassing, if they could get it to stick, would be a misdemeanor at best. If he went to trial, he'd pay a fine and walk away.

Deputy Barney Fife, at least that's what Zane called him because he seemed to enjoy throwing around his weight and Zane couldn't remember his name . . . finally got in the SUV. "We've called a tow to take your truck impound. I'm taking you to the Utah County Jail in Spanish Fork."

"How long is the drive there?" Zane asked.

"From here, forty-five minutes to an hour."

Zane realized he would not get home before morning.

"Deputy, I'd like to call home and let my mom know I'll be late."

"You can make your call to your mommy when we get to the jail."

Zane sat quietly as they drove out of Provo Canyon and then south on Interstate-15. The ride was uncomfortable with his arms behind him and the cuffs biting into his wrists. He knew it would do no good to complain.

When they arrived at the jail, the deputy walked Zane to a security door and punched a code into a keypad. There was a click, and they went through the door. Deputy Fife removed Zane's cuffs and put him in a holding cell.

"I'll be back for you," Deputy Fife said, then disappeared through another security door.

Zane stretched his arms and sat on a metal bench attached to the floor, taking in his surroundings. There was a standard stainless steel jail toilet with an attached wash basin. He leaned back, his head against the wall, and closed his eyes.

A clank on the door woke him up. He did not know how long he'd been there. The door opened, and Deputy Fife took him out and down a hallway.

"We checked up on you. Seems you had some trouble before you retired," Fife said.

"You should have also been told that I was cleared of everything."

"That's the information we have. I'm going to give you a professional courtesy and not book you yet. If the homeowner wants to press charges, then things will change. We're trying to get ahold of him now. I thought you'd be more comfortable in the squad room."

Deputy Fife showed him to a chair next to the desk. "Tell me about this Christian guy you were checking up on. Is this connected to the rich guy who was murdered and the wife arrested?"

"Yeah, Brian Christian is the person I'm looking into. He and the victim, Will Massey, were once business partners. I still don't have a clear story of what exactly happened between them, but Christian either left on his own or was forced out of the company; Massey then sold it for a lot of money, and Christian didn't get a dime. I talked to him last week in Silicon Valley, and he has no love for Massey."

"Your hunch is he killed this Massey guy?"

"He told me he was alone at his cabin the day of the murder. I'm trying to find out if he was actually there. It still wouldn't prove he's the perp, but it would be enough to raise reasonable doubt, especially if I can then place him in Mathoni."

"So what's your connection to all this?" Fife leaned back in his chair.

"Mrs. Massey was my girlfriend in high school. That was back in the Stone Age."

"Let me get this straight. You move back to your hometown just before Massey is murdered, then think you can get back together with his rich widow?"

"That's what the Smith County Sheriff thinks, but there's no truth to any of that. I'm actually out to solve the crime to clear my name."

"I'm betting the sheriff there is not happy to have you sticking your nose into his investigation."

"But he's not investigating. He arrested the victim's wife."

Another deputy walked over. "We talked to someone at the Christian home in California. Seems Mr. and Mrs. Christian are on a plane. Something about an anniversary trip."

Fife stood. "Looks like you get to experience our hospitality overnight."

"I was afraid you'd say that. I'd like to make a call. Tell my mom I won't be home tonight." Deputy Fife handed Zane the handset from the desk phone.

"Dial nine for an outside number."

"Hello?"

"Hi, Mom."

"Zane, what's wrong?"

He would not tell her where he was. "This is going to take longer than I thought. It'll be late before I'm done. I'll get a hotel room down here."

"Thanks for letting me know. I'll be fine. See you in the morning."

Zane hoped that would be true. "Night, Mom."

After Zane hung up, Deputy Fife took Zane to a cell. "We're putting you in solitary. It'll give you some extra privacy. Someone will get you in the morning."

Zane lay on the thin mattress as the door swung shut with a clank.

Chapter 29

LOUD VOICES, METAL HITTING METAL, and clanking sounds woke Zane. He rubbed the sleep from his eyes and looked around, unsure of where he was. Bright light from far above him flooded the room. Then he remembered. He sat up and stretched and wondered what time it was. His stomach growled. How long until breakfast? Would he even get breakfast? Had they forgotten him?

He didn't know how long he had worried about not being found when the door opened. Deputy Fife appeared.

"Grayson, you can go."

"What about the charges?"

"I talked to Mr. Christian. He wasn't happy, but he declined to press charges."

Zane looked at the deputy's name tag as he was led out: Hollister. He preferred Fife. "What time is it?" Zane asked.

Deputy Fife looked at his watch. "06:37."

"What about my truck?"

"That's going to take some time. We need to send notice to the DMV that your vehicle can be released. Then you'll need to get a copy of the release from them. They'll require proof of ownership. Once you get the release, take it to the tow lot and pay the tow and storage fees. The state has a website where you can get all the information."

Zane worried that he'd never see his new truck again.

IT WAS MID-AFTERNOON BEFORE ZANE got back home. He hadn't wanted to bother his mom, so despite the cost, he took a rideshare. Marcia made him a sandwich, and he made coffee, then told her the entire story of his long night in jail and that his truck was in impound.

"I'm sorry I lied about last night, but I didn't want to worry you."

"It's awful you had to go through that," she said.

"It would have been worse if Christian had pressed charges." Zane took a sip from his mug.

"Even so, you were in jail."

"They never booked me, so it didn't happen." He stood and rinsed his dishes and then sniffed his armpits. "I need a shower. How can you be in the same room as me? I smell awful."

Mom laughed. "Seems you forgot about all those long days your father put in and then came back in the evening smelling of sweat and manure. That was much worse."

After a shower and a change of clothes, Zane got back to his investigation. He had a suspect who looked good. Now, he needed evidence Brian Christian had been in Mathoni. To do that, he would ask people around town if they might have seen his suspect on the day of the murder. He had two probable places to begin with, so he set out to get the proof. He drove Marcia's Wagoneer into town.

Lou-Lou's was busy with the usual mix of locals and tourists. As Zane expected, Emmett Young and Charlie Snow were at the back booth, playing checkers. Zane pulled a chair over and sat at the end of the table. He said, "Who's winning?"

The two men looked over at Zane. Charlie Snow looked back at the board. He was heavy set and wore a blue T-shirt, bib overalls, and an old, heavily worn, brown cowboy hat. "I am." He picked up the red king, jumped two of Emmett's black checkers, and laughed.

"Dang-it, Charlie. That's the second time today you've done that," Emmett said. He pushed his glasses up his nose and then counter-attacked by jumping Charlie's king. He was thin, with a large mustache, a black and white checked shirt, and a green baseball cap with a John Deere insignia. "Ha! That'll teach ya."

"Looks like your luck is ending, Charlie," Zane said. "But I wonder if you two can help me." He took out the picture of Brian Christian and handed it to Emmett. "Did you see this man around here a couple of weeks ago? It would have been the same day Will Massey died."

Emmett looked at the picture. "You still trying to prove Tiffany didn't kill her husband? The Sheriff arrested her, you know."

"That doesn't mean she did it. This man," he tapped the picture, "could have slipped into town and done it."

"I haven't seen him," Emmett said. He passed the picture to Charlie.

"Who is this guy?" Charlie said.

"He's someone who holds a grudge against Will. Take a good look at him. Did you see him around?"

Charlie looked at the picture. "Can't say if I did or not. These dang tourists. They all become a blur."

Zane picked up on his comment. "Sounds like you don't want all these people around."

"I could go back to when you were a kid. Yeah, the tourists came in here, but not as many." He handed the picture back to Zane.

"So, you must have been opposed to Will's plans to build a guest ranch."

"Guest ranch—that's just another name for a fancy hotel," Charlie said. "We don't need it. It would only bring in more tourists."

"You's against it. Maybe you killed him." Emmett grinned.

"Now just shut your yap, Emmett. You know darn well we were both sittin' right here playing checkers that day."

"Don't mean I can't razz you about it."

Zane laughed. "Thanks for your help. I need to ask around a bit more, and Charlie, watch out for this one," he pointed at Emmett, "he cheats."

He went to the counter and showed the picture to both Lou and Louise and the two high school girls working there. They all said they hadn't seen the man in the picture.

Homer Bass came in while Zane was watching the checker game. Homer saw Zane and said, "Well, if it isn't Mr. Philosophizer."

"How are you, Homer?" Zane said.

"I'm about as good as a fuzzy peach in August."

Zane laughed. "I've never heard it put that way. I may steal it." He handed the picture to him. "Did you see this guy about the same time Will Massey was killed?"

Homer took a long look at the picture. "I can't say yes, and I can't say no."

"Well, thanks for your help." As Zane was leaving Lou-Lou's, Bruce Colby walked by on his way to his office. "Zane. I haven't heard any updates from you in a while. What happened to that guy I tracked down?"

"He didn't do it, but thanks for locating him for me."

"You still trying to find the killer or did Tiffany's arrest put a stop to it?"

"If anything, it brought new leads, so still working on it." He told Colby about Brian Christian and showed him the picture.

Colby took it and looked at it carefully. "Maybe?" It was more of a question than anything. He handed it back to Zane.

"But maybe not?" Zane said. "Thanks, Bruce." He headed toward the Wagoneer.

"Let me look at that again," Colby hollered.

Colby looked at it again. "You know, I might have seen this guy down at the Gas & Guzzle."

"Are you sure?"

"Not 100% but I'm pretty sure."

"The guy I'm interested in may have had a bike rack with a bike."

Colby thought for a moment. "Yeah, I think he had a bike. It was just one up on top of the roof."

"Thanks Bruce. I'll head down to the Gas and Guzzle. Maybe they remember him."

When Zane drove past the bank, he saw Tiffany walk in. He thought about what she might learn and hoped she came back with a list of accounts that could match up with the codes.

At the Gas and Guzzle, he filled the gas tank on the Wagoneer and looked around for security cameras. He spotted three outside and then went in, stopping at the counter. "Is Jeremiah around?"

"He's not here right now. Can I help you?"

"I guess I need to talk to whoever is in charge."

"That would be me." Evan was printed on his name tag.

"Well, Evan, I'm investigating Will Massey's murder and am wondering if your cameras caught someone who may have been in the area that day."

"You must be working for Mrs. Massey 'cause you ain't a deputy sheriff. I know all of them."

"Actually, I'm working for myself. Now, about those cameras. I'd like to see the video from the day Will was murdered."

"Don't got it."

Zane's heart sank. "Are you saying the sheriff took it?"

"Nope. The sheriff never asked for it. Everything gets recorded over after a week."

"Even the cameras inside?"

"They're all on the same system."

"Well then," Zane said, taking the picture out of his pocket, "maybe you saw this guy in here on that day." He pushed the picture across the counter.

"Yeah, I seen someone who looked like him. Can't say what day though. Can't even say fer sure if it was this guy. Coulda been someone else. Coulda been him."

"Did he have a bike on the car?"

"I'm not sure. We get lots of people through here, with and without bikes."

BACK HOME, ZANE SAT AT his dad's desk and entered his notes from the past couple of days into his laptop. He planned to send a report to David Miller, Tiffany's attorney, and he finally felt good about where the investigation was at, and Christian was a good suspect. He knew it would take weeks but still hoped Miller could subpoena credit card records to show Christian actually came to Mathoni. Maybe he could get cell phone records as well. Just a ping from a tower in Mathoni would be enough.

When he finished, his eyes were tired from looking at the screen. He rubbed them, then pulled out another random journal.

Friday, May 23, 2014

The town is talking about Mountain West Energy wanting to build a pipeline through the area. It is supposed to carry natural gas from wells northeast of us all the way to Vernal. They say it'll be safe, but some of us aren't sure. And because it will be underground, it will scar the landscape where they have to dig the trench. We have enough of that on the way to Vernal from the strip mining going on there.

I'm against this pipeline. It will ruin the beauty of our mountains and could keep visitors away. Some neighbors have asked me to lead the group against it, and I've stepped up and accepted. Marcia says I'd be successful at it. I think there are enough people against it to put a stop to the company tearing up our beautiful valley and mountains.

Zane had never heard about this, so he asked his mom about it.

"It was a big deal," she said. "And it's a good thing it never happened. It would have run right across our property. Robert led the group against it, and the county pushed back on it as well. Almost no one liked the idea. When they couldn't get all the permits and access they needed, the company finally canceled it."

"When did they change their minds?"

"Oh, we fought it for years, but it was after your dad passed when they finally said it would not happen."

Zane was going to ask more about it but a knock at the front door pulled him away.

"I have news about the bank accounts," Tiffany said as soon as Zane opened the door—her voice full of excitement.

They sat at the kitchen table. "What did you find?" Zane said.

"There are a lot of different accounts. Two are personal—savings and checking, one is for the ranch property, another is for the cattle business, one for the guest house, and one is for investments. I knew about these. The others are new to me. I almost didn't get the info because my name isn't on them. I guess I convinced the bank manager because he finally gave them to me. One account was opened here in Mathoni for a business called WM Industries. There's another at Zion's Bank in Vernal for WM Holding."

"That's strange. Why go to different branches? I don't get it."

"I thought the same thing, but what if Will *was* hiding something?"

"It's not even really hidden. They're all the same bank, all with his name on them."

"Well, the Mathoni and Vernal branches both had multiple deposits in the last six months for $150,000 each. I saved the best for last. Someone named Sal Giovanni is also on both accounts."

"I know about Sal, and even checked up on him. He went missing about the same day Will died."

"Who is he?" Tiffany asked.

"He's a criminal defense attorney in Sandy. Apparently, kind of shady."

"And he's missing?"

"He was supposed to go to the Caribbean with his girlfriend. She's still here in Utah. I talked to her. However, Sal is nowhere to be found."

"You think he killed Will and is on the run?"

"That's a possibility. I'm sure the police have an alert out on his credit cards. It's pretty standard when you think someone has skipped town. Let's get back to the codes."

Zane got the papers he'd worked on for the codes. "So 84ZBV is definitely Zions Bank Vernal, and 84ZBM is Zions

Bank Mathoni. What does the 84 mean?"

"I do not know."

"Do the other numbers in the code names mean anything to you?"

She looked at them and shook her head.

"Look at the code names with a B. What do you think of those?"

"Nothing. Just letters."

"What if B stands for Bank?"

Tiffany looked at the list again. "It still makes no sense."

"All right, I'll assume the letter B is for banks and look into it."

"Zane, what was Will into?"

"I don't know, but I'm trying to find out."

After Tiffany left, Zane began spelunking the Internet to find anything related to the two company names. It didn't take him long to find a Utah state government site listing them as foreign corporations registered in the Cayman Islands. That meant he would not get very far. It also pushed him further into thinking Will was into something illegal. Sal Giovanni was listed as an agent for each of them and was heading to the Caribbean. They were registered in Utah seven months earlier.

Payouts, the Cayman Islands, and a missing attorney. Zane wanted to know more about Will Massey's business interests. The only person who might know was Jacob, but he was dead.

Zane stared out the window and wondered what he'd stumbled into. He poured his bourbon and went to sit on the porch. *Will was obviously into something shady, but what exactly was it? Did Sal or Brian Christian murder Will? And where was Sal now?*

Chapter 30

LAVELL BATEMAN ANSWERED THE KNOCK at the door and then sneered. "What are you here for? I have nothing more to say to you."

"But I have something to tell you."

"Get out of here. You're nothing but a crook. And after I talk to the sheriff tomorrow, you'll be in jail for what you've done," Bateman growled.

"Hear me out. You need to understand why I did it."

Bateman tried to close the door, but it was pushed open, knocking him to the floor.

There was a struggle. An end table knocked over a table, shattering a lamp that was on it.

The older Bateman was no match. The assailant yanked the lamp's power cord from the wall socket and wrapped it around Bateman's throat, pulling it tight.

Bateman coughed, his eyes wide with fear, and his hands flew to the cord, trying to pull it away. He looked over at the picture of his wife.

The cord was pulled tighter, even after Bateman stopped breathing, to make sure the job was completed. The house was ransacked, and the glass in the back door smashed to make it look as if someone had broken in.

Then—silence.

Chapter 31

THE HOSPITAL WAITING ROOM WAS quiet on Tuesday morning. While Marcia was getting her treatment, Zane worried about the investigation. Red week would start in a couple of days, which meant his mom would need more help, and he'd have less time to work on the case. While he felt he was closer to solving Will's murder, he still didn't have concrete evidence to show any of his suspects were guilty.

He ran through what he knew. Brian Christian was at the top of the list now. He had motive and opportunity. He was staying a short drive away at his cabin and may have been in Mathoni on the day of the murder.

There were the accounting ledgers with coded account names that Tiffany found that sure looked like criminal activity, and it appeared Brian Christian got some of that money.

The small amount of solid evidence frustrated Zane, and he didn't know how to get it. If he were a cop, he could use warrants and subpoenas, but he was just a regular citizen without those tools.

Zane walked to the check-in desk and talked to a nurse. "If Mrs. Grayson finishes, I may be outside making a call."

Once out of the hospital, Zane found a bench under a tree

and sat there. He pulled up the directory on his phone and hit call. Maybe his old partner, Terrell Morris, could help. Morris had been his training officer when he made detective. He had retired and moved to the Central California coast five years earlier.

"Hello Zane," Terrell said.

"Terrell, how's the fishing in Morro Bay?"

"I catch what I can eat, and I eat *very* well. How is retirement treating you?"

"That's why I called."

A hospital employee wearing scrubs walked past, sat at the other end of the bench, and opened a lunch box. Zane walked away.

"I'm involved in a murder investigation."

Terrell laughed. "I knew it wouldn't take you long to get back into law enforcement."

"I'm not in law enforcement." Zane laid out the entire case, including information on all his suspects.

"Sounds like you've got yourself a problem. Are you asking my advice again?"

"I'm out of ideas."

"Are there any other security cameras in town?" Terrell said. "Maybe there are some doorbell cameras?"

"I checked the gas station. They don't have any video from the day of the murder. The bank has cameras. Maybe Tiffany's attorney can get video from there. I don't know of any other cameras, but it's possible there are some. I'll nose around a bit."

"You can keep working on the dude ranch guy. Also, can you re-interview everyone?"

"I don't think Hubbard will come around. I've already started follow-ups on interviews."

"Have you been through social media, government records, maybe even paid for a Lexus-Nexus report on all of them?"

"I hit up a lot of public sources. Guess it wouldn't hurt to dig some more."

"It's a bitch not having a badge, isn't it?"

"At times like this, yes, it is."

Zane saw his mom exit the hospital and look around.

"My mom's done with her treatment. I need to go. Thanks, Terrell."

"Anytime, Rookie."

Zane ended the call.

He walked to the hospital entrance. "How'd it go?"

"Just like normal. Let's get some lunch. I'm treating this time."

BACK HOME, ZANE SAT AT the desk, still working on the codes when he got a call from Bruce Colby.

"I know you've been talking to Lavell Bateman," Colby said. "Did you hear what happened to him?"

"I haven't heard a thing."

"He was killed yesterday. According to the sheriff, someone broke the window in the back door and entered. He believes they thought the house was empty, but Lavell was there."

"So, Lavell encountered them, or they surprised him?"

"The sheriff didn't say, but the place is a mess. From what I heard, it appears there was a struggle. The sheriff told me an Amazon driver found the front door open and Lavell lying on the floor. He had the power cord of a lamp wrapped around his neck. The medical examiner has the body and will let us know."

"A burglary way out there? That seems odd. It's quite isolated."

"I'm just reporting what the Sheriff told me."

"Do they have a TOD?"

"What's a TOD?"

"Sorry, old habit. Time of death."

"Sheriff Richman said it was mid-afternoon yesterday. He didn't have a more exact time."

"The M.E. won't give an exact time. They always say something like 'between 1:00 and 5:00 p.m.' I know he didn't have kids, but does he have any family?"

"I think there's a sister somewhere. The sheriff will find out all of that. In other news, I heard you got arrested," Colby said.

"Bad news travels fast. They released me and there were no charges. However, my truck is still in impound. I hope to get it out tomorrow."

* * *

ZANE WANDERED OUT TO THE milk barn. "Levi, I need your help tomorrow if you can get Chilo and Miguel to do the milking."

"I'm sure I can. What do you need?"

"Looks like I can get my truck out of impound. I need you to drive me to Provo and then run me around town."

"Sure, I can do that. By the way, there was a note taped to your front door today after you left. It has your name on it. I left it on my kitchen table. You can just go in and get it. The door's unlocked."

Zane stood in Levi's kitchen and looked at the envelope. His name was handwritten with a black marker. He groaned. The last time he got one of these, it was a threat. He sensed it wouldn't be any better this time either.

He opened the envelope. Inside was a single sheet of paper. He pulled it out and unfolded it.

STOP INVESTIGATING. THIS IS MY LAST WARNING.

The message was printed using a laser printer.

He went back to the milk barn.

"Levi, did you see who left this?"

"No, I was out doing the chores. When I came back for lunch, I found it on your door."

Zane showed him the note.

"Another one? Someone isn't happy."

"Yeah. Considering all that's happened, it's not surprising. The big question is, which suspect left this?"

"What are you going to do?"

"Same thing I did after the last one and the beating. I'm going to ignore it and keep poking around."

ZANE AND LEVI WERE OUT the door early Wednesday. They did not know how long it would take to get the truck, but Marcia had assured him the night before that she was feeling fine. It ended up taking most of the day. And what annoyed Zane more than having to go all the way back to Provo was that he'd now gone the past two days with zero progress on the case.

Chapter 32

MARCIA CALLED ZANE ON THURSDAY morning. She wasn't feeling well and needed some help. However, it was help he couldn't give her. She wanted to take a bath and would need help to get in and out of the tub. He went to the plan they made specifically for this situation and called Ruby.

Less than half an hour later, Ruby was there. That meant Zane could take care of some other items, like getting to the General Store for groceries. They had forgotten a few items when they shopped in Vernal.

As he walked out to his truck to drive into town, a shot rang out and hit the rear quarter panel. He ducked for cover behind the truck. Another shot went into the tailgate.

He peeked out, hoping to see where the shots were coming from and who was shooting at him. All he saw was a black pickup with a temporary registration tag in the rear window heading toward the highway. It was a truck he recognized. The new truck owned by Bruce Colby.

At first, Zane thought he was seeing things. Colby was the murderer? It didn't add up. Then he remembered the BC entries in the ledger that he had assumed meant Brian Christian. It made more sense if Will had been paying off Bruce Colby.

He thought about calling the sheriff, but quickly ruled out the idea. Richman had bungled the investigation, and there was no way Zane was going to let him take credit for solving the case. He had to figure out the best way to do it. Sure, he could waltz into Colby's office and accuse him, but he needed something that would give him the upper hand. Something that would trap the killer at the moment.

He got in his truck and headed to town, groceries now less important than catching a killer. If he could find Colby in his office, he might take him without incident. The insurance company was dark, and the doors locked tight.

Zane continued to Colby's house and rang the doorbell when he got there. Bruce's wife answered, holding the baby against her shoulder.

"Annette, have you seen Bruce? I want to see if he's available to go to the shooting range later today."

"He left for the office some time ago," she said.

"I was just there. The lights are off and the door locked."

She put the baby in the playpen. "I'll try his cell phone." She tapped and held the phone up to her ear. From deep inside the house, a phone rang.

Zane followed Annette down the hall to a bedroom. Bruce's phone sat on the dresser.

"That's odd," Annette said. "He never forgets his phone. He must have had something important on his mind this morning."

Something important like shooting at me. Now he's on the run.

"If Bruce wanted to get away, where would he go?"

"Now, why would he want to do that? Besides, he'd tell me if he was going to the cabin."

"What cabin?"

"He and his brother have a hunting cabin up above Altamont towards Mount Emmons. They named it Hunter's Hideaway."

How appropriate.

"Can you give me directions or draw a map?"

"Goodness, you must really want to go shooting. Come on, I'll draw a map for you."

They went to the kitchen. Annette drew the map on a yellow

legal pad, then tore the page off and gave it to Zane.

"Thanks, Annette."

Back home, Zane found Levi in the field inspecting the alfalfa crop. "Levi, I need your help to catch Will's killer."

"So, you figured it out. Who is it?"

Zane told him about being shot at earlier, the black pickup, and the map he got from Annette.

"I never would have thought that Colby was a murderer. What do you need me to do?"

"It could be dangerous, so don't agree until I tell you the plan."

Zane explained the plan to Levi and then ended with a warning. "If possible, I want to take him without incident. We know he is armed, so we'll need to be armed as well. There's a possibility he'll fire on us."

"I can't let you go alone, so I guess I'm in," Levi said.

Levi headed to The Cottage to get his weapons and Zane into the house for his. He stopped short. Marcia was collapsed on the living room floor at the bottom of the stairs. A laundry basket, tipped on its side, was near her, and laundry scattered across the floor.

"Mom!" he screamed.

Zane dropped to his knees, his hands shaking as he checked for a pulse.

Chapter 33

ZANE PACED THE WAITING ROOM at the hospital in Vernal, his phone glued to his ear while Mary Elizabeth chewed him out. Levi watched from a chair in the corner.

He eventually got a word in. "You're right about all of it. Yes, I feel terrible about what happened, but don't jump on the first plane down here until we know more. I'll keep you posted . . . Alright. Bye, Sis."

He shoved his phone into his front pants pocket and sat in the chair next to Levi, exhaled a big breath, and ran his fingers through his hair.

"That looked painful," Levi said.

"Yeah, it was. Despite her telling me she would fly down, she'll hold back for now. However, it wouldn't surprise me if she shows up in the next few hours."

"There's nothing any of us can do right now but wait for the doctor to give us an update."

"It *is* my fault. I called Ruby, and she said that after she helped Mom with her bath, Mom told her she'd be fine, so Ruby went back home. I should have given my evidence to Richie and stayed with her. What the hell was I thinking? On second thought, I shouldn't have been involved at all. I had a solid alibi." He stood and paced again.

"Quit beating yourself up; it won't do no good," Levi said. "And you told me your mom green-lighted your solving Will's murder. Which you did, by the way. Maybe two others, to boot."

"But now Mom's in the ER, unconscious. What if she never wakes up?"

"Zane, you're beating yourself up again. Maybe I should see if I can get us some coffee."

"Caffeine, just what I don't need. I'm wound up enough."

"Then how about a sodey pop?"

"Yeah, that would be good. Diet Coke. No, not that. It has caffeine. Sprite. Or root beer would be better, if they have it."

Levi wandered down the hall as Zane returned to wearing a path in the carpet, then sat again, wringing his hands.

Levi soon returned with a coffee and a root beer. Zane popped open the can and then set it on the table next to him without taking a sip.

A door opened. Zane looked over at it. Dr. Zobell, wearing a white coat, stethoscope in a pocket, walked through. Zane and Levi both stood.

"Mr. Grayson, your mom's lucky."

"How is she?"

"She's conscious now. She hit her head pretty hard, and she has a mild concussion. There's no sign of broken bones or internal injury."

Zane exhaled. "So, she'll be alright?"

"We want to keep her for a couple of days. Not just because of the concussion, but she just had her chemotherapy and her body is already weakened. So, as a precaution, she should be here."

"I want what's best for her. Can I see her?"

"Yes, but she's groggy."

Zane looked at Levi. "Go home and get some sleep."

"I'm stayin' right here for now. Miguel and Chilo can take care of the milking. You come tell me how she is after you see her."

The doctor led Zane down the hall to an elevator, then to the second floor and her room. The lights were dim.

"Mrs. Grayson, your son is here to see you," Dr. Zobell announced.

Marcia looked as if she were sleeping. Zane sat next to her bed and considered how their roles had reversed in just a couple of weeks, when he had been knocked out and beaten.

He took her hand and squeezed it and was relieved to feel her squeeze back.

"Mom? I'm sorry I wasn't home."

She looked at him, blinked, and smiled. "Zane, I'm glad you're here. Did you call your sister?"

"Yes, I did. She wants to get on the first flight from Portland, but I told her to wait until we had more news."

"It doesn't surprise me she wants to rush down here. The doctor said I'll be fine. Tell her . . ." She dozed off.

Zane sat with her for a few minutes and then went to update his farm manager.

"She didn't say much," he told Levi. "She knew I was there. Squeezed my hand, and asked about Mary Elizabeth, then fell asleep. They won't let me stay the night, so we might as well head back home."

Zane called Mary Elizabeth with an update, and he and Levi headed back to Mathoni.

"I missed a step," Marcia told Zane the next morning. "I remember falling, but nothing after until I woke up here."

"You don't remember talking to me last night?"

"No, but if I had been unconscious, then I wouldn't remember it, would I?"

"Well, yes. I'm here now and not leaving."

"What about that killer?"

"I figured out who it is. Richie can deal with it now." He squeezed her hand and then filled her in on Colby shooting at him at the farm.

"Wow. Just wow. Colby? I'm thankful you weren't hurt when he shot at you. Even if you had been in the house, I still could have fallen. I only needed Ruby there to help me in and out of the tub, so I sent her home when I was done. Don't blame yourself for what happened."

"I need to be here for you," Zane said.

"Remember when you were growing up and wanted to go off and play with your friends instead of doing your chores? What did your father and I teach you?"

"Finish what you start."

"So, finish it. I'll be here for a couple of days. Nothing will happen to me with all these nurses fussing about."

"I understand your logic, but Colby's on the run. He has a cabin above Altamont. He may be there. I learned my lesson. I came back home for you, and that's where I'll be from now on."

"You also said you didn't want Rich to get the credit." Marcia's voice was stern now. "Go check out that cabin. I'll be fine here."

Zane raised his eyebrows and looked over at Marcia. "Are you sure? What if you're released before he's caught?"

"We'll deal with that later. Right now, you're wasting time you could use to find Bruce. Now go."

He leaned over and gently hugged her. "Alright, but I'm going to check in often."

Zane got up and walked to the door, then paused and looked back. "I love you, Mom."

"Love you too, Zane."

Chapter 34

ALL THE WAY BACK TO Mathoni, Zane thought about the task ahead. Part of him still wanted to track down and capture Colby. Another part just wanted to call the sheriff and let him handle it. But once he arrived at the farm, Zane found Levi and the two of them gathered their guns and extra ammunition.

When the truck was loaded, Zane went back into the house to get his cell phone. There was a voice mail from an unlisted number. He tapped the play button.

"Hello, Zane. I'm safe in a location where I can be holed up a long time," Colby said. "If you would have stopped snooping around when I warned you at Founder's Day, everything would have worked out. But no, you had to stick your nose in where it doesn't belong. You'd better keep watching over your shoulder because I'm still coming for you. See you soon, Zane."

Zane stood there as he absorbed the threat. *He hasn't run. He's still nearby. He must be at the cabin.*

"Colby left me a threatening voice mail," he told Levi when he went back outside. "I'm ready to find that scumbag. Let's go."

ALTAMONT WAS A TOWN OF about two hundred people an

hour west of Vernal. Mount Emmons was a 13,000-foot peak about another hour north in the High Uintas Wilderness Area. Some peaks in the Uintas were a forty-mile hike from the nearest road. Zane knew they wouldn't have to go that far as there were no roads in the wilderness area, and he was happy he wouldn't have to hike.

They stopped at a grocery store in Vernal for bottled water, protein bars, and other things to keep them going, then continued their journey. It was approaching evening when Zane and Levi got to Altamont. Zane assumed there would be no cell service in the area of the cabin, so he checked in with Marcia before heading any further.

Looking at the map, the tricky part was to find the correct turn off the main road to get to the cabin. The map Zane got wasn't precise, and they made several wrong turns on dirt roads, some taking them for miles before the road ended, forcing them to turn back and try another side road.

Zane was losing faith they'd find the right cabin, but he and Levi pressed forward. They took a fork on the right that looked more traveled. They passed three cars parked on the shoulder. Likely they were hikers or campers. They soon came to another road that led off to the right. If this was the correct road, it was about a quarter mile up to the cabin, but it didn't fit the description he had received.

Night settled in when they got to the next cabin. The sign in front read 'Hunter's Hideaway'. It was the right place. Smoke rose from the chimney of the log cabin, and they could see lights on inside. They knew Colby was armed, so they fell back to make their plan.

Sitting in the truck, they snacked on protein bars. Zane worked out a plan. They would have to wait for Colby to go to bed. It was after 1:00 a.m. before they walked back. They couldn't risk the sound or lights of the truck alerting Colby to their presence. A full moon lit up the area. It would be difficult to get to the door undetected unless Bruce was asleep.

Zane approached the door first. A bat flew overhead. He cautiously stepped onto the wooden porch that ran along the front of the cabin.

A board creaked.

He froze.

Not hearing any sounds from inside, he crouched down next to the door and signaled for Levi.

Doing much the same as Zane, Levi was soon on the porch, but on the other side of the doorway. Zane turned the doorknob. It wasn't locked. He worried that Bruce was expecting them.

He pushed the door open a bit. The hinges squeaked.

They both froze.

There were no sounds from inside, but they waited a few minutes for good measure.

Zane slowly opened the door a couple of inches, again stopping to listen for any sounds coming from inside the cabin. He was still crouched against the wall next to the doorway and pushed the door open a bit more with his foot. The sound of a tin can falling shattered the silence. Zane jumped back just as a shotgun blast tore a hole in the door. Seconds later, another followed.

Zane looked over at Levi, who was safely crouched away from the door. The only sound was of the shotgun being cocked.

No one moved. They didn't even dare take a breath.

Lying flat on the porch, Zane glanced through the doorway. The little light inside came from the moon shining through the open door. He could see some cans scattered across the floor. An inexpensive warning system had alerted Colby to their presence.

Zane slid back behind the safety of the wall and put his finger to his mouth, telling Levi to keep quiet. He needed to distract Colby so he could get inside and signaled Levi to go around back and tap at a window.

Levi nodded and crawled off the porch and around the cabin.

A few minutes later, Zane heard a rustle in the cabin. He peeked around the doorway and saw Colby pulling back a curtain on a window. He must have heard Levi.

Zane lay prone in the doorway, his 9mm Glock in his hand pointing toward the figure at the window.

"Drop it, Bruce," he said.

Colby swung around and fired the shotgun, but hadn't

expected Zane to be lying on the floor. The shot went high.

Zane fired and hit Colby in the ankle. He screamed and collapsed; the shotgun sliding across the floor.

"Zane!" Levi yelled.

Jumping to his feet, Zane ran into the room. In the dim light, he saw Bruce lying, writhing in pain, on the floor, the shotgun just out of reach. He kicked it away, then checked Colby for additional weapons.

"You shot me," Colby screamed at him.

Levi burst into the room. "Zane," he yelled.

"I'm alright, Levi. I shot Bruce. He's down but alive. I need some help to patch him up."

Levi came in and helped bandage Colby with the first-aid kit they had brought. Zane covered him with a blanket from the bed, hoping he wouldn't go into shock.

"You go down to Altamont and call 9-1-1. Tell them what happened. Wait for the sheriff and an ambulance, then bring them up here. Tell them to hurry."

"You okay here alone?" Levi said.

"There's nothing Colby can do. I'll be fine."

After Levi left, Zane questioned Colby about the crimes. "Why did you kill Will Massey?"

Colby didn't answer.

"Bruce?"

"Why should I tell you anything. You shot my ankle!" He winced.

"Did he pay you off to get your vote? Is that what the 75 grand was for?"

Colby's eye's opened wide. "How did you find out about that?"

"Will wrote it all down."

He looked at Zane and sighed. "Fine. The guilt has been eating away at me, so I just as well tell you. I didn't mean to. And you were right. He paid for my vote. We just needed one more from the county commission. I knew Jared would never budge, and I thought if I could get more money for Lavell, that I could swing him. Will refused and laughed at me. I was so angry by then and grabbed the closest thing I could. There was so much blood. I got in my car and drove away, then saw that I still had the hay hook with me."

"How did you get the hay hook into the Massey home?"

"I told the sheriff to keep me updated on the investigation. He called me when they finished there. I drove over and found the house unlocked. It was easy to hide it." He tried to sit up. "My ankle is killing me."

"I can't do anything about that. We'll have to wait for help," Zane said. "The house was locked the next morning when I was there. Did you lock up when you left?"

"Yeah. I needed a solid clue implicating Tiffany. It feels good to get this off my chest."

"Tell me about Jacob Faust."

Colby breathed through the pain. "He called and said he had seen me that morning and demanded half the money. I couldn't have any loose ends. We met where I thought we'd be alone. He didn't leave alive."

"And Lavell Bateman? You killed him too?"

"He threatened to turn me in for trying to bribe him. If he did that, everything would come out."

"It did anyway." Zane took a pillow from the bed and put it under Colby's head. "Why did you take the money?"

"My business is barely making it. I thought if I could get some money from Will for my vote that everything would be fine."

They were quiet for several minutes before Colby said, "How did you know it was me?"

"When you shot at me, I saw your new truck."

"That could have been anyone. There are lots of black trucks here."

"But only one with a temporary registration in the rear window. I made a guess that it was yours. The voice mail you left for me confirmed everything."

Chapter 35

THE NEXT TWO DAYS WERE a whirlwind. Zane spent several hours on both days being interviewed by two different sheriff's departments and the FBI. In the end, they decided he wouldn't be charged with any crime but would be required to testify at Colby's trial.

Three days after the showdown with Colby, Zane stopped for breakfast at Lou-Lou's before going to Vernal to pick up Marcia from the hospital. The restaurant was buzzing with talk about Colby's arrest. When Zane walked in, he received a hero's welcome. He shook many hands, had lots of pats on the back, and even some diners took selfies with him.

Maybe the saying is wrong. You can come home again.

Later that night, Zane sat on the porch swing on the front porch with his cigar and bourbon. It was just after 10:00, the night cool from an incoming storm. He sipped his bourbon and set the glass on the table.

Marcia and Levi sat near him in the rocking chairs.

"How did you know it was Bruce?" Marcia asked.

"That day someone shot at me here, I saw a new black Ford F150 heading down the lane to the highway. It still had a temporary tag in the window. I knew Colby had just got one. Then I remembered the code names list, and there was a 'BC' who got $75,000."

"Could have been another BC," Levi said.

"Yeah, it could have been. I was looking at Brian Christian as BC. The amount was small compared to what Christian should have got."

"What about that lawyer who disappeared?" Marcia asked.

"You didn't see the news? The police arrest his partner for his murder and for embezzling client funds. He directed the police to where he had hidden Sal's car in the west desert. His body was in the trunk. Turns out, Sal was a good guy all along."

"And Wayne Hubbard?"

"Innocent. I still don't know why he wouldn't talk to me. Someday maybe I'll find out."

"How did Colby plant the hay hook in Tiffany's house?" Mom asked.

"Colby went to the Massey home after the sheriff finished there, found a back door unlocked, wiped the hay hook clean, and stashed it in the linen closet."

They watched headlights come up the lane. The lights briefly blinded them, but Zane could tell who it was.

"Hey hero," Tiffany said as she stepped onto the porch.

"Tiffany, I didn't expect you. Looks like you lost some jewelry," Zane said.

She lifted her foot, showing off her ankle. "I'm so happy to get rid of that thing. I'm even happier that they dropped the charges." She sat next to Zane and put her hand on his knee.

"But I don't get it, Zane," Marcia said. "Why did Bruce murder Will?"

Zane looked at Tiffany. "You okay hearing this again, Tiff?"

"Yes, I've come to accept it," Tiffany said.

Zane related the story Colby had told them.

"That was quite a risk you took," Tiffany said. "I'd hate to lose you again." She leaned over and kissed his cheek.

"Well," said Levi, "I think I'll be moseyin' to bed. Night, Mrs. Grayson, Zane, Mrs. Massey." He downed the rest of his bourbon and handed the glass to Zane, then headed across the yard.

Marcia stood up. "I'm going too. Now, you two kids behave yourselves." She winked at them and smiled, then went into the house.

"Night, Mom."

Zane and Tiffany were quiet for some time, just listening to the crickets and the cows and an occasional coyote. She finally broke the silence. "Sooo . . ."

"We need to talk about us," Zane said.

"There's no us, Zane. At least not for a while. Then we'll see where things go."

"I was going to say the same thing." He put his arm around her.

"I'm selling the ranch and building a smaller house closer to town. Up there, in the hills," she pointed with her chin, "with the cattle. That was all Will's."

"Sounds like a good idea."

A light rain started falling, and they sat there quietly until it got too cold.

"I should go. Thank you for believing in me." She gave him a long kiss. On the lips. Then, she got in her car and drove away.

The next afternoon, Zane was on his way back to the house after finishing the milking. A car drove slowly down the lane, as if the driver was lost. He stood and watched as it stopped in front of him, and the driver got out. A tall, dark-skinned woman walked toward him. He smiled at her.

"Hello, Zane. I've missed you. I made a huge mistake leaving you."

"Jade. I never expected to see you again."

"Can I come in?"

Acknowledgements

While I've written two books and many magazine articles on software engineering, I got interested in writing fiction nearly twenty years ago after I read The Otherworld series by Kelley Armstrong. It differed totally from what I usually read and gave me the impetus to write a story. Since then, I have devoured three of her other series. Thanks, Kelley. I hope we meet someday.

The idea for MURDER COMES HOME came from the desire to write about my home state. I wanted to write about a small, rural, conservative town, faced with a heinous crime. Because this is Utah, the Church of Jesus Christ of Latter-Day Saints, commonly called the Mormon church, had to play a part. Mathoni is a fictional location but an amalgamation of several actual towns that I have visited, some many times. I needed to give the town a name that sounded like it could be an actual place. During an Internet search for names from *The Book of Mormon*, I found Mathoni, a minor character from the book.

The idea that a writer sits alone in front of their keyboard in a dark room in the middle of the night is only partially true as many people take part in the production of a book. I need to thank the people who helped contribute to this book.

First, Melissa Meibos for sharing her experience fighting off breast cancer. Check out her books under her pen name, Lysandra James.

The experts of the Cops and Writers, Writer Detective Bureau Q&A, and Legal Fiction Facebook groups, and the Book Passage Mystery Writers Conference for helping me get facts straight.

The staff at High Point Coffee. I'm not a coffee drinker, but thanks for providing me space to write when I needed to get out of the house. And for making a great hot cocoa.

Many thanks to my critique group and beta team, Tami Casius, Lou Cook, Meghan Cochran, and Chris Dreith. Your input has made everything better.

My accountability group — which one member calls 'The

Monday Murder Club': Claire Thomas, David Pingitore, and Alicia Stallings. We didn't organize until I was late in the editing process, but having you there helped me stay on track.

The professional editors who helped me so much. Zoe Quniton, for the story support and advice, and Lisa Mangum, who encouraged me at all those writing retreats at Capitol Reef National Park.

A huge thank you to Johnny Worthen for the classes he taught, the advice he gave, and the inspiration to keep going. Most of all, your friendship. Love you like a brother. Be sure to check out his amazing books across multiple genres. I highly recommend his Tony Flaner mystery series. You should check it out.

My dad, who every time we talked, would ask how my book was coming along.

Most of all, thanks to my wife, Laurie, for helping with plotting, hearing out ideas, providing valuable input, and her continual support in everything. You're the best.

About the Author

Craig Kingsman spent many years working in the tech industry, where he was globally recognized as a thought leader and for his tech community work. He wrote two books and dozens of magazine articles on software development and spoke at tech conferences and other events across North America and Europe.

A career executing programs and killing bugs turned into writing crime fiction. He is a member of Sisters in Crime and Private Eye Writers of America.

Craig lives in northern Utah with his wife and their two cats. You can find him as @kingsmanbooks on social media or at his website, craigkingsman.com.